THE WEREWOLF WHOOPS

A CHARLIE RHODES COZY MYSTERY BOOK 3

AMANDA M. LEE

WINCHESTERSHAW PUBLICATIONS

ONE

"*I* love you more than life itself."

Millie Watson, her cheeks flushed with color, gave our co-worker Jack Hanson a poke in the side before grabbing the video game controller out of his hands and practically dancing with glee.

Jack merely shook his head and offered a hint of a smile as the gregarious woman mimed disco dancing with the precious item in her hand. He ran a hand through his dark hair – it was so black it almost looked as if stars twinkled between the strands when the light hit it the right way – and shifted from one foot to the other, clearly uncomfortable being the source of Millie's unrequited love. "You don't have to thank me."

"Oh, but I do." Millie was adamant, her eyes sparkling as she met Jack's reticent gaze. "You fixed my controller. That means I can play the new *Resident Evil* game as soon as it arrives. That means you're my hero. In fact … come here, I want to give you a kiss."

Jack's eyebrows flew up his forehead and he looked as if he was going to jump out of Millie's reach. She was too fast for him, though, and grabbed his arm before planting a noisy kiss on the side of his face.

Jack's cheeks turned crimson to the point he almost appeared sunburned, but he accepted the affection. I wanted to laugh at his response, but the warning look he shot me clearly expressed exactly how bad an idea that would be.

Once she was finished fawning over him, Millie offered up a half wave and disappeared toward her office. She was the only person on the basement level of The Legacy Foundation – the place where we all worked – who could get away with playing video games rather than conducting research or looking for a new case. Because her former husband was co-owner of the company – and appreciated not having to pay huge amounts in alimony to make Millie happy – Millie was essentially allowed to do whatever she wanted, and say whatever came to mind, while complaining bitterly when something she didn't like arose.

I was only mildly jealous of her situation. Yeah, it surprised me, too. Millie was so likable that I couldn't even muster legitimate envy. It was something of a modern miracle.

Charlie Rhodes – that's me, for the record – absolutely loved Millie and her motor mouth. I didn't see it coming, but I would never regret bonding with the woman. I didn't have a grandmother (and Millie would melt down if she realized I thought of her in that manner, because she thought she was too young to be anybody's grandmother) but Millie was the first person I bonded with when I joined the crew at The Legacy Foundation several weeks ago.

Sadly, the other person I bonded with was the only one who remained once Millie scampered off to play her zombie game. Jack blessed me with a shaky smile as he smoothed his hair. Our bond was much more tenuous and fraught with unexplained feelings and considerations. I had no idea what to make of it, so I chose to ignore the situation entirely.

"How are you feeling?"

The question was out of Jack's mouth before I had time to warn him to steer clear of the subject. Two weeks ago I'd been injured when a case we were working went sideways. I fell down a flight of stairs, saw the Chupacabra before I passed out from the pain, and somehow managed to survive the machinations of two evil individuals looking for a payday they didn't earn. The events were fresh in my mind, as was the sense of calm and happiness I'd felt when I woke in the hospital to find Jack sitting at my bedside.

He wasn't calm, of course. I tumbled hard and fast and hit my head ... and back ... and twisted my knee. I was essentially a black-and-blue mess who fought terrible headaches for several days and hobbled around for another week. Jack was close for the convalescence period – something that mortified me. I was pleased about his actions, but once he was sure I was on my way to recovery he took a pronounced step back.

That hurt almost worse than the fall.

The truth is, I didn't want to like Jack. He was often rude and surly, he didn't believe in the paranormal – and we were a group of paranormal monster hunters, for crying out loud – and he treated me as if I were a child. Sure, I was the youngest member of the group. I was fresh out of college when I joined and I had a lot to learn. That didn't mean Jack, who was only a few years older than me, was so much more knowledgeable about ... well, everything. That's how he treated me, though.

I was furious when he backed away after being so sweet and attentive while I was in the hospital. That fury switched from him to me when I realized exactly why I was so angry ... and even a little hurt. I can be brutally honest when searching my own motivations, and I didn't let myself off the hook when it came to Jack. No, instead I debated the source of my emotional upheaval and explored exactly why I felt the way I did. That's when I realized I liked him. Er, well, maybe it was more apt to say that I had a crush on him. Either way, I didn't like the answer, so it turned me belligerent. That reaction only magnified on the rare occasions when Jack asked me how I was doing.

I fought to bite back a sigh and forced a smile for Jack's benefit. "I'm fine."

"You keep saying that, but you're still a little pale for my liking," Jack noted, folding his arms across his chest. It had been weeks since we had a new assignment – I wasn't the only one who needed to recover, after all – and everyone was getting antsy. "You should get some sun."

"Does a tanning salon count? If I suddenly come in bronzed and pretty – maybe add some sun streaks to my hair – will you stop asking me how I'm feeling?"

Jack's expression was hard to read, but annoyance clearly seemed to be one of the emotions he grappled with. "I'm not trying to irritate you."

I didn't believe that. I was convinced he'd been trying to irritate me from the start. Sure, I was brutally honest with myself when I tried to ascertain exactly what I was feeling when it came to Jack, but I was also happy to put the blame firmly on his shoulders when I finished the round of self-examination. He shouldn't have spent so much time with me when I was in the hospital. He shouldn't have checked on me repeatedly when we returned home and I was supposed to be taking it easy. He certainly shouldn't have disappeared without a word the second he decided I was better. I was angry with him for all of those things. So angry, in fact, I wasn't sure which one agitated me most.

Okay, fine. I knew exactly which one bothered me the most. No one needs to dwell on it, though. No, really. What? I just said I don't want to think about it. Wait … what were we talking about again?

"I know you're not trying to irritate me." I kept my voice level and met Jack's steady gaze even though I wanted to look anywhere but his dark eyes. "You're checking on your fellow co-worker because you're head of security and you feel that's your job. But I'm fine."

Jack's expression was unreadable. "When was your last doctor's appointment?"

"Five days ago. He cleared me then."

"And you have full range of motion?" Jack didn't wait for me to respond, instead moving closer and grabbing my arm so he could lift it over my head. He rested one hand on my hip and the other wrapped around my wrist as he stretched and contorted my body.

"What are you doing?" I tried to yank my arm away from him – and it wasn't simply because his proximity made my head go fuzzy – but he ignored my attempts. "I just said I was fine."

"Does that hurt?" Jack lifted my wrist higher. "You bruised your ribs when you fell. I want to make sure you're at one-hundred percent before we go on another assignment."

I was furious when I jerked away. "I'm fine!" The words came out shriller than I expected. "Why can't you get that through your thick head?"

"Because you were hurt." Jack's response was simple. "You fell down a flight of stairs. You knocked your head. You thought you saw the Chupacabra."

I narrowed my eyes. "I did see the Chupacabra."

"The Chupacabra isn't real."

Oh, it's real. I saw it. I'll never forget the vision of the magical beast that smelled like garbage while reminding me of a mutant rat that grew to the size of the one in those *Teenage Mutant Ninja Turtles* movies. Yeah, the Chupacabra would definitely be cuter if it had hair.

"Whatever." Jack rolled his eyes. "I know what you think you saw – and I honestly don't blame you for believing that, because your adrenaline was pumping and you were hurt – but it's time to put that story to rest."

"I'll never put that story to rest."

"Why not?"

"Because I saw the freaking Chupacabra and it was the coolest thing ever!"

Jack rolled his eyes and heaved out a sigh. "You are so much work."

"You have no idea." I grinned as I took a step away from him. Moments like this were rare between us. Actually, that wasn't quite true. They were actually frequent. What was also frequent was Jack's insistence on pulling away and creating a tense situation the second he realized we were engaging in a moment that could be construed as intimate.

The thing is, I get it. He doesn't want a personal relationship between us. He's torn because I'm the youngest member and he's the head of security. He feels he has to take care of me even though I irritate him on almost every level. That simple fact strains our relationship. I could only hope things didn't stretch so far that they'd break. No one wanted that.

I stared hard into Jack's eyes for a beat as he regrouped. I could tell he was debating pushing the Chupacabra issue with me, which would turn disastrous (like always). He didn't get the chance, though, because one of our co-workers picked that moment to join the party.

"What are you guys talking about?"

Laura Chapman, she of the auburn hair and the body that models would covet, glanced between faces as she tried to gauge the temperature of the room. She was something of a pain – okay, she was essentially the kidney stone wedged in the bladder of our operation – and she knew which buttons to push when she wanted to irritate someone. Unfortunately for us, Laura always wanted to irritate someone. Jack was a frequent target, mostly, I believe, because they'd had a fling of sorts that went south before I joined the group. That meant I was a frequent target, too, because she didn't like knowing Jack was spending time with me (even if he was playing overprotective big brother and nursemaid at the time).

"We're not talking about anything," Jack answered smoothly.

"We're talking about the Chupacabra," I countered at the same time.

Laura arched an eyebrow, clearly amused. "I see. So, basically, you guys are having the same discussion you've been having for the past three weeks." She rubbed her hand over her narrow chin. "Doesn't that get boring?"

"You tell us," Jack drawled, his expression going lazy. "You've been having the same conversation for much longer – you know, the one where you're center of the universe and everyone should fall at your feet – and you don't seem bored."

Laura clearly wasn't in the mood for a fight because all she did was shrug. "I was simply trying to have a conversation with you. I wasn't trying to do ... whatever it is you think I was doing. We're all a little agitated when it comes to the job. We want to head out and we can't help but wonder when that will happen. You're not alone, so ... chill."

Jack had the grace to look abashed. "I didn't mean to snap at you."

"You always mean to snap at me." Laura folded her arms over her chest and adopted an aggressive stance. "I don't see why we have to constantly be enemies. We could be friends. Stranger things have happened."

"I think that sounds like a good idea," I offered, smiling. "We should all start over and be friends."

The corners of Laura's mouth curved down. "Oh, honey, I can't be friends with you. I was talking to Jack – and only Jack – because you're far too annoying to be friends with. I simply don't want to keep fighting with him. I don't mind fighting with you."

I made a face. "Oh, well ... ."

"Don't say things like that to her," Jack admonished, his temper flaring. "She might be too nice to call you on your crap, but I'm not. You're only over here because you're bored and want someone to mess with. Charlie is always an appealing target because you feel threatened by her. I'm not going to sit back and watch it happen."

I glanced between Jack and Laura, nervousness forcing me to shift from one foot to the other, and briefly wondered who would win if it came down to a physical fight between the two. Jack was clearly stronger and boasted a muscular frame, but he wasn't the type to hurt a woman. That gave Laura the advantage. There was no rule she wasn't likely to obliterate in her attempts to win at life.

"You're a complete and total killjoy," Laura said after a beat, making a tsking sound with her tongue as she shook her head. "You realize that, right?"

"I'm considering adding it to my business cards," Jack deadpanned. "I'm thinking 'Jack Hanson, security specialist and killjoy extraordinaire' has a nice ring to it."

Jack had a very dry sense of a humor that he rarely let out to play when we were in the office. I couldn't stop myself from barking out a loud laugh as Laura frowned.

"You're really starting to annoy me," Laura snapped. "Do you even care about that?"

I shook my head. "I'm over it."

Laura shot me a withering look. "I was talking to Jack."

"Oh, I care." Jack patted her shoulder in an exaggerated gesture. "Why do you think I work so hard at it? I want to be the absolute best at everything I do."

"Oh, whatever." Laura didn't stomp away – her normal mode of retreat – and instead focused her attention on the small area in front of the elevator. Our boss, Chris Biggs, had disappeared to the top floor almost an hour before. Whispers spread fast that we were finally getting a new assignment and everyone excitedly waited for his return. I wouldn't believe it until I heard the words come out of his mouth, but that didn't stop me from dreaming. "Where do you think they're going to send us?"

Jack shrugged. "I don't really care. I just know I'm sick of being in the office."

"You and me both," Laura said. "I don't see why the whole group needed to be sidelined while Chris, Millie and Charlie recovered. They should've sent the rest of us out while they were laid up. That would've been the smart thing to do."

I balked. "Chris is our leader. You can't go on a job without him."

Laura snorted derisively. "Chris has his head in the clouds. The only reason people like him is because he's a relatively easy boss. He's hardly the end all and be all of this company."

"I disagree," Jack countered, licking his lips. "Chris is the heart of this operation."

"I agree," I added. "He's the reason we're all here."

"He's an idiot who believes you actually saw the Chupacabra during our last case," Laura fired back. "I mean … he actually believes your story. That proves he's mentally unbalanced."

"No, it proves that he's convinced Charlie saw something in that basement," Jack argued. "There were footprints all over that place, prints no one could identify. Just because the Chupacabra didn't kill someone and it turned out humans did doesn't mean Charlie didn't see exactly what she said she saw."

I cast him a keen look, dumbfounded. "But you said … ."

Jack cut me off with a wave. "Stop attacking her, Laura. Stop attacking Chris while you're at it. If you don't want to be here you're free to leave. In fact, I think if we took a vote the rest of the group would be happier if you weren't here. Why don't you take a hint and find another job?"

Laura's glare turned hot. "Oh, you'd like that, wouldn't you?"

"I believe that's what I just said."

"Well, it's not going to happen." Laura planted her hands on her hips and bobbed her head in a manner that reminded me of an angry chicken. "I'm part of this team and you can't get rid of me. It's not going to happen."

"Then try shutting your hole," Jack suggested, holding Laura's challenging gaze for a measured moment before flicking his eyes to the elevator as it dinged to signify someone was about to land in our department. "Here we go."

I lifted my eyes, expectant, and watched as Chris strode off the elevator with a spring to his step.

"Pack your things," he announced. "We've got a job ... and it's a doozy!"

I smirked as I glanced at Jack. "I guess our rest and relaxation period is over, huh?"

"Yup. We're back to Operation Adventure. Brace yourselves, because I have a feeling this one is going to be big. Chris looks too happy for it to be anything but something huge."

I could only hope he was right.

TWO

*C*hris waited until everyone was in the conference room to explain our next assignment … and unveil our upcoming destination.

"We're going to Michigan."

I could barely hide my disappointment. "We've already been to Michigan."

Jack's eyes lit with amusement as he shook his head. "You don't like Michigan? I would've thought that was your favorite spot after you bonded so thoroughly with the Winchesters during your first job."

He wasn't wrong. I had bonded with the owners of the northern Lower Michigan inn where we'd stayed. It wasn't exactly for the reason he thought. They were witches. Sure, they hid it in a unique way by living in a town that had rebranded itself as a paranormal destination. The Winchesters were essentially witches pretending to be humans pretending to be witches. Did you follow that? I know, it's convoluted.

Jack found my interest in the Winchesters amusing. I guess I couldn't blame him. It did look a little like hero worship. The thing he didn't realize is that the Winchesters boasted real magic, the kind that comes with curses and muttered spells. They could make things happen, which I found interesting because I could do the same.

Oh, did I forget to mention that? Yeah. I'm magical too. It's a big secret, though. I'm telekinetic and I draw the occasional psychic flashes and dreams. I'm exactly the sort of thing The Legacy Foundation is looking to discover, so I'm hiding in plain sight. It's either genius or incredibly stupid. I haven't decided which.

"I loved our time in Michigan when we visited the Winchesters," I said. "I'm still in touch with Bay. We email. As for Michigan itself, I just thought we'd be seeing more than one state."

"We go where the reports take us," Chris interjected, leaning back in his chair and fixing me with a quirky smile. I would've melted at the smile the day I met him. I thought for sure he was the one I'd develop a crush on. He was gung-ho when it came to the paranormal (just like me) and he was eager for a grand adventure (also just like me). Instead, for some reason I still couldn't fathom, my heart decided to become attached to the taciturn jerk of the group. I was still internally cursing my bad luck. "It just so happens that we've stumbled across a very interesting case out of Michigan. I don't think it's something we can ignore."

I bobbed my head without hesitation. "I wasn't complaining." That's not what I wanted to be known for, after all. "I just thought we might go somewhere new."

"Well, we'll be going to mid-Michigan instead of the same area we were before, so it's not exactly the same location." Chris's grin was contagious, and I couldn't help returning it. He was an enthusiastic soul, and even though he'd been kidnapped and seriously injured weeks ago, he was ready for another adventure. I had to give him credit for his strength and bravery. "This is an entirely new investigation, and I have to admit it's one that's near and dear to my heart."

"Oh, geez," Laura muttered, refusing to hide her disdain.

I spared her a glance and wrinkled my nose at her grimace. When I risked a look around the table I found amusement flitting across the now-familiar faces. The rest of the team looked resigned rather than upset. I was clearly missing something.

"I guess I don't understand," I said. "What's near and dear to your heart?"

"They're all near and dear to his heart," Millie explained, casting a fond look to her nephew. Chris was technically a relative only while she had remained married to his uncle, but she loved him all the same, and divorce didn't stop her from doting on him. "It's Michigan, though, so I'll hazard a guess that our next job involves paws … and sharp teeth … and tails."

"Bigfoot?"

"Not Bigfoot," Chris corrected, agitation showing. "I told you, I prefer referring to that particular creature as a hominid."

I held up my hands in a placating manner. "I'm sorry. I forgot."

Chris was back to smiling. "It's fine. I understand. Anyway, we're not technically going after a hominid this time. We're going after something else."

"What?"

"Wolves."

"Wolves?" I furrowed my brow. "Like gray wolves? I didn't know they had wolves in mid-Michigan. I thought that was an Upper Peninsula sort of thing."

"Not those kinds of wolves," Jack offered, shifting on his chair.

It took me a moment to realize what he was saying. "You can't be serious." The words were out of my mouth before I thought better about saying them. "You think we're dealing with werewolves?" I corrected quickly.

If Chris was offended, he didn't show it. Instead he eagerly bobbed his head. "That's exactly what I think we're dealing with. But I prefer calling them lycanthropes."

Of course. I should've seen that coming. Chris was nothing if not a stickler when it came to scientific names. "So we're going after a lycanthrope?"

Chris rubbed his hands together, eager. "We are. It seems Michigan might have more than one running around. Maybe, if we're lucky, we'll run across a whole pack."

Laura cleared her throat to get everyone's attention. "I don't want to be the naysayer ... ."

"But you will be," Millie muttered, her expression going dark. She hated Laura most of all, which was saying something because the woman was pretty much everyone's least favorite member of the group.

Laura ignored the dig. "We've been down this road before. I believe this is the third time we've been to Michigan looking for the Dog Man."

I stilled, rubbing the tender spot between my eyebrows as I rolled the words through my head. "The Dog Man? Why does that sound familiar?"

"It was brought up when we were visiting the Winchesters," Jack replied. "Landon – he was the FBI agent on the case – mentioned that there was a Dog Man legend that everyone gossiped about when we thought we were looking for a hominid. He suggested that was our killer rather than Bigfoot."

"Did he really?" I was intrigued. I remembered the FBI agent well, and he seemed more pragmatic than that. Of course, he was also dating a witch – and seemed to not only know about but embrace her abilities – so perhaps he was more open than I realized. "I didn't hear him mention that."

"You didn't spend as much time with him as I did," Jack pointed out. "We ran a few errands together and discussed the case while you were busy running around the golf course."

I wasn't sure if he meant it as a dig, but I took it that way. "If you're suggesting I didn't do my job ... ."

"I'm suggesting nothing of the sort," Jack snapped. "I'm simply trying to relate what Landon told me so we can move this meeting along and not trip over issues no one cares about."

Annoyance was evident in his voice, and my cheeks burned hot when I realized he was right. "I'm sorry. Continue."

Jack opened his mouth as if he was about to say something, and then clearly changed course as he rubbed the back of his head and gathered his thoughts before speaking. "So, back to the Dog Man. Landon told me he'd heard the legend not long after he started spending time in Hemlock Cove. Apparently it's so prevalent that a local radio station plays a song around Halloween every year to remind everyone of the phenomenon."

"I believe I've heard of the song," Chris noted. "It's actually historically accurate, if I remember correctly."

"I can't confirm that either way," Jack countered. "I will say that Landon was ... I guess the word would be 'open' ... to the possibility that the rumor was part of some mass hysteria hoax put forth by a group of people several decades ago."

I frowned, and when I glanced up I found Chris's expression matched mine. "Mass hysteria? Why must it be mass hysteria? Why can't the Dog Man story be real?"

Jack didn't meet my gaze. "I'm just telling you what we discussed. I'm not here to make judgments on the story."

That was rich. I'd been on exactly three jobs with him before injury struck, and he made judgments on every single one of them. "Right. That's you. Non-judgmental Jack. We're thinking of having that added to your business cards."

Jack slid me a sidelong look. I couldn't infer what he was thinking, but I was fairly certain it wasn't good. "So, we were talking about your case, Chris," he prodded, turning back to our boss and fixing him with his full attention. "What do you have that suggests we're dealing with a lycanthrope? I'm guessing it's another body."

"That's where you'd be wrong." Even though Jack was a naysayer at heart and Laura was a pain in everyone's posterior, Chris was the sort of guy who didn't let anyone dampen his enthusiasm. That's why I was certain I'd develop a crush on him from the start. It wouldn't have gone anywhere even if I managed to control my stupid hormones, because our resident medical expert Hannah Silver was clearly more his speed – and he only had eyes for her. But Chris's eager nature was a constant reminder that Jack was nothing more than a wet blanket. "We don't have a dead body."

"So, what do we have?" Jack clicked his pen and focused on the notebook sitting open on the table. "Paw prints? Howls? Claw marks on a door?"

"We have two missing campers, a community panicking about howls in the night, and various paw prints and claw marks." Chris beamed. "We have a perfect storm of evidence and events that leads me to believe we're finally going to be able to prove that lycanthropes are real."

The fact that Chris was excited about the prospect wasn't out of the ordinary. I was new to the group, but even I recognized that Chris would always be this way. He couldn't help himself. What was out of the ordinary was everyone's responses to Chris's excitement. No one else seemed remotely interested in the possibility of seeing an actual dog man. I leaned closer to Millie, who sat on my other side, so I could whisper.

"Why is everyone acting so weird?"

Millie arched an eyebrow as she scanned the table, blasé. "Chris loves the idea of werewolves. He's, like, ... obsessed with them. When he was a kid, he was bitten by a dog and told everyone he turned into a werewolf under the full moon."

"Did he say 'werewolf' or 'lycanthrope?'"

Millie chuckled. "Werewolf. He was six."

"That's an elaborate story for a six-year-old."

"He's always been obsessed with werewolf stories," Millie admitted, making sure to keep her mouth shut when Chris cast the occasional glance while giving a brief history of Michigan's mitten. "I don't know why. I think it's because he wanted a dog and his mother wouldn't let him keep one in the house. Chris was too much of a kind soul to have a dog and keep it chained outside. That's probably why he has five dogs now and has in-house dog sitters when he's out of town."

The tidbit surprised me. "He has five dogs?"

"And two cats ... and three rats ... and some ferret thing that smells like stinky feet. The boy is a complete and total animal lover."

I fancied myself an animal lover too. Still, I couldn't imagine having that many pets. "So you think Chris is focusing on this lycanthrope possibility because he wants it to be true and there's no chance we'll run into the real deal while we're there?"

Millie licked her lips, cocking her head to the side as she debated how to answer. "I think that Chris has been desperate for an outing since he started feeling better. He was down for the count longer than you or me, as you know, and he wants to prove to everyone that he's back to his normal self. That means not allowing anything to hold him back."

"So we're going to hang out in Michigan while the locals look for missing campers and we simply go through the motions." I couldn't help being disappointed. "That's what you're saying, right?"

"I'm saying that Chris is excited and it's a good thing," Millie clarified. "If this turns out to be nothing, I won't complain. That will allow him to ease back into work without wearing himself out. I'm fine with that."

Seeing it through Millie's eyes, I realized I was fine with it too. "I'm sure everything will work out. It might turn out to be a learning experience on top of everything else."

Millie chuckled as she patted my shoulder. "I wouldn't get your hopes up."

I pursed my lips as I tuned back to the main conversation flowing around the table.

"What can you tell us about the missing campers?" Jack prodded. "What do we know about them?"

Chris consulted the file sitting open on the table. "It's a missing couple. Lisa and Ethan Savage. They've only been married a few months. High school sweethearts with a long history together. They're both outdoor enthusiasts and know each other well. My understanding is they love the outdoors and enjoy spending time together under the stars."

Laura involuntarily shuddered. "Ugh. You mean there's more than one person who likes stuff like that? Why?"

Chris ignored the question. "Three days ago they went to a special nature preserve recently opened to campers. For years it was owned by a private entity that didn't allow hunting, fishing or camping on the property. It was recently opened for camping and fishing … but no hunting, and from what I can gather from this report the police have been busy enforcing that rule. Hunters apparently feign ignorance and wander into the area with weapons anyway."

"Is it even hunting season?" Jack asked, typing on his phone. "According to this, you can't hunt deer until the fall. The same for certain grouse. Umm … it says that nothing most people would find valuable can be hunted this time of year.

"Of course, you can hunt opossum, porcupine, weasel, red squirrel, skunk, ground squirrel, woodchuck, feral swine, feral pigeons, starling and house sparrows any time of year," he continued, reading from a list. "I don't see anyone going to formerly-protected land to hunt any of those things."

"No, I'd agree on that." Chris thoughtfully stroked his chin. "The police report says the tent was found in tatters, as if something with long claws cut through the nylon to get to the people inside."

Jack's face remained impassive. "Okay. Did they find any blood?"

"No."

"Any signs of a struggle?"

Chris shrugged. "Things were tossed around the campsite. That seems to indicate a struggle. I don't think we can know if that happened during the attack or after. There are bear in that area. One of them could've torn up the campsite."

"Good point." Jack scratched the back of his neck. "When did they go missing?"

"They were reported missing when they didn't return from their trip at the appropriate time yesterday morning. One of the fathers – I believe it was the husband's father – assumed they just lost track of time, but filed a report anyway just to be on the safe side.

"The Department of Natural Resources had representatives banding birds in the area and sent someone to the spot where the couple was believed to be camping – everyone who wants to camp on the land has to register for a parcel. He's the one who found the place completely torn up," he continued. "He called for search dogs and volunteer personnel right away, but as of about an hour ago there's still no sign of either of them."

"Okay." Jack was all business. "What's the prevailing hunch that the DNR is working under?"

"The report doesn't really say, but if I had to guess I'd go with bear attack."

"So why do you think it was a lycanthrope?" Jack questioned pointedly. "It could very well be a bear."

"Bears don't usually attack tents out of more than curiosity," Chris pointed out. "If they come into your campsite, it's because they're looking for food. It's summer. There's an abundance of natural food in that area. The bears are hardly starving."

"What if there was something wrong with the bear?"

"I'm not ruling that out." Chris was earnest. "But in addition to the shredded tent there have been numerous police reports filed in that area about howling wolves and shadowy monsters running around on two legs ... monsters that look like men with dog heads. I was already monitoring the situation when the story of the missing campers popped up.

"I'm not going in there assuming it's a lycanthrope," he continued. "But I'm not ruling it out either, because this is what we do. We take cases like this and tear them apart looking for clues. That's what I want to do."

Jack's lips curved. "Okay. As long as you're not already convinced it's a werewolf ... ."

"Lycanthrope," Chris automatically corrected.

"Lycanthrope," Jack gritted out. "As long as you're not already convinced it's a lycanthrope, I think we can work with what we've got."

Chris beamed. "Great. Everyone grab your bags and meet at the airport in two hours. We're heading for Michigan."

Even though Michigan wouldn't have been my preferred destination, I couldn't entirely tamp down my excitement. The idea of actually finding a werewolf – er, a lycanthrope – was exciting. Even if it turned out to be a mutant bear, it was better than hanging around the office.

"I can't wait," I announced, hopping to my feet. "That werewolf had better look out because I'm totally coming for it."

"Lycanthrope, Charlie," Chris chided.

"Right. I'll get right on committing that word to memory."

"Do that. I don't like it when people think we're kooks. Crazy people look for werewolves. Scientists look for lycanthropes. Get it right."

THREE

The flight to Michigan wasn't long – a little less than two hours, to be exact – and even though Chris and Hannah seemed excited to be getting back on the adventure train I couldn't help but notice everyone else seemed rather reticent.

I chose a seat in the back of the jet so I could conduct some research on werewolves without looking like a dolt – all my knowledge came from movies, after all – so I expected to be alone for most of the flight. Imagine my surprise, then, when Laura decided to sit with me.

"Are you looking at porn?"

Laura waited until we were in the air to comment. The Legacy Foundation has its own private jet, which made trips more comfortable, and meant I could search the internet to my heart's content on the Wi-Fi.

I slid a dark look to Laura, who held up a small compact and stared at her reflection so she didn't see my glare, and shook my head. "I'm researching lycanthrope sightings in Michigan."

Laura stiffened before lowering her mirror and shooting me an incredulous look. "Are you serious?"

"Last time I checked."

"But … ." She broke off, wrinkling her nose. "You don't really think we're going to see a werewolf?"

"I believe Chris wants us to use the word 'lycanthrope.'" I hated how prim and proper I sounded, but I didn't back down. "As for seeing one, I would be massively excited if that were the case."

"Uh-huh." Laura didn't look convinced. "Well, I hope you and your werewolf have a good time together. I think it's good you're going to focus on that. After what happened in Texas, I was worried you were going to start focusing on Jack. That would be a mistake."

I wiggled in my seat but somehow managed to keep my face impassive despite the fact that her words jolted me. "Excuse me?"

"You heard me." Laura snapped the compact shut and pinned me with a weighted look. "I came over here to play nice and ease you into my way of thinking, but I've decided you're too slow for that."

"This is your way of playing nice?"

Laura ignored the question. "I don't really like you. I don't think that's a secret."

"Do you like anyone?"

Laura pretended she didn't hear my question. "After what happened in Texas, I was forced to do some soul searching."

"Did you find yours?"

This time Laura scowled at my feigned incredulity. "Don't push me right now. I'm trying to do the right thing by you, even though it goes against every fiber of my being."

I didn't bother to hide my eye roll. "Whatever. I don't really care why you're here. I'm trying to actually work, so if you could move things along that would be great."

"Good. We understand each other." Laura let loose a smile that set my teeth on edge. "After the disaster that resulted in me almost dating a murderer in Texas – I still can't believe Zach was evil and I'm seriously reconsidering my screening process when it comes to meeting new men – I've decided that I need to set my sights a little lower."

"Oh, I can't remember where I heard it, but I think it's illegal to date animals," I drawled. "You can adopt a cat, but dating a dog is out of the question."

My sarcasm clearly didn't make Laura happy. She flicked me between the eyebrows, causing me to rear back. "Stop being you," she ordered. "I don't want to hang out with you any more than you want me to. But I have something to talk to you about, and I need to get it out of the way before we land."

I ruefully rubbed the space between my eyebrows and glared at her. "What do you want, Laura? I'm already sick of this game."

"I just want you to know that I've decided that Jack and I deserve another go." Laura's voice was smooth, like liquid gold, although the statement caused my blood to run cold. "That means you can't hang around with him. I don't consider you competition, but you're going to seriously slow my efforts with that wide-eyed ingénue thing you do, and I don't want to deal with it."

I was flabbergasted. "I'm not standing between you and Jack."

"Oh, I know." Laura gave her manicure a good stare before shaking her fingers and returning to the conversation. "But you tend to get in trouble, which means Jack has to run to the rescue. I don't like it, but it's in his nature. I want you to stop doing that."

"I don't want Jack to run to my rescue." That was true. I preferred the idea of being a self-rescuing heroine. Laura wasn't wrong about me finding trouble, though. Apparently the ability was etched into my DNA. "As for you and him, I thought you'd never really dated. I heard that you wanted him but he didn't want you."

Laura turned haughty. "Everyone wants me."

"Everyone but Jack, apparently."

Laura narrowed her eyes until they were nothing but glittery slits. "You don't want to push me, Charlie." Her tone was frigid. "I only came over here because I thought it was the prudent thing to do – the nice thing, really – and I didn't want you to get hurt when I decided to implement my plan."

What was that supposed to mean? "Why would I get hurt?"

"I see the way you look at Jack. You have a crush on him. Everyone knows."

Even though I didn't want to give Laura the satisfaction I could feel my cheeks burning and knew I'd flushed red. "I do not!"

"You do. I find it adorable because you're a geek and he's ... well, he's not. I just want to make sure that you stay out of the way, because I've got something planned for him and you're not invited to the party."

"Oh, there's going to be a party?" I swallowed hard as I tried to regroup. "I don't have a crush on Jack."

"You do. Everyone knows. It's fine." Laura waved her hand imperiously, as if she were the queen and I her handmaiden. "It doesn't really matter. I just want you to know that your presence will not be necessary when Jack and I officially start dating. Do we understand each other?"

I had no idea how to respond. "Sure. I can guarantee I don't want to hang around with you and Jack."

Laura slowly got to her feet, giving me a pitying look before shaking her head. "As long as we understand each other. You need to stay out of my way. If you don't, you'll regret it."

"The only thing I want to get in the way of is a lycanthrope."

"And the sad thing is I think you believe that." Laura made a clucking sound with her tongue. "Have fun with your werewolf. I know I plan to have fun on my end."

I watched her sashay down the aisle, my molars grinding when she pretended to drop something and bent over in front of Jack. To my surprise, Jack didn't as much as look at her. Instead, his eyes were focused on me as Chris nattered along at his side. Jack's gaze was piercing, something clearly on his mind.

He simply stared, leaving me wondering exactly what was going on in that busy mind of his.

WE LANDED AT A DIFFERENT airport. I wasn't surprised – Michigan is a big state, after all – and within thirty minutes we were loaded into two Jeep Grand Cherokees, headed toward a hotel located between Midland and Bay City. That was the extent of the information I knew about the area.

"There's not much here," I noted from the back seat as I stared out the window. "It's pretty much flat forestland."

"What were you expecting?" Jack asked from behind the wheel. He seemed intent on the road, even though, Laura, from the passenger seat, kept asking inane questions that he deigned to answer with the fewest words possible.

I shrugged. "I don't know. Hemlock Cove had hills and water. This is just ... blah."

"Michigan is one of those states that can be more than one thing," Jack explained. "The southeastern portion is urban. Everything else is rural. There are different types of rural, though."

"I think Michigan is a dumb state," Laura offered. "I much prefer a sunshine state – like Florida or California ... or even Hawaii – because Michigan gets snow and I hate snow. How about you, Jack? Do you like sunshine states?"

Jack clearly wasn't expecting the question, because the look he shot Laura was one that reflected dumbfounded confusion. "Um ... Michigan is fine. I like all the rivers and trees. I happen to like seasons, too."

"Not me." Laura was prim as she showed off perfect posture and rested her hands on her knees while offering Jack a pretty smile. "I like places where it's okay to wear a bikini year-round. I look good in a bikini."

Jack blinked several times in rapid succession before looking to the rearview mirror in an attempt to meet my gaze. All I could do was shrug before turning back to the window. When Laura announced at the airport that she was riding with Jack, the other members of our group scrambled to climb in the second vehicle. That left me to ride with them, even though I was certain (especially after our plane discussion) that was the last thing Laura wanted. There wasn't much I could do about it, so I pushed it out of my mind.

"How far is the hotel?" I asked after a beat.

"Close. It's right down the road here," Jack replied. "It's supposed to be one of those log cabin deals."

Laura pushed her bottom lip into a sultry pout. "Does that mean there's no spa?"

"I definitely don't think there's a spa," Jack replied. "It shouldn't matter, though. We're here to do a job."

"We're here to look for a werewolf," Laura corrected. "But they don't exist, so this will be a waste of time."

"You don't know they don't exist," I argued. "They could be real."

Laura snorted. "Can you believe her?" She jerked her thumb in my direction and smiled seductively at Jack. "There's a sucker born every second, huh?"

Jack stared her down for a long moment before speaking. "She's right. You don't know that we won't find ... something."

Laura balked. "But you're usually the first one to laugh at Chris's werewolf talk."

Jack didn't back down. "That doesn't mean there isn't something to discover here."

"But ... ."

Jack shook his head, firm. "Part of our job is keeping an open mind. You should keep an open mind, Laura."

I couldn't stop myself from getting involved in the conversation. "Yeah. You should keep an open mind."

Laura snapped her head to glare at me. "Perhaps you should shut your mouth and go back to staring vacantly out the window. I think we'd all enjoy that."

I held up my hands in mock surrender. "Absolutely. Your wish is my command." I barely managed to contain my smirk as I focused on the foliage blurring on the other side of the glass. Perhaps Laura's determination to snag Jack – a man who hated her more than I did – would turn out to be fun after all. There were worse ways to spend a day than watching Laura act like an idiot, after all.

THE HOTEL WAS NOT what I'd expected and I couldn't hide my dismay in the lobby as I tried to avert my eyes from the multitude of animal heads mounted on the wall. I felt as if they were staring at me – the deer with their glass eyes, the wolf with his snarling snout and the bear with his sad grimace – and I felt mildly guilty for their deaths even though I obviously had nothing to do with them.

"It kind of makes you want to eat nothing but vegetables, huh?" Jack asked, sidling up to me and regarding the wolf with a sad smile. "I bet he was beautiful back in the day."

"You mean before they shot him and stuffed cotton in his neck and made his nose do that thing it's doing?" I challenged. "Yeah, I'll bet he was beautiful too."

Fred Pitman, the hotel owner, caught us staring and beamed as one of his workers ran Chris's credit card and gathered room keys. "Nice, huh? Shot him myself."

I couldn't decide if that was supposed to impress me. "What was he doing when you shot him?"

"Wandering through the woods hunting for prey." Fred, who looked to be in his fifties and did that thing where he combed his hair over a bald spot and pretended that it looked normal, puffed out his chest. "He didn't even see me coming."

"That hardly seems fair." The words were out of my mouth before I realized how they would be received. "I think it's only fair if you give the wolf a gun, too, and then see what happens. That sounds more sporting."

Fred made a derisive sound in the back of his throat as he folded his arms over his chest. "Let me guess … you're a vegetarian."

I immediately started shaking my head. "I'm not. I eat meat. Sometimes I wish I could be a vegetarian, but I like a burger too much to go without one for the rest of my life. I simply don't understand the point of killing this wolf."

"Hunting is a sport."

"It doesn't seem sporting."

"Well, it is. It's a sport I'm good at." Fred swaggered out from behind the desk, ignoring everyone else and focusing solely on me. "Hunting is the sport of kings … and by that I mean actual kings did it. I killed every animal you'll see mounted in this place."

I couldn't hide my horror. "There aren't animal heads in the rooms, are there?"

The woman behind the counter – I think she introduced herself as Harley – offered a sympathetic smile. "I'm afraid so."

Ugh! That was the last thing I wanted to hear. "Well ... great."

Jack rested a sympathetic hand on my shoulder. "You must have one room that doesn't have a head in it." He flashed a smile for Harley's benefit because she seemed the helpful sort.

"No, they all have heads." Harley risked a look at her boss before pasting what could only be described as the world's fakest smile on her face. "They look over you while you're sleeping."

"Yeah, I think that's what Charlie is worried about." Jack's expression was rueful as he snagged my gaze. "Just remember they're already dead and not really staring at you."

"I'll do my best," I sighed. "Maybe I'll sleep in the bathtub or something."

"The werewolves won't be able to get you there," Laura supplied. "Maybe you should turn on the water while you're in there and see if you can join the animal heads in the great beyond."

Jack glared at Laura. "What is your deal? You've been in a mood since we left the office."

Laura adopted an innocent expression. "What makes you think I'm in a mood?"

Jack didn't get a chance to respond because Fred decided it was time to take over the conversation. "Werewolves, huh? I bet you guys are here to look for that missing couple."

"What do you know about that?" Chris looked eager to change the subject. "Have you heard reports of lycanthropes in the area?"

Fred was puzzled. "What's a lycanthrope?"

"Werewolf," Jack supplied. "Do you have a lot of werewolf legends around here?"

"Oh, we definitely do." Fred enthusiastically nodded. "I'm looking to find one to add to my wall."

My stomach twisted. "A werewolf would be half human," I pointed out.

"That's why I'll only kill it when it's fuzzy and hunting." Fred was blasé ... and deathly serious. "It's not against the law to kill an animal

27

… and a werewolf is definitely an animal. I go out hunting for one at least once a week. I think I'm getting close to finding one."

I didn't like the sound of that one bit. "And what about when it's a man? What about the people who love him or her, the ones left behind?"

Fred shrugged. "If it didn't want to die, it shouldn't have become a monster. It's not rocket science."

"No, definitely not." I grabbed the handle of my suitcase and spared a glance for Jack. "I already hate this one."

Jack was sympathetic. "You'll perk up when we get to the scene." He lowered his voice as he leaned forward. "This guy has been hunting for years and never killed a person. I wouldn't worry too much about it. Do you see that head over there?" Jack jerked his chin in the direction of the bear. "He says he killed all the animals, but there's a tag on that one, just under the chin, that suggests he bought it in Canada."

I brightened considerably. "Really?"

Jack nodded. "Not everything is what it seems. You need to remember that."

He didn't have to remind me. I was a prime example of exactly that. For now, I was merely happy that Fred didn't appear to be the famed hunter he claimed.

"I'll remember." I forced a smile. "Let's drop off our stuff and hit the woods. I'm dying to see this campsite."

"There you go." Jack returned my grin. "Now you sound like yourself. We'll take twenty minutes to get settled and then go. We want to take advantage of the light."

That was, thankfully, something we could all agree on.

4

FOUR

*J*ack already had Millie and Bernard, our equipment
manager, secured in his Jeep when I walked out of the
hotel. He grabbed my arm and shoved me toward the
passenger door before I realized what was happening.

"My vehicle is full," he announced. "Laura, you'll have to ride with
Chris."

Laura, who had apparently been distracted when Jack carried out
his maneuver, made a face. "But ... ."

"I'm sorry." Jack shrugged as if signifying weakness and regret. "I'm
full."

"I could ride with Chris," I offered, keeping my voice low enough
so only Jack could hear. "I mean ... if you want her to ride with you."

Jack made a face. "Don't even suggest it." He opened my door and
gave me a small shove. "Get in. You're riding shotgun."

I smiled, amused. The feeling lasted only until I saw Laura's dark
glare. She clearly thought I'd manipulated the situation, and I doubted
very much she would let it slide. Ah, well, that was a concern for later.

I waited until I fastened my seatbelt and Jack had navigated to the
main highway to speak. "Do you know where we're going?"

"It's programmed into the GPS."

I glanced at the small dashboard computer, which was directing us toward what looked to be an isolated spot about fifteen miles away. "I'm surprised we didn't get a hotel closer to the scene," I said after a moment. "I guess it probably wasn't possible given how sparse the population is out here, huh?"

"It only looks sparse." Jack eyed the GPS for a moment before turning his full attention to the highway. "There are three small cities not too far away, and if we find we need something bigger Saginaw is about a thirty-minute drive."

My knowledge of Michigan geography was limited. "That's where the airport is, right?"

"Yes."

"Do you think we'll need a bigger city?"

"I have no idea what we'll need," Jack replied. "Chris is gung-ho on this one. He might insist we camp close to where the incident happened. I need to look over the scene before I agree to that. After what happened last time we went camping, I'll probably put up a fight regardless."

"If you don't believe it was a lycanthrope, why does it matter?"

Jack arched an eyebrow. "What makes you think I don't believe it was a lycanthrope?"

"Because you don't believe in anything."

"I believe in things," Jack countered. "I just don't believe in werewolves."

"Or Bigfoot ... or the Chupacabra ... ."

"Or psychics and telekinetics," Millie offered from the back seat. Her tone was teasing, but the comment felt pointed and caused sweat to break out on my brow. Several weeks ago, Millie was present when I let loose my magic and fought off not one but two deranged murderers who were bent on destroying her, Chris and me. I was never certain what she saw – or if she saw anything – but I was nervous enough that I squirmed in my seat. Even though I wanted to turn and meet her gaze, I was too much of a coward to do it.

"Just because I don't believe in those things doesn't mean I'm the enemy in our little group." Jack was philosophical. "I'm simply the sort of person who needs physical proof to believe in something."

I cleared my throat to dislodge some of my discomfort. "So what do you believe in?"

"Human nature. People are most often the answer when it comes to any mystery. Sometimes nature itself is the answer. I've yet to run across a situation where magic is the answer. And I doubt I ever will."

"Well, I hope that works out for you." I stared out the window. "At least the scenery is pretty. I can see why people choose to live out here."

"Did I say something wrong?" Jack asked, confusion evident.

I shook my head. "No. Just focus on the road. There's nothing wrong."

WE HAD TO HIKE from the road to the campsite-cum-attack scene. I figured that would be the case, but it turned into a fifteen-minute hike, which was more than I wanted to bear given the oppressive heat and humidity.

"I thought Michigan was supposed to be cool," I grumbled, wiping the sweat from my brow as I stopped to drink from my water bottle. "Isn't Michigan supposed to be a cold-weather state?"

Millie's gaze was unreadable as she stopped next to me, her face red from exertion. She looked unhappier than I felt. "I'm right there with you. Where is the snow when we need it?"

I offered a small smile, trying to hide my discomfort as she met my gaze. Millie was the first member of The Legacy Foundation I'd bonded with. I liked her a great deal. She was like the kooky grandmother or weird aunt I'd never had. The problem was I couldn't decide if she knew my secret and decided to keep it to herself or was so overwrought during the fight for our lives that she'd never considered the obvious answer. Part of me was nervous to know the truth, but the other part recognized it would be easier to know – no matter the outcome – so I could deal with it, even if it meant fleeing in the night and never looking back.

"We're almost there," Jack offered, casting a glance over his shoulder and pursing his lips when he realized Laura was bringing up the rear ... and heading directly toward him. "Pick up the pace. I want to get there."

"Hey, some of us are old," Millie argued. "I'm moving as fast as I can."

Jack, who was genuinely fond of Millie and not afraid to show it, merely shook his head. "And some of us are trying to keep harpies at bay. Pick up the pace."

"I'd rather kick her in the face than pick up the pace."

"You're a poet and you didn't even know it," I teased, amused.

Millie chuckled as Jack scowled. "We're coming, Jack. Chill out. There's no reason to melt down. Just tell Laura to back off."

"I've told her." Jack was adamant. "It's as if she suddenly can't hear. I have no idea what's going on with her."

I thought of my conversation with Laura during the flight. "She's decided that she can't trust men she doesn't know – I think Zach turning out to be a killer was a crushing blow to her ego – so she's decided that Jack is the safest choice."

Millie slid me a sidelong look. "How do you know that?"

"She told me on the jet." I saw no reason to lie. It wasn't as if I was loyal to Laura, or ever would be. "She wanted to make sure I didn't insert myself into the situation and distract Jack by becoming a damsel in distress."

Millie snorted. "Did she really say that to you?"

"Yup."

"What a troll." Millie was never one to hide her opinion. "I wish she would cross paths with a werewolf. Then we'd never see her again."

I didn't bother to hide my surprise. "You want her to die?"

"No. I want her to be like one of those chicks in the werewolf romance books who gets all hot and bothered for a hairy guy and takes off to live happily ever after."

"You read werewolf romance books?" I honestly had no idea that was even a thing, but now that I knew I kind of wanted to read one, although I'd never admit that out loud. "Are they like … hot?"

Millie nodded without hesitation. "So hot."

"I can't believe we're having this conversation," Jack muttered, stalking ahead of us and pushing through the trees. "This is what I get for surrounding myself with weirdos."

Millie and I exchanged amused looks.

"I just know he's going to buy a werewolf book to check it out now," Millie supplied. "He's got that look."

I chuckled. "He's not the only one. I want to read one now."

"I've got a list I can email you."

"Awesome."

THE CAMPSITE WAS ROPED off with yellow police tape, which Jack and Chris brazenly crossed. I remained rooted to my spot as I watched them, momentarily waiting to see if law enforcement officers would come charging from the trees brandishing handcuffs and Miranda rights.

Eventually everyone else crossed, too, leaving me as the only standout. Jack's expression reflected amusement when he snagged my gaze.

"We have permission to be here. It's okay."

"Oh, well, I knew that." I had no idea. I sucked in a breath and slid under the tape, exhaling heavily once on the other side. I wasn't in handcuffs, at least for the moment, so that was a good thing. "Where should I start?"

"Just look around," Chris instructed as he crouched on the far side of the tattered tent. "We need to photograph everything. In fact, why don't you check the perimeter of the site for prints that we can cast? That would be a good task for you."

"Okay." I intended to do as Chris asked, but the shredded tent seemed to be calling me and I couldn't stop myself from heading there first. I glanced around to see what everyone else was doing – they all seemed intent on a chore I couldn't quite identify – and then focused on the shredded fabric.

I touched my fingers to a particularly savaged spot and barely managed to swallow a gasp when a kaleidoscope of images pummeled my mind. It was hardly the first time I'd been accosted with psychic images, but there was a reason I preferred for the episodes to occur when I was alone.

There was nothing I could do about it now, so I did my best to commit the flashes to memory without looking as if I was having some sort of fit requiring medical assistance.

Screaming.

A man calling for a woman, panic evident in his voice.

Sharp teeth, the sort that would belong to an animal.

Blood. I could smell it, not see it.

Another scream and then an overwhelming burst of anguish punching me in the stomach.

I jerked back my fingers and sucked in a breath, working overtime to slow the rapid beat of my heart. I pressed the heel of my hand to my forehead and stared into nothing, my vision blurring at the edges as I tried to regain my senses.

It was a tough battle, but I managed it thanks to a variety of coping techniques I'd acquired over the years. When I was breathing normally again – and my heart didn't feel as if it was about to burst from my chest like the creature in *Alien* – I shifted my gaze to the left and found Millie staring at me, her gaze thoughtful and intense.

"I was just thinking how terrifying it must have been for them," I lied gamely. "I have no idea what happened, but it must have been something that frightened them."

"Uh-huh."

Rather than remain close to Millie, and perhaps answer questions I wasn't ready to tackle, I moved away from her and headed straight for the perimeter. "I'll look for those prints now."

"Be careful," Chris called out, oblivious to my episode. "Don't step on anything that might be useful."

"I'll do my best."

. . .

TWENTY MINUTES LATER I SAT on the ground and waited for the fast-drying plaster I used to make three casts to solidify. This was the second time I'd made casts since joining the team, but the first I was trusted to do alone. I was mildly excited about that … but still bored because I had to wait. I wasn't exactly known for my patience.

That's where Millie found me, her hands dirty from digging in the soft soil near what looked to have been the fire pit. I wasn't sure why she sought me out until she glanced over her shoulder to make sure we weren't in hearing distance of everyone else and then dropped to the ground next to me.

"We need to talk."

My heart lurched and a pain I was certain would lead to imminent death coursed through my arm. "About what?" I seriously thought I might pass out I felt so lightheaded. I'd been waiting weeks for her to broach the subject and now she appeared ready to do so out of nowhere, with our colleagues close enough to eavesdrop, no less.

"Wipe that look off your face." Millie leaned closer and pinned me with a glare. "You are, like, the worst person ever when it comes to subterfuge. It's a good thing you didn't want to be a spy. You would've died on your first mission."

The comment was enough to calm me, but only a little. "I … you … we … what do you want to talk about?"

"Try to pretend we're talking about the casts," Millie hissed, risking a glance back at our colleagues before continuing. "No one will be suspicious unless you make them suspicious."

I wrung my hands and did as she instructed, hoping beyond hope that my world wasn't about to implode. "Whatever you think happened … well, it didn't. You're imagining things."

Millie rolled her eyes. "Good grief. Stop fretting and pay attention. I get that you're panicking, but there's no need to. I figured there was something different about you before you did … whatever it is you did … in Texas. I wasn't going to say anything about it because that's not my way, but you're wound too tightly to let it go. It's apparent you need reassurance, so here it is.

"I'm not going to tell anyone what you are," she continued, her voice low and calm. "I recognized there was something different about you from the beginning and figured you would eventually get comfortable enough to come out on your own."

I swallowed hard. "What do you think is different about me?"

"You're magical."

"I ... ." I broke off and licked my lips. "I didn't think you believed in stuff like that."

"I'm not Jack. Don't mistake me for a non-believer. Just because I happen to be practical in nature when it comes to this stuff doesn't mean I'm not a believer. You need to pull yourself together, though. I'm not going to tell anyone else – and I mean *anyone* – so there's no reason for you to be such a nervous wreck."

And here I thought I'd been hiding my terror so well. "What did you see?"

"I'm not sure what I saw," Millie admitted, brushing off the knees of her jeans before twisting the cap off her bottle of water. "I know you used magic. I saw you fighting, and then I saw things flying through the air. I looked to you because I thought I might be imagining it, but you were calm, not surprised even a little. I knew you did it."

"Why didn't you say something sooner? I couldn't decide if you actually saw anything or missed it because you were so worried about Chris."

"Why didn't you say anything?"

"Because ... ." I thought about my dead parents, about the way they'd stressed that I was never supposed to let anyone in on the big secret. They were always so worried when I was a kid that someone would try to take me for government research ... or maybe to use as a weapon. Sure, I thought they were overreacting and perhaps watched a few too many science fiction movies, but I knew spreading my secret far and wide was a bad idea.

"Because you were afraid," Millie finished, bobbing her head. "I figured. You've kept this secret for a long time. Is that why you studied what you did in college? Is that why you joined The Legacy Foundation?"

I nodded. "I don't know what I am."

"Do you want to know?" Millie's voice turned soft. "Just because you can do things doesn't mean you're not the person you've always believed yourself to be."

I gave her question careful consideration. "I want to know," I answered finally. "I've always wanted to know. After we met the Winchesters a few weeks ago, that need kicked into overdrive."

Millie pursed her lips. "And what were the Winchesters?"

I realized my mistake too late. "I didn't say they were anything," I answered hurriedly. "I didn't mean they were anything. I just ... they were nice and open, and it made me want to learn more about myself."

It was the lamest lie ever, and Millie saw through it. "They were real witches, weren't they?" Millie smiled to herself when I didn't answer, the expression lighting her amused features. "I wondered once I heard about the nude dancing. That's a pagan thing – a *real* pagan thing – and they weren't exactly subtle about some of the things they were doing."

"You can't tell anyone." I gripped Millie's arm tightly. "I made a promise."

"Calm yourself, girl." Millie patted my arm. "I won't tell anyone. It's not my place. I'm glad you found someone in that family to talk to, though. If anyone can help you get through whatever it is you're going through, it's people who have similar secrets to hide."

I hadn't even considered that. "I don't think their secrets are the same as my secrets."

"No." Millie turned philosophical. "They're real witches and they can't do the same things you can. I wouldn't mind a demonstration of exactly what you can do if we get a chance down the road, by the way. No pressure."

My smile was rueful. "You really won't tell anyone?"

"Honey, it's none of my business."

"But ... I'm exactly what we're looking for."

Millie winked, causing the tension rolling through my body to dissipate. "That's what makes this so much fun." She sobered as she leaned forward and grabbed my hand. "I won't tell. You can trust me. It'll be okay."

I wanted so much to believe her. For now, I embraced relief because I was no longer alone and felt as if I had someone in my corner. "Thank you."

"Don't thank me yet. I'm still going to want a demonstration."

"Sure. Once we don't have an audience."

FIVE

I felt better after my conversation with Millie. Once I gave it some thought, I knew it was ridiculous to worry about her spreading my secret. I didn't know her well, but she was the sort of person who stood up for the little guy ... or girl, in this instance. She was also ridiculously loyal, whether she knew someone well or not, and there was no chance she would talk out of turn when it came to my abilities.

I should have realized that. The whole thing made me feel stupid.

After finishing the casts, I stacked them toward the front of the campsite so we wouldn't forget to take them with us, and then expanded my search. Even though two people went missing from the area – and were presumed dead or in grave danger – I didn't feel afraid. I knew that if a real threat presented itself my inner alarm would signal in plenty of time to alert me.

That's why I allowed myself to wander farther and farther from the campsite. I didn't even realize I was doing it at first. I was too intent on the ground, looking for more prints or scraps of fabric. Heck, I thought there was an off chance I might stumble across a body.

I was so far from the group that I could no longer hear them when

I finally realized my mistake. Unfortunately for me, I heard something else.

"I'm not doing it."

"You are."

"I'm not."

"You are."

"No, I'm not!"

The first voice belonged to a young girl. I was sure of that before I saw her face. I made out the distinctive sound of a foot stomp before straightening my shoulders and jerking to a standing position, my head popping above a bush.

On the other side of the ragged foliage stood a woman and a girl who looked about twelve or thirteen. The woman, a blonde who looked young, but with a wary countenance that made me think she'd seen a lot in this world … and she wasn't overly happy with any of it.

She wore cargo pants and leather sandals, the sort that you can hike in for short walks. Her eyes were so blue they were almost unnatural, although a hint of mischief lurked in their depths, making her seem approachable.

The young girl was something else entirely. Unlike her mother – and I was certain they were mother and daughter because the blonde went from irritated to protective in the blink of an eye when she saw me – the girl boasted shiny black hair and matching eyes. She was slim, narrow at the hips and shoulders, but I could tell she was a handful simply from the look on her face.

"Who are you?" The question was out of the girl's mouth before I had a chance to realize how weird I looked crouching behind a bush. The mother probably thought I was some sort of freak, perhaps even that her daughter was in danger. The arm extended in front of the child told me the mother was ready to put up a fight if necessary.

"I'm so sorry." I held up my hands. "I didn't mean to frighten you."

"I'm not frightened." The mother spoke evenly, keeping her arm in place as she looked me up and down. "What are you doing out here?"

"I'm with friends." I gestured over my shoulder even though my group wasn't within sight. "They're not far."

"Uh-huh." The woman didn't look convinced. "You know two people disappeared from these woods, right? Most people believe something bad happened to them."

"I know. I'm with a group investigating the disappearances."

"You are?"

I nodded and extended my hand, even though it seemed a lame gesture in the middle of the woods. "I'm Charlotte Rhodes. Er, Charlie. Everyone calls me Charlie. I'm with The Legacy Foundation."

The woman slowly took my hand and shook it, her eyes never leaving my face. For a brief moment I was convinced she'd somehow managed to hop inside my head. I felt a niggling pressure that didn't belong there, and then it was gone almost before I had time to register it.

"I'm Zoe Lake-Winters," she said after a beat, lowering the hand she held in front of the girl. "This is Sami."

"I'm Sami Winters." The girl puffed out her chest. "I don't have the same last name as my mother. I think that's because the world is trying to tell me that I don't belong with her."

I thought it was an odd thing to say and was going to point out exactly that but then I realized the girl was simply trying to agitate her mother. From the looks of it, I had to believe it was a regular occurrence. Zoe's eyes filled with enough fire that I inadvertently took a step back.

"You don't belong with me, huh?" Zoe basically turned her back on me as she focused on the kid. "Fine. Why don't you head home then? You don't need me to get there."

Sami balked. "I didn't say that. I just said ... well, you know what I said. I didn't mean it the way you think I meant it."

"Uh-huh."

"It's true!" Sami's eyes flashed. "I don't see why you have to be so sensitive all the time. Not everything I say is meant as an insult to you."

"Everything you say *is* meant as an insult to me," Zoe countered, running a hand through her long flaxen hair. "You're my penance from the universe. I was a rotten kid so I got you as part of that whole karma thing. I'm still trying to figure out what I did that was so bad to deserve you."

"Oh, whatever." Sami rolled her eyes as she folded her arms over her chest. "You're a pill. That's what Grandma says, and I believe it. You're a total pill, and I'm sick of hearing you complain. I thought you said we were going for ice cream. That's the only reason I agreed to come out here with you."

"We are going for ice cream." Zoe's eyes returned to me," just as soon as I'm finished talking to our new friend, I'll be ready to go."

If I didn't know better, I'd think Zoe meant the statement in such a way that she'd been out in the woods specifically looking for me. That was ridiculous, though. Why would she possibly want to meet me?

Sami flicked her disdainful eyes to me. "Okay. If you're sure. But I want sprinkles on my ice cream."

Zoe made a face. "Do I ever not get you sprinkles? I mean … seriously. When do I withhold sprinkles?"

"You haven't yet, but you could."

"I'm going to actually do it if you don't shut your mouth," Zoe grumbled, shaking her head as she held my gaze. "So, you're with a group investigating the disappearance of those campers. What kind of group?"

"It's called The Legacy Foundation. We're part of a paranormal think tank. We investigate unexplained phenomena." I got that right off the brochure and didn't realize how ridiculous it sounded until I said it out loud. "I mean … we look for things that can't be explained."

"I see." Zoe didn't appear puzzled by my fumbling words. If anything, she was preternaturally calm. I couldn't rationalize that given the fact that we were standing in the middle of the woods, miles from civilization as far as I could tell, and she didn't seem all that surprised to see me. Sure, I jolted her when I popped out of the bush, but other than that she appeared to find our meeting normal. "And what do you think is abnormal about this case?"

I wasn't sure how to answer. "The Savages – that's their names – were camping out here and disappeared. Their campsite looks as if an animal barreled through, ripped things apart and then dragged them off."

Zoe's eyes lit with keen interest. "You've seen the campsite."

"Yes."

"And what kind of animal do you think attacked? I mean … was it a bear? We have bears in this area."

"I doubt it was a bear." Zoe's attitude was striking, but that didn't stop me from discussing the case with her. I couldn't fathom why, but it seemed somehow natural to tell her what she wanted to know. "I can't say I've seen a lot of bear attacks, but that campsite looked as if it had been systematically destroyed."

"What do you mean by that?"

I held my hands palms up and shrugged. "I mean the tent was shredded. It looked like claw marks."

"A bear could've done that."

"A bear standing on two legs could've done that," I conceded. "But why that way? I've never heard of a bear going after humans unless food was scarce or its cubs were threatened. This was a very obvious attack."

"Hmm." Zoe absently smoothed Sami's hair as she considered the statement. "Do you know anything about the couple who disappeared?"

For the first time since she started asking questions I realized the entire situation was surreal. "Wait … what are you guys doing in the middle of the woods?"

Surprise momentarily flashed through Zoe's eyes, but she shuttered it quickly. I had no idea what part of the question knocked her off course, but her answer was smooth and easy. "We live close to here."

"You live on a land preserve that was recently opened to campers?"

Zoe shook her head. "We live in a house about a mile that way." She pointed for emphasis. "We're outside the preserve. My husband's father has a position with the group that owns the preserve, so we're not entirely separate from it."

"Oh." Her explanation caught me off guard. "So … um … you really live out in the middle of nowhere?"

Zoe chuckled. "Our house is just off the highway. We can get to town in less than ten minutes. It's not that bad."

"That's easy for you to say," Sami groused. "You're not alienated from all your school friends and forced to listen to Dad's awful singing voice when he drives me to town or to sleepovers."

Zoe snorted. "Your father has a lovely singing voice. I like it when he raps."

"You're only saying that because you guys are disgusting and gooey with one another. I think it's gross."

"You'll live." Zoe patted the top of Sami's head, an action that clearly irritated the child, who jerked away from her mother and glared. I'd known Zoe for exactly five minutes and I could tell that was exactly the reaction she was going for. "As for what we're doing out here, we heard about the disappearances and wanted to take a look around."

"You wanted to look around a potential murder scene?" That didn't make much sense to me. "That seems … fun."

Zoe merely shrugged. "Curiosity is something I've never been able to overcome. It's not something I can shake. I simply wanted to see the campsite everyone in town is talking about."

Now it was my turn to be skeptical. "From what I understand, a lot of people believe it's an animal attack … or something worse. Doesn't that frighten you?"

"Not particularly. I've never met an animal I couldn't take. There are no sharks here, so I think I'm good."

"But what about the other stuff?" I persisted. "Some people claim there's something called the Dog Man living in these parts. Local legend has it that the Dog Man attacks people and kills them. Aren't you afraid of that?"

Sami opened her mouth to answer, but Zoe quieted her with a quelling look before shaking her head. The child's reaction was enough to make me suspicious, so I decided to do a little probing of my own.

"I've learned throughout the years that legends aren't always natu-rally occurring," Zoe explained, making a face as I poked inside her brain. "Some legends are created to scare people. I'll never be afraid of those legends."

"I see." There was some sort of barrier in her head. I'd never come across anything like it before, and I was fascinated as I tried to break through, practically desperate to see what was on the other side. "That sounds ... um ... logical."

"What is it you're trying to do?" Zoe challenged, causing me to jolt.

"I'm not trying to do anything." I was surprised she called me on my actions and yet that didn't stop me from probing. "I'm just standing here."

"No, you're doing more than that. In fact ... ." Zoe's eyes widened to saucer-like proportions when I finally managed to break a hole in the wall. Then, even though I had no idea how it happened, our minds joined in what can only be described as a powerful flash.

I saw a thousand things in an instant, although I could make sense of none of them.

I saw Zoe when she was younger, standing next to an unbearably attractive man. They were clearly flirting.

I saw me as a child, crying because I'd accidentally discovered information about my teacher that I wasn't supposed to know, and I was certain it would give me nightmares.

I saw Zoe fighting ... something ... in the woods. She looked deter-mined. Then she was afraid until the man from the first vision barreled into the scene and attacked another man, all the while screaming her name as he fought to protect her.

I saw myself hiding from the other kids in high school.

I saw Zoe crying as she walked away from the dark-haired man. He looked wrecked, but let her go.

Then things started hitting me even faster.

Me shopping for a prom dress, Zoe's hands glowing blue as she tried to save the same man from all her visions, me fighting off a would-be mugger in an alley, her unleashing a mountain of power on what looked to be witches, me reading minds, her healing people, me causing a branch to fall from a tree and hit what very well could've been Bigfoot, her unleashing holy hell on an army of what looked to be gigantic wolves.

On and on and on. Then, finally, one vision almost knocked me to the ground. Zoe on the ground, perhaps dying. Sami crying as the man who shared her coloring and facial features howled – yes, howled – into the night sky.

It was replaced by a vision of me fighting Zach in the abandoned Texas town as I tried to make sure Millie and Chris were spared a terrible fate. The vision of my powers threw me so hard that I managed to slap up a weak barrier and take a shuddering breath as I turned away from Zoe. For her part, the woman looked just as shaken.

"What the heck was that?" Sami asked, her eyes wide.

That was a very good question. I wasn't sure how to answer.

Zoe opened her mouth to say something, but whatever it was died on her lips as Jack appeared out of nowhere.

"There you are!" He stormed to my side and grabbed my arm, ignoring my shaking shoulders as I forced myself to regain some semblance of calm. "You scared the crap out of me, Charlie! What were you thinking?"

"I … ."

"It's my fault," Zoe volunteered, taking me by surprise with her poise as she stared down Jack. "She heard my daughter and me tromping through the woods and came to help. She thought we might be in trouble. Don't blame her."

Jack furrowed his brow. "I … um … and you are?"

"Zoe Lake-Winters." Zoe extended her hand.

"Okay. Nice to meet you." Jack shook her hand, his eyes keen as he slid his free hand up and down my back. "You're shaking, Charlie. What happened?"

"Nothing happened." I sounded calm, normal even. I had no idea how I managed it, but somehow I pushed through the panic threatening to swamp me. "We were just talking and I thought I saw a bee. I don't like bees."

"Uh-huh." Jack didn't look convinced as his eyes bounced between us. "And you just ran into each other?"

"We came to see the campsite," Zoe explained. "There are a lot of rumors flying around about the disappearances. We wanted to see if the scene was as bad as everyone said."

"Her father-in-law works for the company that owns the land," I volunteered.

"Oh." Jack's unfriendly demeanor lessened. "I don't see why you would take your daughter to see that, but ... well, it's none of my business."

"No, it's definitely not," Zoe agreed, briefly locking gazes with me. "Either way, we should be going. We have a lot to do ... ."

"Ice cream," Sami interjected excitedly.

"Ice cream," Zoe conceded. "We won't get in your way. I hope you find those people. I hate to think of them being lost and confused out here. If you need anything, our house is that way." Zoe pointed for emphasis as she focused on me. "I hope to see you around again. It was nice talking to you."

I wanted to repeat the words back to her – or at least some variation – but she was already walking in the opposite direction. Jack's eyes were dark when I glanced at him, suspicion evident.

"What?" I felt as if he was trying to peer into my soul.

"Nothing," Jack said after a beat, his expression unreadable. "Are you sure you're okay?"

"I'm fine. I just hate bees."

"Well, we should get back. The others are probably looking for us. They might send out a search party if we're not careful."

"Yeah, we don't want that."

"Definitely not."

SIX

I was shaky after my encounter with Zoe Lake-Winters and her mouthy kid. In truth, it took everything I had to focus on Jack's back as he led the way to the campsite. If he hadn't found me I was doubtful that I could've remembered how to get back, genuinely feared I would've roamed the woods endlessly until I either fell down and died or the werewolf got me.

Jack cast the occasional glance over his shoulder to make sure I still followed, but otherwise remained silent. That lasted only a few minutes, until he either got fed up with my slow pace or figured we were far enough from Zoe that she wouldn't overhear us.

"What just happened?" Jack grabbed the front of my shirt and held me still as I struggled to put my thoughts in order.

"What?" I was confused. Keeping my mind in the game was more difficult than I'd imagined. I had no idea what Zoe Lake-Winters was … but she was something. That something was clearly more powerful than me. I had no idea what to make of it. "What did you say?"

"Charlie, what is the matter with you?" Instead of anger I saw worry on Jack's features as he let go of my shirt and cupped my chin, his eyes searching my face. "You look like death."

The simple statement caught me off guard and I did my best to focus on the here and now rather than the lifetime of memories I saw in Zoe's head. "I'm fine. I just ... freaked out a bit. I'm sorry."

"Freaked out about what?"

It was time to lie. I wasn't keen on it, but Millie finding out my secret was vastly different from Jack doing the same. He would turn me over for experimentation in a heartbeat. He might not have been a believer at heart, but he was loyal to the company. That meant he would turn on me if necessary. I couldn't risk it.

"I didn't mean to get turned around."

Jack's eyes momentarily darkened. I couldn't decide if it was because he knew I was lying or he was upset that I'd wandered off. Both options worried me. Finally, Jack merely shook his head and briefly pressed his hand to my forehead.

"You shouldn't have wandered off, but it's my fault because I wasn't watching you."

I felt like myself enough to wrinkle my nose. "You think it's your job to watch me?"

Jack nodded without hesitation. "Oh, and then some." His lips curved as he pulled back his hand. "You don't have a fever."

"Why would I have a fever?"

Jack shrugged, noncommittal. "I've been worried ever since you were hurt in Texas. One of the things the doctor warned me to look for right after he released you was fever."

Something occurred to me, and it wasn't an altogether friendly feeling. "Because you think I'm crazy. I said I saw the Chupacabra and you think I'm nuts."

Jack extended a warning finger. "That is not what I said. It's just ... you hit your head hard. You fell a long way. Before that you were fighting for your life. I'm understandably worried about you."

"Right." I dragged my hand through my hair and took a step back. I needed to expand the distance between us. "Well, I'm sorry that my mental capacity is such a worry for you. I promise to never bring up the Chupacabra again. Is that what you want to hear?"

"Oh, don't do that." Jack made a face as he tapped his foot against the ground. "That's not why I came after you. I was legitimately worried when I couldn't find you. I didn't want to alert the others right away because I knew you would be embarrassed when I dragged you back. I'm trying to be a good guy here."

He was. I didn't doubt that for a second. "I'm fine. I was trying to see if I could find some footprints, maybe a path, when I lost my sense of direction and started to worry. I was crouched low when I heard voices and popped up. It was Zoe and her daughter. They frightened me – and I think I frightened them – and that's why I'm out of sorts. I didn't want to admit it because I thought it would make me look goofy, but ... there it is."

Sympathy creased Jack's forehead. "I'm sorry."

"It's fine. You didn't do anything wrong."

I made to move around him, but Jack grabbed my arm before I could take the lead for the walk back to the campsite. "You don't have to be embarrassed."

"I'm not embarrassed." Mortified was more like it. "I just feel a little silly about letting myself get lost. It won't happen again."

"You weren't very far from the group. Next time ... um ... next time tell someone before you take off to explore a strange forest. In fact, if you could grab a partner before wandering off that would be great."

"Are you giving everyone the same advice?"

"To have a partner? Absolutely."

"Okay, well, I'm sorry I made you worry." I attempted to pull my arm from Jack's grip, but he refused to let me go. "Is there something else you want to say?"

"I want you to be careful." Jack licked his lips, choosing his words carefully. "This might not be a safe area. I don't want you to put yourself at risk."

"You don't believe in werewolves, so what does it matter?"

"It matters to me." Jack was firm. "And just because I don't believe in lycanthropes doesn't mean I don't believe something is out here. I don't want you to fall victim to whatever that is."

"I'll do my best to keep from disappointing you."

"That's not what I meant." Jack carefully released my arm before heaving a sigh. "I know you don't want to listen to me because you feel that I don't listen to you, but that's not true. Just ... try to be safe."

"That's the plan." I forced a smile for his benefit, but only because I wanted to ease the tension. "So, after listening to Zoe and her daughter I've decided that tween age must be the absolute worst. I thought for sure there were a few minutes when Zoe wanted to kill her own kid. Do you think that's normal?"

Jack took me by surprise when he chuckled. "I think that's entirely normal. I think the people you love and care about the most are the ones who set you off the easiest. That's definitely the case for parents."

Hmm. I hadn't considered that. "You must care about me a great deal."

Jack's cheeks flooded with color before he quickly covered whatever emotion he was feeling. "Why do you say that?"

"Because I set you off constantly."

"Yes, well, there are different types of worry."

"I'll try to refrain from being the source of your worry." I offered a chipper smile that I didn't necessarily feel. "I don't want you to get an ulcer or anything ... and you strike me as the sort who would definitely get an ulcer."

"Why do you say that?"

"You're wound really tight."

Jack balked. "I am easygoing and a delight to be around."

I snorted, genuinely amused. "Yes. You're the calmest man I know."

"I am."

"You are."

"I really am."

"I know you are." I picked an easy pace as I strode toward the campsite. "You're not high strung at all."

"I know exactly what you're thinking," Jack grumbled as he trailed behind. "By the way ... you're wrong."

"Of course I am."

"Ugh. I hate it when you say things like that."

"Why do you think I do it?"

I WAS EAGER TO get away from the campsite so when Hannah mentioned she'd made arrangements to stop in at a local lab to test samples, I volunteered to go with her. Bernard served as chauffeur, and I'd barely glanced over my shoulder as we said our goodbyes. When I did, I noticed Laura cozying up to Jack – whispering something to him that was probably filthy – and it took everything I had to tamp down my agitation. I needed time to regroup, and a quiet laboratory environment sounded heavenly.

That's not exactly what I got.

I wasn't used to a lab setting, but clearly Hannah was. I considered her the quietest member of our group and I genuinely liked her because she didn't pretend to be anything she wasn't. Unlike Laura, she wasn't over-sexed and she was mostly interested in the work.

The woman behind the desk showed Hannah and me where we could work. Bernard opted to conduct research on his phone in the lobby, so he remained at the front of the building. I thought we would be alone in a tiny room, but the space the secretary ushered us into was large … and bustling with activity.

I looked to Hannah to see if she was surprised, but she barely paid attention to the other lab technicians, instead heading straight for a microscope and dropping her purse on the floor before sliding on the provided stool. "I'm going to sit here unless it's someone else's station," she announced.

When no one answered, she immediately set about her work. I couldn't help being impressed with her fortitude. "You're a lot more forceful when it comes to being in a lab, huh?"

Hannah smirked as she dug in her bag for the plastic bags she secured before leaving the campsite. "You seem surprised."

"I am. You're usually the quiet one."

"That's because everyone else is so loud. I don't want to simply be another voice in the void."

I pursed my lips as I watched her remove a baggie full of dirt before grabbing a pair of rubber gloves and tugging them into place. "I guess I never thought about it that way. There are a lot of loud voices in the group."

"I don't mind the noise," Hannah said hurriedly. "I'm simply not a noisy person."

"No, you're definitely not." I grabbed an empty stool so I could sit without crowding her, and watched her fast hands as she doled out samples onto slides. "What do you expect to see with the soil samples?"

"Probably nothing, but you never know what you'll find when it comes to stuff like this," Hannah replied. "The big thing I'm looking for is traces of blood in the soil. I took samples from eight different spots."

"Wow!" I'd been wandering around looking for paw prints so I hadn't noticed what Hannah was doing. "Do you think you'll find blood?"

"I have no idea. That's why I'm looking." Hannah took a moment to smile. "You seem quiet yourself today. Is something going on?"

I chuckled at her earnest expression. "I simply got distracted in the woods, which meant I ended up turned around. I was getting close to panicking when Jack found me." I'd already told the lie once so it made sense to keep repeating it, even if it did make me feel like a ninny. "I guess it kind of freaked me out more than I expected."

"I can see that." Hannah was pragmatic, so there was nothing accusatory about her tone. "You were alone when you fought off Zach and Naomi. I'm sure that's still fresh on the surface for you. I don't blame you for being afraid."

"I wasn't afraid," I said hurriedly. "I just ... don't like the feeling of being lost."

"I don't believe anyone likes that feeling." Hannah tied her long hair into a ponytail as she looked me up and down. "I never got a chance to thank you for what you did."

The simple statement threw me. "Why would you thank me? I was simply doing my job."

"You did more than that. You saved Chris ... and Millie. Somehow you managed to keep yourself alive, too. No one else may be saying it, but I know they're all thinking it. What you did that day was impressive."

Hannah wasn't naturally verbose so I felt uncomfortable with her rather obvious scrutiny. "I wasn't trying to be impressive. I was simply trying to get everyone out alive."

"And you managed to do it despite being outnumbered. I don't know anyone else who could've done that. Okay, maybe Jack. No one else, though."

"Jack probably would've done it without falling down the stairs."

"Yes, well, Jack is trained." Hannah was matter-of-fact. "You're barely out of college and you saved three lives. You made it so Chris came back to us ... and I'm extremely thankful for that."

One of the first things I noticed upon joining The Legacy Foundation was the tight bond Chris and Hannah shared. It was one of the things that made me realize harboring a crush on my boss would be a mistake. "Have you considered asking Chris out on a date?" The question was out of my mouth before I realized how idiotic it sounded. Of course, that was the story of my life.

Hannah's cheeks flushed crimson as she lowered her gaze. "Why would you ask that?"

I considered taking a step back and apologizing for overstepping my bounds, but I simply couldn't. When else would I have an opportunity like this? "Because it's obvious you like him."

"It is?" I didn't think it was possible, but Hannah's cheeks turned even redder. "I didn't think anyone realized how I felt about him."

Her voice was so soft I took pity on her. "I think everyone knows but you two."

"Two?" Hannah's puzzled expression made me understand exactly how oblivious she was.

"Oh, you're so cute." I patted her forearm as I searched for the right way to drop the bomb on her. "Okay, here's the thing: Everyone in our group seems to realize that you and Chris are gaga for each other. Everyone but you two, that is. We know you're attracted to him and it's clear he adores you ... even though you clearly don't see it."

Hannah's eyes widened to comical proportions. "You think he adores me?"

"Of course he adores you." I was caught between pity and frustration. "Have you looked at yourself in the mirror lately? Every guy with a pulse would fall all over himself just to get close to you. I swear I'm not making it up."

"She's definitely not." A bearded man stepped to the open work station to our right and offered a grin for Hannah's benefit. He wore a lab coat, and there was a mischievous twinkle in his eyes. "If you want a test date or something, I'm open for offers."

"Oh, well, um … ." Hannah, clearly uncomfortable, shifted from one foot to the other.

I scalded the newcomer with a dark glare. "Don't mess with her. She's already nervous enough."

The man held his hands up. "Sorry. I was just kidding. I couldn't help hearing the tail end of your conversation. I thought I'd take a shot. After all, it's not often that we have two such cute scientists in our midst."

It took me a moment to realize he was including me in that statement. "I'm not a scientist. I'm only here to help out my colleague, who really is a scientist."

"That doesn't mean you're not cute." The guy winked, causing my mouth to drop open.

"This would be an example of the flirting I've heard so much about, right?" Hannah asked, glancing between us. "Is he doing it right? Should I try to emulate him if I'm going to ask Chris out?"

Well, that was a loaded question if I ever heard one. "No, you most definitely shouldn't emulate him," I replied when I found my voice. "His approach is an acquired taste. You won't need it. Chris is already head-over-heels for you."

"So … what should I do?"

"Just ask him out." I opted for honesty. "Hannah, you could ask Chris to spend a day searching through dirt for specific bugs and he'd say yes because he's that enamored with you. The problem is you're both too timid to do anything about it. One of you has to be the brave soul and take a chance."

"And do you think I should be that brave soul or wait for Chris to do it?"

"I think you should do it," I answered without hesitation. "Chris is a fraidy-cat and it will take him forever to get up the courage. Heck, it might take him forever and a full fifth of whiskey to get up the courage. You should do it."

"But … how do I do it?" Hannah was earnest. "I've never asked anyone out before."

"But you have been on a date, right?" I couldn't be sure. Hannah was beautiful, but closed off.

Hannah nodded. "I went out with people when they asked during college – and even a little after – but I stopped agreeing to the requests because I didn't like any of them. I already like Chris."

"And he already likes you. I promise that's true." I licked my lips as I debated what plan I should offer. "I think you should just be calm and self-assured. Wait until he's alone, ask him about his day, and then suggest a quiet dinner with just the two of you. I think you'll be amazed at how fast he jumps at the chance."

"Really?" Hannah didn't look convinced, but I knew I had time to bring her to my way of thinking.

I nodded. "Really." I flicked my eyes to the amused man who continued to watch us as he organized slides. "What is your name?"

"Kent Logan. Why? Are you going to ask me about my day and then invite me to dinner?"

"No."

"That's too bad." Kent's smile was so wide it split his entire face. "I like Mexican, and you happen to be too cute for words."

Despite my determination not to fall victim to his charm, I couldn't stop myself from smiling. "Just out of curiosity, are you local?"

"Will that help my chances for dinner?"

"No. I want to know if you're familiar with someone I met this afternoon, someone I find very intriguing."

"Does this person have a name?"

"Zoe Lake-Winters."

Kent's smile grew even wider. "Oh, well, how much time do you have? Zoe Lake-Winters is famous. So is her husband. As for that kid? She's young, but she's building quite the reputation, too. Who do you want to hear about first?"

That answer was easy. "Zoe … and don't leave anything out."

7

SEVEN

*H*annah's soil samples were a bust, but my mind was bursting with gossipy goodness when we returned to the hotel. I retreated to my room to shower and change – the Michigan humidity was murder – and by the time I returned to the lobby I found almost everyone hanging around and talking.

"So there was no blood or anything?" Jack was focused on Hannah when I sidled up to the couch. I could tell he was doing his best to ignore Laura, who insisted on sitting next to him, and instead glean more information about why we were actually here.

"No blood in any of the samples," Hannah confirmed as she stiffly perched on the arm of the chair in which Chris sat. What she couldn't see was the way his eyes kept drifting to her rear end. She was too nervous to even look at him. I figured I would need another talk with her before the night was over. She had to loosen up if this was going to work.

"That basically means no one died there, right?" Laura interjected, angling her body so Jack had a better view down the vee of her shirt … but only if he wanted to look. Apparently he didn't, because he absolutely refused to look in her direction.

"We don't know that," Chris argued. "We only know that no blood was involved."

"How would your werewolf kill without blood?" Laura challenged. "Do you think he's walking around with poison or taking the time to strangle people?"

"You know I don't like that word," Chris shot back. "Use the correct word or ... ."

Laura cocked an eyebrow. "Or what?"

"Don't speak at all," Jack finished for our boss, his discomfort obvious. "I don't care who uses what word. I care about being helpful. If you can't be helpful, Laura, then shut your trap."

Laura had the audacity to look affronted. "I was trying to help!"

Jack ignored her screech, pushing himself to a standing position before stepping over the glass coffee table in the middle of the furniture arrangement. He glanced around for a moment and then grabbed my arm to drag me to the middle of the second couch – the one across the table from Laura – before he sat at the end. I realized right away it wasn't because he wanted to be close to me, but rather that he wanted to ensure Laura couldn't sit next to him and continue her relentless flirting.

"So what do we have?" Bernard asked, leading the conversation toward something constructive.

"We have two missing people who haven't been seen in days," Jack answered. "Their cell phones are off. They haven't pinged on a tower in more than three days. We have no idea when they went missing because they were supposed to be camping for three days. We have no idea how they went missing. That's basically it."

Chris stirred. "That's nowhere near everything we have. You're forgetting the prints on the ground, which were definitely canine in nature. You're also omitting the claw marks on the tent and the way the campground was trashed. We very clearly have the makings of a lycanthrope attack."

Jack managed to keep his temper in check, but just barely. "No, we have a disturbed campsite. You can't prove that damage wasn't faked in an attempt to cover up a crime."

"How would that even happen?"

"They're rich, right?" I asked, drawing several sets of eyes to me as I worked through a scenario. "Maybe someone knew they were going to be isolated, followed them out there, and waited for them to let down their guards to attack."

"To what end?" Millie asked.

I shrugged. "Money? Perhaps kidnappers took them for a ransom."

"The police have talked to the parents," Chris argued. "No ransom demand has been made."

"Maybe something else happened," I offered. "Maybe the husband – his name is Ethan, right? – maybe he put up a fight. Maybe they killed him during the fight and they panicked and then killed Lisa. There are a lot of variables we can't account for."

Jack pursed his lips. "I can't believe you're the one agreeing with me," he muttered.

"Oh, I didn't say I agreed with you. I simply said we have no proof it was a lycanthrope attack. We need more information."

"Do you have any idea how to get that information?" Millie asked.

That question led to thorny answers I wasn't keen on exploring. "I don't know. People live out there, though. That woman I ran into – who has quite the saucy reputation, for the record – is only one of a handful of people who live in the area. Maybe a hunter ran into them in the woods, accidentally shot someone and then messed up the campsite to make people think it was a lycanthrope. The legend about the Dog Man might simply have been a handy tale."

"And here I thought you couldn't be logical," Jack said, shaking his head. "Both of those scenarios are possibilities. While you guys were at the lab, I did some research on the families in the area. The one that lives closest is the Winters family."

Jack grabbed a folder from the coffee table and flipped it open, withdrawing a large photograph that featured three faces. "This is Aric Winters." He tapped on a strapping man I recognized from the memories in Zoe's head. "He's the son of Senator Winters, who has a financial stake in the company that owns the land where the Savages were camping."

"Well, isn't he just a tall drink of water." Laura's eyes sparkled as she stared at the photograph. "He's rich, too, right? If he's a senator's son he'd have to be."

Jack shot a quick look to me, something unsaid passing through his eyes, and then he shook his head. "He's also married. See the blonde in the photo? Her name is Zoe Lake-Winters. They've been married for thirteen years."

Laura wasn't about to be deterred. "That doesn't mean they're happily married."

I thought about the images from the shared vision. "I'm guessing that their life isn't always happy, but they're dedicated to one another."

Jack shot me an odd look. "Why would you say that?"

I realized I'd said more than I'd intended and quickly crashed back to reality. "She briefly talked about her husband in the woods. She didn't mention problems."

"Why would she?" Laura let loose a derisive snort. "It's not as if you two bonded after talking for thirty seconds. She doesn't know you. She's not going to confide in you."

We might not have bonded, but we shared something profound, and I couldn't (no matter how hard I tried) force the images from my mind. "No. I guess you're right."

"I think you should totally move on him," Millie suggested.

Laura preened. "Because I'm prettier than her, right?"

"Because I want to see you get your ass kicked and I'm pretty sure that woman can do it without breaking a sweat," Millie countered, rolling her eyes. "Focus on the problem at hand, Laura. No one cares about your non-existent love life."

Laura growled and folded her arms across her chest. Thankfully she opted to remain silent so we could continue talking about the Winters family. I was anxious to hear what Jack had discovered.

"It's not easy to find information on Aric and Zoe Winters," Jack continued. "They attended Covenant College together. Aric graduated. No graduation records for Zoe can be found, yet it appears she actually matriculated there and perhaps someone paid a lot of money to make that information go away."

Now, that was interesting. "Why would someone do that?"

Jack shrugged. "I don't know. They lived off the grid for five years after what should have been her college graduation. Their life on paper isn't easy to track. Suddenly, five years after they apparently went into hiding, they came out of hiding."

"Is that when they moved here?" I was enthralled by the story.

Jack shook his head. "They lived here while they were in hiding. They kept to themselves and didn't broadcast their whereabouts. Apparently they just decided to stop at some point. Samantha Winters was born about eight months after they stopped hiding. They seem to mind their own business and stay out of trouble, although there's some … um, I guess colorful would be the word … stuff in some of the notations I've been able to find."

Now we were getting somewhere. "Like what?" I was practically salivating.

Jack slid me a sidelong look. "Why are you so interested in Zoe Lake-Winters?"

"I found her fascinating in the two minutes we spent together." I opted to leave out the part when I magically saw flashes of her life and knew her to be so much more than she appeared to be. "I just want to know what you know. I heard a bit of gossip this afternoon at the lab, too."

"Okay." Jack cleared his throat and turned back to the file. "Aric Winters heads his father's lumber company. It's a very lucrative business."

"Ha! I knew he was rich." Laura was triumphant. "What else can you tell me about him?"

Jack stared at her for a long beat, his distaste on full display. "I can tell you he's married and almost every story in his wife's dossier features a cameo by him."

"Which means there's probably strain on the marriage." Laura rubbed her hands over the knees of her jeans. "Go on."

I wanted to challenge her regarding her insistence on chasing Jack right up until the moment when she thought there was a potentially eligible rich guy hanging around, but I stopped myself from making a scene. Laura didn't have a chance with Aric Winters. There was no reason for me to point that out.

"Wow." Jack made a face before handing me the photograph and focusing on the typed information beneath it. "Sami Winters goes to the local middle school. Her parents seem interested in her studies and attend events. Their house is supposedly magnificent. It's a log cabin deal that Aric designed and had built for them. It's located off the main highway."

"That's great. The house sounds awesome." Laura beamed. "Has the wife been locked up for mental problems or anything? That would be really helpful now."

"I don't believe Zoe Lake-Winters has ever been locked up in a mental ward," Jack said dryly.

"I don't think so either." I stared at the photograph. "She's famous around here, though."

"How so?" Millie asked. "Does she do a special dance to entice men or something?"

"No, she simply doesn't put up with any crap," I replied. "We met this guy at the lab, Kent Logan. He was very talkative. He's local and had a lot of information."

"He tried to trade that information to Charlie for a date." Hannah giggled at the memory. "He was totally hot for her. Charlie played it cool, though. I was very impressed, because he was cute and seemed really good at the flirty stuff."

Chris furrowed his brow. "You thought he was cute?"

Hannah bobbed her head, clearly missing his distress. "He had a beard."

"Yes, he looked like Grizzly Adams," I agreed. "Except younger … and a little more manscaped. More important than his looks is the fact that he had a lot of information on the Winters family."

"Let's hear it," Laura prodded. "And, for the record, I'm more interested in the gossip about him, but if there's something I can use against her I'm all for it."

"Whatever." I blew out a sigh and shifted my eyes to Jack. I expected him to be eager to hear the gossip, too. Instead I found him glaring. "What?"

"You spent your afternoon picking up a date? You were supposed to be helping Hannah."

I balked. "I didn't pick up a date."

"It wasn't for lack of trying on his part," Hannah countered.

"You were supposed to be working with Hannah." Jack's voice was sharp and laced with annoyance. "This is not play time. It's work time."

I shifted on my seat. "I was working."

Hannah turned earnest. "She really was, Jack. She helped me as much as she could. Kent did all the talking. He inserted himself in our conversation and asked Charlie out a few times. She refused, although was nice enough to him to secure some information."

"Oh." Jack pressed the heel of his hand to his forehead. "I guess that's okay then."

"Oh, gee, Dad," I drawled. "Thanks for your permission."

Jack ignored my snarky response. "What did you learn? I mean ... I don't think the Winters family is necessarily guilty or even believable as suspects, but they're the nearest ones to the location so we can't rule them out."

"I heard a lot of stories. Some of them are sort of fantastical," I replied. "The first is that they used to have some sort of electrified fence surrounding their property. I guess that would've been active during the years you said they were hiding. Apparently they don't use it much now, but there have been occasions when they've turned it on."

"And how did your buddy Kent know that?" Jack challenged.

"I guess it's common knowledge; hunters know to be on the lookout for it."

Hannah nodded. "That's what he said. People are afraid to get electrocuted, so they watch for it."

Jack was mollified, but only slightly. "Well ... what else?"

"There are a lot of rumors about them." I worked hard to keep Jack's harsh words from settling like an anchor around my neck. He was brittle when he wanted to be. He was also good at his job. I tried to remind myself that he was simply trying to be diligent and not a really big turd. "For one, apparently a woman and her child went missing in this area about a year ago. Some people claim the last place she visited was the Winters house. She was never seen again."

"And people think the Winters family had something to do with that?" Chris asked, intrigued.

I shrugged. "There's a lot of gossip about the Winters, Zoe in particular. There's a little bit about Aric. Apparently he's been known to run around the woods naked. A few hunters claim to have gotten a gander at … well, everything … near dawn a couple of times. Kent says there's a rumor that he and his wife are into some freaky stuff."

"Like freaky sexual stuff?" Laura asked.

"I have no idea."

"As fascinating as I find romping naked in the woods, I'm more interested in stories that will lead to a motivation for murder – or at least kidnapping – so let's focus on that," Jack ordered. "What else did you hear?"

"I heard that last summer the kid was at a special camp when something happened and Zoe got in a fight with the other mothers and threatened to kill them," I answered. "That's not the first time she laid down the law with people she didn't like. Apparently she's one heck of a brawler."

"Maybe she's the lycanthrope," Chris suggested. "Maybe she was in the woods looking around because she wanted to make sure she'd covered her tracks."

That didn't sound likely to me. "Why would she take her kid into the woods with her to cover up a murder?"

"She's probably too young to be left home alone."

"She's thirteen," Jack corrected. "She's more than old enough to spend a few hours watching herself. I have to agree with Charlie on this one. I don't think it makes much sense for a mother – even if she is some sort of weird killer – to take her kid on a search of the woods. I think something else was going on."

"What did she say?" Millie asked. "You're the only one who spent time with her, Charlie. She must have said something to you."

In truth, Zoe said very little to me during our brief conversation. Most of what I learned was from the visions we'd shared. It wasn't just me seeing flashes of her life. She saw things from my past as well. That left me unsettled, even though part of me couldn't help but want to trust the woman.

"She didn't say much. She said they lived close by and went for a walk because they'd heard the news in town. They wanted to look around."

"That's it?"

I nodded. "That's it."

"Well, we're going to need more than that." Chris slowly stood. "We need to find a way to get more information."

I wholeheartedly agreed, although there was no way I intended to share my plan for getting that information. "That sounds like a good idea," I lied. "We should get some dinner first, though. I'm starving."

"You and me both." Chris beamed. "Let's hit the dining room and we'll start making plans from there. We're going to have a busy few days."

That's exactly what I was hoping for. If everyone was busy, it would be easier for me to slip away and confront Zoe. Right now, that was essentially the only thing on which I could focus. Everything else would have to take a back seat.

EIGHT

*D*inner was full of energy and conversation.

Hannah planted herself next to Chris and stared at him adoringly whenever he wasn't looking. Then, when she glanced away, Chris did the same to her. It was beyond frustrating. I figured one or both of them would need a little push to get things going.

Fred Pitman, the annoying owner of the inn, had a few stories of his own about Aric and Zoe Winters. His tales seemed bitter and mean – especially the one in which he swore up and down that they were nymphomaniacs because he was certain they once had sex in a vehicle parked on a downtown street – but he also had interesting tidbits about the family as a whole. My one takeaway was that Aric and Zoe Winters seemed to protect their child above all else, even if it made them appear wacky and overprotective.

I was fairly certain I knew why.

I said my goodnights early, claiming I had a headache, before retiring. Then I sat in my room for a full hour before pressing my ear to the door. I heard some of my colleagues return from dinner, laughing gregariously in the hallway before separating to their rooms for the night. Once I was certain that no one remained in the hallway, I let myself out and headed to the main floor.

One of the things I found most interesting about the inn is that Pitman had a key board and insisted that guests register their vehicles, leaving the keys on the board when not driving. That made things easier because I planned to "borrow" one of our rentals and drive to the Winters house.

That was the only thing on my mind as I crossed the lobby and focused on the girl behind the desk. That's why I didn't see Millie until she stepped directly into my path and cocked her head, forcing me to pull up short.

"I … um … what are you doing here?" As far as greetings go, it wasn't my best attempt.

"The same thing you are," Millie replied, keeping her voice low. "I'm going to spy on the Winters family."

I tried to play it cool, but my gaping mouth wouldn't allow me that small pleasure. "W-what?"

"Oh, don't do that." Millie made a tsking sound with her tongue. "I saw you over dinner. I could practically hear the gears in your mind working. You're fascinated with the woman. You might be able to hide it from everyone else, but not me. If you're fascinated with her, there must be a reason."

Oh, there was definitely a reason. That didn't mean I wanted to drag Millie into my espionage excursion. "Well … ."

Millie held up a finger to silence me. "I'll make this easy for you. I'm going. If you try to sneak out without me, I'll make a fuss. Jack was adamant about no one taking off alone this afternoon. It shook him a bit when you disappeared."

"It shook him?" That's not exactly how I remembered things. "Why would it shake him? I'd think he'd prefer it if I disappeared in the woods and was never seen or heard from again."

"You only think that because you're an idiot. You'll figure out the truth on your own going forward."

I had no idea what that was supposed to mean. "Millie, I'm not sure you should be involved in this," I said. "I'm about to break some really big rules."

"You are," Millie agreed. "They're the same rules we broke a few weeks ago, in fact. That's one of the reasons I'm going with you."

"How will that help?"

"I can't get in trouble," Millie reminded me. "Given my position with the family, I can essentially do whatever I want. You don't have that luxury. This way, if I steal the Jeep and force you to go along you're in the clear."

It made sense, which only forced my worry to grow exponentially. "I don't know. What if they are dangerous? What if they really are lycanthropes and they try to kill us?"

"I don't think you believe they're werewolves."

I didn't. At least as far as Zoe was concerned, I was almost certain she was something else. That didn't mean I felt good about potentially sharing her secret with Millie. It didn't feel fair. It wasn't something I'd expect Zoe to do to me if our roles were reversed. Of course, she could be sharing what she saw during our brain meltdown even now. I had no way of knowing.

"Well . . . ."

"We're going together." Millie was firm as she lifted her hand and jangled the keys. "I already secured us a vehicle and everything."

Well, great. It looked as if I had no choice. "Okay, but if I sense something is about to go wrong and I tell you to run, you'd better do what I say. I know you're older and technically the boss, but something really weird happened this afternoon and I'm desperate for answers."

"You'll get no argument from me." Millie was smug as she fell into step with me. "So, just out of curiosity, what did happen this afternoon?"

"I'm not sure you'll believe me if I tell you."

"Try me."

WE WERE PARKING ON THE ROAD that led to the Winters house, making sure to hide the Jeep the best we could before proceeding on foot, when I finished the story.

"I don't know what to make of it." I zipped my black hoodie, hating the sweat that rolled down my back thanks to the stifling fabric and high humidity. "I want to talk to her, but I can't do it with Jack and the others around."

"Wow! That's quite the story." Millie shrugged into her own black hoodie before pocketing the keys. "Did she seem as surprised as you felt?"

I searched my memory. "She did. She seemed really curious, too. Unlike me, though, she wasn't afraid."

"How do you know that?"

I shrugged. "It's a feeling. I can sometimes read emotions. She didn't seem all that surprised at what she saw in my memories, while what I saw in hers completely threw me. I mean … I swear I saw magical power beams flying through the air at one point. I can't figure out where they were coming from, but they were definitely there."

"Now I really want to meet her." Millie beamed as she followed me into the woods. "She sounds like she's extremely powerful."

"She does," I agreed. "I think she's the most powerful being I've ever come across."

"More powerful than you?"

"I'm not that powerful. I can do, like, two things, my parlor tricks, if you will. If what I saw in those flashes was any indication, Zoe Lake-Winters can do a heckuva lot more than I can."

"Which probably means her husband is aware of her abilities, and that's why they went into hiding in the first place," Millie mused, her eyes focused on the ground so she didn't accidentally trip over a branch. "I'm going to guess they've led a rather interesting life if what you saw in those visions is true. Was there any one part that stood out?"

I nodded without hesitation. "Yeah. The part where she died."

Millie came to a complete standstill. "What?"

"She died," I repeated. "It wasn't just that I saw it. I felt it. It was almost as if I was there with her."

"If she died, how is she here now?"

"I don't know." I thought about my parents and how they died so young. "I want to know how she did it. She cheated death. Although – and I know this is going to sound strange but I swear it's true – she seemed almost surprised when she realized she was still alive."

"How do you know that?"

"I felt her emotions. She was ready to let go. I mean ... she was unbelievably sad. The husband was practically screaming he was so upset and the girl ... well, she was a mess of tears and fear. Whatever happened was big enough that Zoe felt she'd done her very best and realized she was okay with dying. It was one of the most profound moments I've ever witnessed."

"Which is part of the reason you're obsessed with seeing her again," Millie surmised. "You want to know if you can learn how to cheat death, don't you?"

I hadn't really considered the question until Millie brazenly asked it. "I'm more interested if I can stop death for others."

"Oh, that's a load of crap." Disbelief flashed in Millie's eyes. "No one wants to die, Charlie. It's okay to be curious about what this woman can do. If you're similar and can do it yourself, that might change things for you."

That was true, but .... "That's not the first thing I thought of when I saw the flash." I opted for honesty. "I thought about my parents. And, yeah, I know they've been gone way too long to help. But if I could've helped back then, perhaps saved them, I can't help but wonder how different my life would've been.

"So, yeah, in theory it would be great to save myself if the opportunity arose," I continued. "But I really am more interested in helping others."

"Then I guess we should see if we can find this magical wonder." Millie flashed a genuine smile. "Just out of curiosity, do you have any idea how you're going to approach this?"

I nodded, causing Millie's eyebrows to wing up her forehead.

"I thought we would hide behind some trees at the back of the property and see if we catch a glimpse of them," I explained. "Once I'm comfortable spying and know where they are, I thought I would make a rash decision on the spot and possibly get us killed."

71

Millie didn't appear bothered by the admission. "Well, at least you have a plan."

IT TOOK US A LONG time to wind through the woods and find a spot that was comfortable to spy from. The back of the sprawling property looked up at a beautiful elevated deck that ran the entire length of the house. The yard was green, lush, and sloped toward the woods. There also looked to be a hot tub off to one side, offset by romantic lights, which offered a pretty place where I was certain Zoe and her husband spent a lot of their time.

We watched in silence for a good twenty minutes, but nothing stirred. I could see lights from the second floor of the house – it made me think someone was in the living room watching television – but there was no movement. I was just about to suggest to Millie that we move closer for a better look when a first-floor door opened and allowed two people to exit.

"I still can't believe you talked me into having a kid." I recognized Zoe's voice right away. She had a certain cadence that couldn't be mimicked. "That was a stupid idea, huh?"

I couldn't initially make out the individual who chuckled as he followed but I wasn't surprised to see the man from the visions once a beam of light from the balcony runners hit his face. "You talk big but you kind of like her," Aric Winters said, his voice full of light and mirth.

"Oh, come on," Zoe countered. "I'm not saying I don't love her, but there are still times I would like to trade her for a cat."

"You don't like cats."

"I like cats," Zoe countered. "They're easy to take care of and they don't chew shoes. That thing upstairs watching Netflix with Sami has eaten at least three shoes in the past six months. A cat wouldn't do that."

"A cat wouldn't protect her from attack either," Aric pointed out as he sauntered toward the hot tub. It was only when he closed the distance that I realized he had towels draped over his arm. Crap! They were hitting the hot tub, which meant there was a very good chance they might get naked. Laura might want to see something like that, but I was fairly certain I'd never get over the mortification. "At least at times like this, times when we want to be alone, we know Trouble will alert if someone tries to get in the house."

"No one will try to get into the house." Zoe stopped next to the hot tub and kicked off her shoes. "We haven't heard as much as a whisper from potential enemies in almost a year."

I risked a glance at Millie and found she was intent on the conversation. She didn't as much as move a muscle or make a sound while breathing. I was so edgy I feared I would fall forward, make a ruckus in the bushes and cause what I was sure would be a terrifying and painful death.

"You can't just assume no one will ever come after us again, Zoe." Aric's tone was gentle but firm. "What happened was amazing – and I'm certainly glad that no one has bothered us since – but I don't think our luck will hold forever. We can't let down our guard."

Aric stripped off his shirt, revealing one of the most muscled chests I'd ever seen. He was tall to the point I swore he could've doubled as a male model – even though records put him at older than forty – and I had to blink several times to believe what I was seeing.

"I didn't say we should let down our guard," Zoe argued, her eyes trained on her husband's face. "I'm just saying that … things are quieter now. The big battle is behind us."

"*Our* big battle," Aric corrected. "I think people have learned their lessons about coming after you. Heck, they better have. You've sent more messages than Western Union. That doesn't mean that Sami won't make an enticing target again at some point. No one knows exactly what she did that day, and if rumors are to be believed, most of the community thinks you're the one who razed the school."

Most of what they said didn't make sense to me. Razed the school? Did that mean they destroyed an entire school? Was that where they were in the vision I saw, the one where Zoe was dying and then suddenly she was alive and embracing her family? If I focused hard on what I remembered from those images, it did sort of look like a school. I made a mental note to do a little research. If they destroyed a school, surely that would've made the news.

"I would rather they think it was me than her," Zoe said, holding out a hand when Aric reached for his shorts. "Don't get naked."

Aric's expression was hard to read, but I was certain the smile on his face reflected surprise rather than disappointment. "Since when don't you want me to get naked?"

"Oh, there have been plenty of times when I haven't wanted you to get naked." Zoe made a face that caused my lips to curve. "You have a big head and assume I always want to see you naked because that means you'll get sex. That's not happening tonight."

"It's not?" Aric's smile slipped. "Why did you get me all excited for a hot tub night if you're going to make me suffer through something else? You said we were going to spend some quality time together. That means hot tub time. What else did you have in mind?"

"I said we were going to do something important outside," Zoe clarified. "I didn't say anything about the hot tub."

"You saw me grab the towels."

"I did. I thought about telling you to put them back, but then I realized they'd make good cover."

Aric knit his eyebrows. "What kind of cover?"

"I wanted to get a feeling for the people hiding in the bushes watching us without them realizing what I was doing," Zoe replied, causing my heart to plummet to my stomach. "If they thought we knew they were out here they would've run, which meant we would've had to chase them. It's too hot to run."

Aric let loose a wild growl as he dropped the towels and adopted a territorial stance, sweeping out his arm to shove Zoe behind him. Zoe easily sidestepped her husband and focused her eyes on the exact spot where we hid.

"Who is it, Zoe?" Aric sounded as if he was about to start ripping out hearts and tongues. "Where?"

"Don't worry about it." Zoe took three long strides in our direction. "They're not dangerous. Er, well, at least I don't think they're dangerous. I guess they could be dangerous, but I don't happen to believe so."

"Ugh. I hate it when you're purposely vague."

"I know." Zoe took another step, narrowing her eyes until she finally snagged my gaze through the heavy foliage. "There you are, Charlie. I've been expecting you."

And just like that my covert mission turned into something else entirely. I really should've seen that coming.

NINE

J was uncomfortable as I stood, my heart hammering and my cheeks burning. I kept my gaze on Zoe and did my best to ignore her large and intimidating husband.

"You knew we were out here."

Zoe pursed her lips and nodded. She looked amused, which seemed completely inappropriate for the situation.

"How long have you known?"

Zoe shrugged. "A little bit. Before we left the house. I'm assuming it was after you parked and picked your way through the woods. That probably wasn't a smart move, by the way. We have roaming security."

I had no idea what that meant. "How does it roam?"

"Very carefully." Zoe folded her arms over her chest and looked to Millie's crouching form. "Your friend doesn't have to hide. I knew you weren't alone. It would've been stupid for you to come here without backup."

"Um ... right." I grabbed Millie's arm and gave it a tug. "Stand up. She knows you're here."

"Fine." Millie grumbled as she dusted off the knees of her jeans and stood. There was something defiant about her stance as she glanced between Aric and Zoe. "Do you have a problem with us being here?"

Aric's face relaxed into something akin to a smile as he shook his head. "You brought your grandmother to eavesdrop with you? I have to say, that's a new one."

Millie was angry. "I'm not her grandmother! We're co-workers."

"It would've been a funnier story if you were her grandmother." Aric was blasé as he flicked his eyes to me. "You're the woman my wife met in the woods this afternoon, aren't you?"

I swallowed hard and nodded. "Yes."

"How did you find your way here?"

"Everyone in town knows who you are." I opted for a false veneer of bravado, as if I weren't terrified of what the couple – especially the woman – were capable of. "You two are famous in local gossip circles, in case you're interested."

"I create a stir wherever I go," Zoe agreed, grinning. "I think you and I should have a talk, Charlie. I was expecting to see you again. I didn't think you'd pull a boneheaded move like this, but I have to give you credit for being courageous even though your survival skills seem to be lacking."

Millie narrowed her eyes before I had a chance to respond. "Was that a threat?"

Zoe shook her head. "I have no interest in threatening her. However, I do have an interest in talking to her. I was considering trying to find her tomorrow, after some sleep and a little more time spent thinking. I'm guessing Charlie is the impulsive sort. That's not necessarily a bad thing. I was that way for a number of years."

Aric made a face. "Are you suggesting that you're no longer impulsive?"

"I'm saying that I've matured with age," Zoe replied. "I think things through now."

"Really?" Aric snorted. "Two days ago, on a whim, you decided you were going to throw a net over the beehive at the back of the property. You thought that would keep the bees inside, allowing you to keep a promise you made to me a very long time ago about not killing the bees while still keeping them from landing on you. What happened?"

77

"I don't think now is the time to bring this up." Zoe sent Aric a pointed glare. "Our guests don't want to hear about the bees."

"Oh, that's where you're wrong," Millie countered. "I totally want to hear about the bees."

"Well, great." Zoe wrinkled her nose. "This is exactly how I saw my night going."

"Since you won't tell them, I will," Aric said. "You threw a net over the hive and the bees crawled through the holes and chased you through the yard. You screamed so loud I thought it was Sami being … well, Sami. I'm pretty sure that was an impulsive decision."

"I thought the netting holes were smaller," Zoe argued. "That would've been a good plan if we'd had the proper netting."

"Whatever." Aric rolled his neck. "I'm simply pointing out that you calling someone else on impulsive behavior is a bit hypocritical. Of course, I married you either because of or in spite of that impulsive behavior, so what does that say about me?"

"You're a glutton for punishment," Zoe answered as she locked gazes with me. "Why don't you take Charlie's grandmother in the house and give her some juice or something? I need to talk to Charlie."

Aric sobered. "Are you sure that's a good idea?"

"I'm not her grandmother," Millie barked. "I'm also not sure leaving her alone is a good idea. I mean … can you promise me your wife won't kill her? We're here looking for a werewolf. I don't know if you realize that or not, but if your wife is a werewolf I don't think it's a good idea to leave her with Charlie. She's young, so Charlie is probably a nice meal for a werewolf. You know, soft and tender."

Aric didn't bother to hide his smirk as he glanced at his wife before focusing on Millie. "I swear my wife isn't a werewolf and won't eat her. She'll be perfectly safe … as long as she doesn't move on my wife."

Now it was my turn to balk. "That's not why I'm here."

"I know."

"How do you know that?"

"Because Zoe has a feeling about you and I've learned to listen when she has a feeling," Aric replied, holding out his arm for Millie to link hers through. "Come on. I'll help you up the steps."

"I'm not old," Millie complained bitterly as she moved toward him. "You're acting as if I'm ancient."

"The steps aren't illuminated," Aric countered. "It's simply for safety, not a reflection of your age."

"I'll have you know I'm only agreeing to this because you're hot and shirtless," Millie offered, causing my lips to curve.

"I'm fine with that. In fact … ." Aric didn't get a chance to finish because a shriek emanated from the elevated deck, causing the hair on the back of my neck to stand on end as I readied myself for attack.

"Daddy!"

I realized it was Sami – she sounded as if she was in mortal peril – and braced myself to run up the stairs in an attempt to help. Neither Aric nor Zoe moved to race to their child's aid, though, so I remained rooted to my spot.

"What's wrong, Sami?" Aric yelled out. "How many times have I told you not to screech like that unless you're actually under attack?"

Sami, her dark hair pulled back in a ponytail, appeared at the edge of the deck and looked down. She registered surprise when she saw us. "How do you know I'm not in danger?" Sami asked her father while focusing on me. "You're the woman from the woods this afternoon."

"I am." I forced a smile for the kid's benefit. "You look like your father."

"And acts like her mother," Aric muttered, glaring at his child. "I know you're not in danger because you have different screams. That was your 'my life is going to end because I broke a nail' scream. It's not the same as your 'there are monsters breaking through the windows trying to eat me' scream."

Sami rolled her eyes. "Whatever. The remote control isn't working."

Aric made a comical face. "Did you change the batteries?"

"I don't know where they are."

"They're in the drawer in the kitchen where everything that doesn't have a specific place to live goes to die," Aric supplied. "Change the batteries."

"Can't you do it?" Sami sounded whiny, and when I risked a glance at Zoe I found her smirking instead of frowning.

Aric growled low in his throat as he ushered Millie toward the stairs and scowled at his wife. "You were right. We should've remained childless."

Zoe shrugged. "Live and learn."

"Yeah, yeah." Aric paused when he hit the bottom step and shifted to face me. "Zoe says you're okay, that you're not a threat. I believe her, but I'm going to throw this out there all the same.

"If you move on my wife, if you try to hurt her, I will rip your heart from your chest and feed it to the first werewolf I find," he continued. "That's after she's finished with you, of course, and she's a lot meaner and more inventive than I am."

For some reason the fact that he even remotely considered me a threat to his wife bolstered my confidence. "I'm not here to hurt her. I just want to ... talk."

Aric nodded. "I know. I get it. But she's my wife, and I will kill for her."

"I understand. You don't have to worry about me." I watched him go, doing my best to ignore the way Millie fawned over him – and the inappropriate things she said about his chest – and waited until I was sure it was just Zoe and me to speak again. "You're being awfully gracious for someone who found two strangers spying from your bushes."

"I guess that's how you'd see it." Zoe gestured toward a set of chairs near a fire pit. "From my perspective, I knew you would come."

"Because of what you saw in my head?"

"What makes you think I saw anything in your head?" Zoe asked. "That's a weird thing to say."

I couldn't decide if she was playing coy to monitor my reaction or if she really thought I'd fall for the lie and opted to say it as a way to discourage me from questioning her further. "Because I saw things in your head, too."

"Really?" Zoe crossed one leg over the other and leaned back in her wooden chair as I did my best to get comfortable in the other. "And what did you see?"

"I saw your husband at various stages of your life. I saw ... at least I think I saw ... your hands glowing blue."

Zoe held up her hands. "Glowing, huh?" She shook them. "They seem to be on the fritz."

I pressed my lips together as I debated how to proceed. "I get that you're trying to protect yourself. You have no idea who I am or what I'm capable of doing. You have a family you need to protect."

"My family is my biggest priority," Zoe agreed. "I'll do whatever it takes to keep them safe. I don't think that's out of the ordinary for most people."

"No, probably not." I scratched my upper lip, convinced angry bees lurked in the area and were ready to strike. "Do you know what happened to the people in the woods? Did you have something to do with their disappearances?"

Whatever she was expecting, that wasn't it. For a brief moment I saw a flash of uncertainty buzz through Zoe's brain. She shuttered it quickly and forced a smile. "Do you think I had something to do with their disappearances?"

"I don't know." I opted for honesty. "The things I saw ... they happened so fast. I couldn't quite understand what I saw. The only thing I did understand was that you and your husband are a unit ... and you're the sort of unit that manages to survive terrible things because you work together."

"I think that's a fair assessment." Zoe tilted her head to the side. "I did some research after our meeting in the woods. I placed a few calls to learn about the people staying in town and came up with a name, one I think you volunteered before I really started listening. The Legacy Foundation is a big operation. It's so big I almost glossed over the fine print of the description. If I'd done that, I would've missed the part that said the group searches for paranormal creatures."

"I think that's a rather simplistic version of what we do," I offered.

"Okay. What do you do?"

"I don't know. This is my fourth assignment with the group. I've only been out of college a few weeks."

Zoe snorted, amusement evident. "That's ... freaking priceless. You're very funny. Back in the day, you're exactly the sort of person I would've surrounded myself with in college. I like to think I have good instincts, and my instincts say I should trust you. Of course, my instincts also had me trusting evil losers a time or two over the years, too, so I never do anything without giving it a lot of thought these days ... no matter what my husband says to the contrary."

"Bees?"

Zoe nodded. "They're evil. He doesn't get it, but I do."

I chuckled as I rubbed the back of my head, weariness threatening to overtake me. "You're not going to tell me why our minds joined like they did, are you?"

"I can't say that I remember that happening." Zoe was a master at controlling a situation. I could see that, sense her determination to remain enigmatic. "If something like that did happen, though, I would imagine it wasn't on purpose. Perhaps it occurred because two like minds crossed paths when neither was expecting it."

"So you don't know why it happened either."

Zoe smirked. "I don't know what you're talking about."

"Right." I briefly pressed my eyes shut. "You're sure you didn't kill the people in the woods? I'd hate to start liking you and then find out you're a murderer."

"I didn't have anything to do with the disappearances." Zoe sobered. "I was out there looking for answers, the same as you. I'm just as concerned about what could have happened as you, maybe more so because it essentially went down in my backyard."

"Did you find anything?"

"Just you."

"Will you keep looking?"

Zoe nodded and leaned forward. "I can't give you what you want, at least not right now. I'm sorry if that's disappointing, but it's another reason I was waiting to seek you out. I don't know you. You could very well be a good person – and I think you probably are – but you said it yourself: My family is my number one priority."

"And you can't trust me because you don't know me." I honestly understood where she was coming from. Her family had to take precedence over the needs of a virtual stranger. "Can I ask you one thing, though, even if you don't answer the question?"

Zoe nodded.

"Did you die?"

Zoe jolted, but regained control of herself relatively quickly. "Why would you ask that?"

"I saw. I saw what looked to be a burning building ... and a gun ... and your crying husband and child. I felt what you felt for a moment. You were willing to go if it meant they'd be safe. All of it overwhelmed me."

"Is that what you felt when your friend arrived?" Zoe asked, not bothering to deny my description. "Were you feeling the aftereffects of death?"

"No." I shook my head. "I was feeling something else. I don't know how to describe it, but I haven't been able to shake the feeling all day. That's why I asked around town about you. Your reputation is out there, by the way. According to the guy I talked to, you're the most hated and feared woman in town."

Instead of being offended, Zoe grinned. "I've worked hard for that reputation. It's exactly what I want."

"Because you've been hunted?"

Zoe shrugged. "I've been many things. Are you asking if I've been hunted because of what happened in the woods? Do you think they were hunted?"

I shrugged. "My boss is convinced that a werewolf got them. Do you believe in werewolves?"

"I believe in a little bit of everything."

"But you're not a werewolf, right?"

"I'm definitely not."

That made me feel better. I got the distinct impression that Zoe tiptoed around questions she didn't want to answer, but when she did offer a sound response it was the truth. That was simply how she rolled. "So, what do you think happened?"

"I don't know." Zoe's expression turned troubled. "If something attacked in the woods – even though it was a mile away – I have to think I would've felt a ripple. I didn't. That means either something else happened or nothing happened."

The two options threw me for a loop. "What do you mean?"

"Perhaps what happened in those woods is human in nature," Zoe suggested. "Or perhaps two people were looking for attention and set up a scene as a way to get the town buzzing. We don't have enough information to move forward with a workable hypothesis yet."

"But ... we have footprints. We made casts of them. They're canine in nature."

"Not everything is as it appears." Zoe brushed off the seat of her pants as she got to her feet. "Whatever is out there – human or otherwise – you need to be careful. I have a bad feeling about this one, which is the only reason I got involved."

"And we're seriously not going to talk about what happened?"

Zoe's lips curved. "Again, I have no idea what you're talking about."

I heaved out a sigh. "You're a lot of work."

"You're not the first person to tell me that." Zoe tilted her head to the deck and smiled when she saw Millie and Aric talking. They seemed to be having a good time. "Sometimes the work itself is fun, though. Just ask my husband."

"He seems fine with it."

"He does." Zoe turned serious as she glanced at me. "Don't make the mistake of wandering around these woods again after dark. If you need to talk to me, knock on the front door. Don't eavesdrop."

I felt sheepish. "I didn't mean to be rude."

"I don't care about that. I care about what could possibly be in the woods. You need to think before you act. I know it's difficult – trust me, if anyone knows it's me – but you need to think hard right now. I don't know what's out there, but I am concerned that something bad could happen if you don't pay attention. Fight your inner urges and pay attention."

"Are you going to fight your inner urges and do the same?"

Zoe shrugged. "I live by my own set of rules. It's basically, 'Do as I say, not as I do,' in this house."

I was definitely starting to believe that.

TEN

*M*illie couldn't stop talking about Aric and Sami for the duration of the drive back to the inn. Apparently Aric left his shirt off for the entire conversation, which was a big bonus, and even though the kid had a few irritating quirks, Millie was in love with the Winters family.

"Seriously, he must work out ten times a day to get a body like that. Hello, hunka, hunka burning love!"

We were walking up the pathway to the inn, so I felt the need to admonish her. "Yes, he was hot," I hissed. "But you've got to stop talking about it, because our trip has to be a secret. We agreed on that."

Millie's expression turned dour. "Do you think I don't know that? I'm not a rookie. I just can't get over that body. Are you telling me you didn't want to run your fingers over that chest?"

I was fairly certain that Zoe was the type to scratch out eyeballs if someone expressed that sentiment, so I merely shook my head. "He was a nice guy."

"And?"

"And his body was nice, too. You have to stop talking about it, though. We need to get the keys back and pretend we were in our rooms all night. If someone finds out ... ."

"You'll be in a lot of trouble," Jack finished, moving from the shadows offered by a set of trees to our right and cutting off our avenue into the building. He stepped under the bright outdoor lights and let loose a glare that would've shriveled the bowels of almost everybody ... except possibly Millie. "Hello, ladies."

"Uh-oh." I shifted from one foot to the other, uncomfortable.

"Uh-oh is right." Jack's expression wasn't hard to read. He was angry. No, he was royally ticked off. "Where have you two been?"

Millie decided to take control of the conversation. "I don't think that's the most important topic of discussion for the night. I think it's far more important to discuss why you felt it necessary to hide in the trees and then ambush us like some sort of self-righteous ninja. That's a lot weirder than whatever we were doing."

I wasn't a big fan of going on the offensive when in the wrong, but for this particular situation it seemed a good idea. "Yeah." I nodded. "Why are you hiding in the bushes like a ... hiding-in-the-bushes sort of guy?"

Jack rolled his eyes and lifted his phone. "Because after your last excursion with the rental vehicles I decided it would be smart to pay for tracking on future trips. There's an app that provides everything there is to know when a vehicle is in motion. It's a good thing I thought ahead, isn't it? This way I knew when you were coming back and didn't have to call the police to find you."

"Huh." Millie moved her jaw back and forth. "Well, if you knew where we were why did you bother to ask in the first place? That seems like a waste of time."

"I didn't ask you." Jack expectantly held out his hand.

Millie slammed her hand into his and grinned, offering a high-five for the ages. "I'm glad all the uncomfortable stuff is over. Let's move on and forget all about it."

Jack narrowed his eyes to the point where I could see nothing but darkness. "Give me the keys."

"Oh." Millie dug in her pocket and returned with the keys. "There you go. No harm, no foul."

"Oh, there was very much a foul."

"How so?" Millie wasn't in the mood to back down. "We had some-place to be so we took one of the Jeeps. As you're well aware, I am always listed as a driver on the vehicles. If you have a problem with me taking one, I suggest you talk to Chris about it. He is the boss, after all."

"Maybe I will." Jack wrapped his fingers around the keys and glanced between us. "As it stands now, I'll keep this to myself. I don't want to see you two getting in trouble and turning into a distraction. It hardly seems conducive to finding answers about our missing couple."

"Thank you," I offered hurriedly. "I didn't mean for this to turn into a thing."

Millie put her hand on my arm to still me. "Don't let him get your panties in a twist. He's only complaining because he likes the sound of his own voice and hates it when he loses control of the situation. He has no reason to be so upset."

Jack's eyebrows practically flew off his forehead. "No reason? You disappeared without telling anyone where you were going!"

Millie refused to back down. "And we're both adults. We don't have to tell you where we're going."

"You do if you take one of the rental vehicles."

"No, we really don't." Millie used her hip to nudge Jack out of the way. "If you have a problem with what I did – and I'm the one who enlisted Charlie's help – then take it up with Chris and I'll talk to him. Don't try to bully me. I don't like it."

Jack took an inadvertent step back. "I'm not trying to bully you."

"That's exactly what you're trying to do."

"It is not."

Millie poked a finger into Jack's chest for emphasis. "You're not the king here. You're the security expert. You're good at your job. That doesn't mean you get to issue proclamations and edicts about how everyone else should act.

"Think about it," she continued. "You spent your evening watching your phone in an effort to spy on us. That says a little something about you … like you're bored and need to get some action. If that's the case, I think Laura is open for offers."

The look Jack unleashed was straight out of a bad horror movie. "Don't ever say anything like that again."

"Then don't force me to say it." Millie grabbed my arm and jerked me toward the door. "You're not the boss of the world, Jack. You need to understand that. We didn't do anything wrong and we're not going to apologize for exercising our rights as adults and taking a little trip. Get over it."

Jack opened his mouth to continue the argument, but Millie shook her head to cut him off.

"We're done!" She gave me a hard shove through the door and waited for it to close, leaving a perplexed Jack on the other side, before speaking again. "Well, I handled that well. Now he'll spend the entire night thinking about what I said and start tomorrow with an apology."

I was dumbfounded. "Do you really think that's true?"

Millie bobbed her head. "He's a man. I just shamed him. He'll apologize."

"But he didn't technically do anything wrong. We were in the wrong."

"Bite your tongue! We were not in the wrong. As far as I'm concerned, I'm never in the wrong. Mark my words, Jack will be calmer and easier to talk to in the morning. That's exactly what we want."

"What if he's not?"

"Then I'll have to walk through door number two to save us."

"And what is door number two?"

"You wouldn't believe the stuff I have on my ex-husband." Millie's smile was evil. "There's a reason I can do whatever I want, and I only pull that trigger sparingly. Don't worry about it. We'll be fine."

I wanted to believe her, but I'm a worrier by nature. "I hope I don't lose my job."

"You won't. You'll be fine. Trust me."

TRUE TO HER WORD, Millie was right.

Jack was waiting in the hallway when I opened my room door the following morning. He leaned against the wall, his hands behind him, and offered a wan smile when I met his gaze. "I'm sorry about last night."

Everything I thought I believed about men flew out the window. "You're ... sorry?"

"I am." Jack didn't seem keen on the idea of delivering the apology, but here he was all the same. "You have to understand, I was worried when I found out you were gone. It took me a bit to realize Millie was with you. That made me feel worse, not better, and I reacted. I'm sorry for yelling at you."

Wow. That was way too easy. "Oh, well, that's okay." I moved to slip around him. "I don't blame you for being upset. We were out a lot later than we thought we'd be."

"Well, I'm still sorry." Jack caught my arm before I could move too far. "I'm also not an idiot." He lowered his voice so no one inside the rooms to either side could hear us. "I know you two were up to something big last night. I want to know what it is."

Hmm. It seemed Jack wasn't the foolish sort who would apologize and walk away after all. "I'm not sure what you mean," I hedged. "We were just out to ... get some air."

"You're full of crap." Jack spun me around so I had nowhere to look but his serious face. "I know very well that you were out in the middle of the woods last night. At first I thought you went back to the campsite – I mean, you were parked kind of close to that location – but when I ran the GPS information I found that you parked near a house. Do you know who owns that house?"

If that was his version of a trick question he needed to work on his timing. "I have no idea whose name is on the deed."

Jack scowled. "Charlie, are you trying to kill me?"

I shook my head. "No. I can't even figure out why you were

looking for me last night. Is it because you wanted to get me in trouble? I wasn't trying to hurt anyone when I left. I simply … needed to get some air."

I had no idea why I kept coming back to that lie.

"Air is outside." Jack gestured toward the wall. "There's plenty of air out there. You don't need to drive to get to it."

"Maybe I wanted a change of scenery. Did you ever consider that?"

"Not even a little." Frustrated, Jack dragged a hand through his long hair. "Charlie, I came to check on you last night because I was worried. You were off the entire day. In fact, you've been off the better part of the last three weeks, ever since you fought off Zach and managed to save the day.

"Now, most people would chalk that up to you coming to grips with your mortality," he continued. "I thought that was a possibility. The thing is, you lost your parents when you were young. I think you've already come to grips with your mortality. I think something else is going on."

"I'm perfectly fine," I lied, averting my eyes. "I don't know why you're worried about me."

"I don't know why either," Jack muttered, "but I am. You've been moping around for weeks. I thought you'd eventually tell me what was bothering you, but so far that seems to have been a fairytale.

"Then, out of nowhere, you perked up yesterday," he said. "You had your little talk with Millie and you were back to your old self. I have no idea what she said to make you feel better, but I was grateful.

"Then you wandered away," he continued. "You disappeared in the woods, and I thought it was a stroke of luck that I managed to follow. You weren't alone, were you? You were with that woman and her kid. And you were pale enough to see through. I know something happened out there. I want to know what it was."

I always knew Jack was the observant sort, but I was flabbergasted by the amount of attention he'd clearly paid to my life the past few weeks. I didn't even notice him watching, which was probably why he was so good at his job. "I'm okay. I'm not moping around or anything.

I've just been ... thinking, I guess would be the best word ... about everything that happened in Texas."

"What have you been thinking about? Have you been having nightmares?"

I shook my head. "I've been thinking about the Chupacabra and how no one believes I saw it." I knew it was petty, but I couldn't stop myself. "As for yesterday, you're right. I was a little off my game. It was hot and I was searching for footprints when that woman and her daughter caught me off guard. I was simply surprised – and embarrassed because I practically jumped out of my skin because of it. Nothing else was going on."

Jack searched my face for a long moment. "I think more than that is going on, but I won't press you. You're not the quiet type, so I figure you'll tell me when you're ready."

"Seriously, I'm fine."

"No, you're going through the motions and desperate to find a way to be fine," Jack corrected. "But you're not fine. As for Zoe Lake-Winters, I'm not sure what's going on with you and her. I saw the looks on both your faces and there was definitely something there. Do you know her?"

"How would I possibly know her?"

Jack shrugged. "I have no idea. There was more than surprise on your face, though. And, as good as that woman is at masking her feelings she was clearly upset about something. The only one who didn't seem to be upset was the kid."

"Well, kids are often mistaken for sociopaths simply because they don't express standard emotions," I offered. "I learned that in a psych class, by the way. It's totally true. Look it up."

Jack rolled his eyes. "Good grief. You're not fooling anyone."

"I'm not trying to fool anyone. I'm simply trying to be a good worker."

"And that's what you were doing last night, right? You were working."

I nodded without hesitation. "We were definitely working."

"Fine." Jack's forehead puckered as he massaged a finger in the spot between his eyebrows. "I am not going to lose the entire day arguing about this. That's not productive."

"I agree. We should drop it."

"That doesn't mean I'll forget about it," Jack sneered. "Did you see anything of interest while you were hanging around the Winters house last night?"

Now that right there was an interesting question. "No. We didn't see anything of interest. Er, well, Aric Winters was shirtless and Millie thought that was pretty much the best thing she'd ever seen in her entire life. Other than that, no."

"And what about you?"

"I thought he was impressive, too. He's very clearly devoted to his wife. They're joined at the hip."

Jack scowled. "Not that. Did you see anything other than a shirtless man that piqued your interest?"

There were so many ways I could go with that question I didn't know where to begin. Ultimately, I merely shrugged. "No. Not so far. We didn't see much."

"Well, I guess that leaves us with an endless pile of opportunities when it comes to planning our day." Jack stroked his chin, thoughtful. "Chris will want everyone to split up and focus on different things."

"Well, I want to be with whatever group goes to the woods and checks on the campsite again," I said. "I think there's more to discover out there."

"That's what you want, huh?"

Uh-oh. I recognized the look on Jack's face right away. "I ... um ... want to do whatever is best for the team."

"That's good." Jack's lips curved. "I think what's best for the team is if you go with me."

"Are you going back to the woods?"

"No."

Crap! "Are you making me go with you so Laura won't want to go with you?"

Jack's smile widened. "That's simply an added benefit."

Crap on toast. "And where are we going?"

"Oh, don't worry. I think you'll really enjoy yourself on our little adventure. I know I will."

That didn't make me feel much better. "You're going to punish me, aren't you?"

"You have no idea."

ELEVEN

"You've got to be kidding me."

I slouched down in the passenger seat of the Jeep and glared at the huge Winters Lumberyard sign that towered over the log cabin building, which felt as if it had been plopped down in the middle of nowhere. In truth, it was located about four miles from the Winters house and five miles from the campsite.

"I thought you'd be pleased." Jack beamed as he pushed open his door and hopped out, pocketing the keys as he fixed me with a pointed look. "Are you ready?"

"Ready for what?"

"We're here to ask questions." Jack was matter-of-fact. "We have a missing couple who disappeared from the woods. This is one of the few businesses in the vicinity."

I wasn't about to fall for his just-business act. "And are you going to question everyone else who owns a business up and down this stretch?"

Jack shrugged, noncommittal. "I haven't decided yet."

"So why focus on this business?"

"The owner is the son of the man who sits on the board of the group that owns the land in question. That means he's doubly of interest."

Huh. I hadn't considered that. It sounded so reasonable. Of course, I knew better. "I think I'll wait in the Jeep while you do the questioning. I'm not really in the mood to hang out with lumberjacks or anything. You can do that on your own since you think they'll be of help."

"Oh, no." Jack made a tsking sound as he shook his head. "I don't think that's a good idea. It's still early, but it's supposed to be a scorcher today. You'll die of heatstroke if I leave you in the vehicle too long."

"You could fire up the engine and turn on the AC."

"I'm not sure that's a good idea." Jack was clearly enjoying himself at my expense, something that set my teeth on edge. "I'm afraid you might take off with the Jeep without telling me – that is your way, after all – and I don't want to be left stranded."

And we were right back where we started. He was good. I had to give him that. "Fine." I heaved out a sigh and threw open the door with some force. "I want you to know that I get what you're doing and I don't like it."

"I have no idea what you mean." Jack closed his door and waited for me to join him, ignoring the way the Jeep shook when I slammed my door. "I'm simply trying to find answers. I think you'd understand that. I mean, if we can find this couple before something terrible happens, that's a win for us all, right?"

"Whatever." I scuffed my shoes against the packed dirt in the parking lot and trudged toward the main office. "This is absolutely ridiculous."

"Yes, well, I thrive on being ridiculous." Jack held open the door for me. I was braced for some sort of explosion when I walked into the cool office. Instead, five heads turned in our direction ... and I didn't recognize any of them.

Hmm. Maybe this wouldn't be so bad after all. Aric Winters was the owner of the company. That didn't mean he showed up to work a shift every single day. That's not how the big boss structures his days, right?

"Can I help you?" A man with the name "Teddy" embroidered on his black polo shirt strode in our direction with a smile on his face. "Are you working on a home project and need some help? If so, you've come to the right place."

"We're not working on a home project," Jack replied.

"We don't share a home," I added, cringing when Jack slid me a questioning look. "What?"

"Do you really think he cares if we share a home?"

I shrugged. "I was just making conversation."

"Whatever." Jack pressed the heel of his hand to his forehead before collecting himself. "We're actually here for a different purpose. Is the owner in? I believe his name is Aric Winters."

Teddy's smile didn't diminish. "He is. Can I tell him what this is about?"

"It's okay, Teddy," a gravelly voice offered from the back of the showroom. I jerked up my chin and recognized Aric right away. His gaze was intent as it bounced between Jack and me, finally settling on The Legacy Foundation's taciturn security chief. "I know why they're here. You guys can come back this way."

"Thank you." Jack nodded at Teddy and then put his hand to the small of my back to usher me forward. I got the distinct impression he thought I might bolt and wanted to make sure that didn't happen. I was well beyond bolting now.

"Hello, Charlie." Aric grinned at me as he held open his office door. "It's nice to see you again."

"You, too," I muttered. "I wish it was under different circumstances." Or no circumstances at all, I silently added.

"I'm sure everything will be fine." Aric didn't appear worried about our sudden appearance. He offered us bottles of water before sitting behind the expansive oak desk in the center of the room. "So, what can I do for you?"

"Well, for starters, you can tell me what Charlie was doing at your house last night," Jack replied, taking me by surprise when he cut straight to the heart of matters.

Aric arched an eyebrow. "I didn't spend much time with her, but I believe she had a conversation with my wife."

"And this would be your wife, right?" Jack gestured toward a framed photograph on Aric's desk. Three familiar faces smiled back from it. "She's the blonde, isn't she?"

"Well, since the other person in the photo is my daughter, and I believe she was ten at the time that was taken, I should hope so." Aric was jarringly calm. He had a presence that wasn't easily discounted. Jack was used to being the strongest personality in the room, or at least the toughest nut to crack. I had a feeling Aric Winters could give him a run for the title.

"You know what I mean," Jack pressed. "This woman is your wife, right?"

"For fourteen wonderful years. She's an absolute joy and the light of my life."

I pressed my lips together to keep from laughing at Aric's expression. It was clear that he understood Jack's reasons for being at the office, but he wasn't about to make things easy for him.

"Okay, well, we saw her in the woods yesterday," Jack plowed forward. "She was with your daughter."

"True?" Aric held out his hands. "I'm not sure what you want me to say to that. Our house is surrounded by woods and Zoe hates working out, so she considers a walk in the woods exercise."

"Yes, but she was near the spot where a couple went missing," Jack persisted. "No one knows what happened to them and the police are considering an animal attack."

"My understanding is that no blood was found at the scene," Aric noted. "If an animal attacked, there would be blood."

"So you're not worried about your wife and daughter wandering around the woods when two people have gone missing?"

"My wife is capable of taking care of herself," Aric replied. "She also has a mind of her own. I learned a long time ago that ordering her around wasn't going to work for anyone, least of all her. Actually,

I should rephrase that. Technically it works least for me because the punishment that woman can mete out when things don't go her way is downright terrifying."

Aric seemed so amiable, so rational, I wanted to believe everything that came out of his mouth. Jack was another story.

"And you don't have a problem with her dragging your daughter along for the ride?"

For the first time since we'd entered his office, Aric showed signs of temper. "Are you suggesting that I don't care about my daughter?"

Jack was taken aback. "No. That's not what I was saying at all."

"Are you suggesting that my wife is somehow negligent and putting my daughter at risk?"

"No."

"Then what are you suggesting?" Aric seemed to grow in stature as he glared at Jack. "We have no idea what happened in those woods. That couple could've taken off together and purposely left their families with unanswered questions because ... simply because that's what they wanted to do. We have no way of knowing what went down without more information."

Jack held up his hands. "I think we got off on the wrong foot."

"I think we did," Aric readily agreed. "I'll give you a pass, though, because I don't believe that you're calling my wife's parenting into question when you ask these questions. What I think you really want to know is what Charlie was doing at our house last night."

"I wouldn't mind an explanation for that," Jack admitted.

"Well, I can't tell you what she was doing there because she talked to my wife in private," Aric supplied. "If you want to know what went down, why not ask Charlie? She's sitting right next to you."

My cheeks burned when I realized I was suddenly the focal point in the room. "I told him I just needed some air."

"Ah." Aric smirked. "Well, that seems fair enough. The heat has been stifling. It gets cooler after dark. Fresh air is always best when it's cooler."

"Oh, come on." Jack made a face. "I know she was there for another reason. Something happened in the woods."

"That's my wife's business." Aric shot me a kind look. "And Charlie's business. Even though you're clearly in charge, I believe she visited on a personal issue. I can't imagine that you're entitled to know everything she does every moment of every day."

"That's not what I said." Jack turned pouty. "Whatever. I can see you're not going to tell me what went down so I'll let it go."

"I can't tell you what I don't know."

"Then let's talk about the land itself," Jack prodded. "My understanding is that your father owns it. Clearly he should want to be involved in the investigation and yet the inquiries I've made seem to suggest he's only made a cursory call."

Aric shook his head. "You're misinformed. My father doesn't own the land. He is, however, something of a caretaker of sorts."

"What does that mean?"

"The property is owned by a consortium," Aric explained, choosing his words carefully. "It's not a public consortium or anything. It's a large group of private land owners, businessmen and even some politicians."

"Like your father?"

Aric nodded once. "I believe the property went up for auction about twenty years ago. I don't know much about it before then, although I can certainly do some research if you think it's important.

"My father didn't have enough funds to buy the land himself at the time, so he joined with some others," he continued. "The idea was to make sure that we had a forest utopia of sorts that could never be touched by industry or business interests. As someone who loves nature, I'm fine with that."

"It was recently opened to outsiders, though," Jack pointed out. "Before that it was closed off."

"I believe that decision was made due to some complaints from locals," Aric said. "They wanted to be able to hunt and fish on the land. The deer population exploded in recent years because our winters are nowhere near as brutal as they once were. There was a lot of a discussion and a compromise was struck."

"And that compromise includes?"

"I'm not sure I know all the nitty-gritty specifics," Aric replied. "I do know that camping is allowed in certain areas June through August, and that a certain amount of limited hunting licenses are granted in November."

"And that's it?"

"That's it." Aric steepled his fingers. "If I understand the information that was communicated to me yesterday, you're with The Legacy Foundation. Is that right?"

Jack leaned back in his chair, something I couldn't quite identify flitting across his features. "How did you learn that?"

"Charlie mentioned it to my wife, so I did some research when she told me what happened in the woods."

"I guess you had longer to talk to each other than I realized, huh?" Jack slid me a sidelong look. "Did you mention that to her?"

I couldn't remember exactly when the information popped up. I knew it wouldn't take a lot of effort for someone with Aric Winters' clout to track down answers, though, so I decided to make things easier on all of us. "Yeah. I just said that I was with The Legacy Foundation and we were investigating the disappearances. I didn't want her to be afraid of me. She had a kid with her, after all."

"And did you get the feeling that she was afraid of you?" Jack pressed.

"I don't know. I was confused because I didn't expect to see her out there, and when she said she lived nearby I thought I owed her some sort of explanation. I honestly didn't give it much thought."

"Right." Jack's expression was hard to read. "Well, I guess it doesn't matter. We are with The Legacy Foundation, though. Is that a problem?"

Aric shook his head. "No. I love a good monster hunt as much as the next person."

"Is that what you think we're doing?"

"I'm not sure you even know what you're doing, but it hardly matters," Aric answered. "My guess is that you want to question business owners and workers in the area to see if they've seen aggressive animals or anything that might explain the disappearances. That's common with investigators, and I have no problem with you questioning my workers."

I was taken aback by Aric's offer. I expected him to put up resistance. "That's good, right?" I glanced at Jack. "He wants to cooperate."

"I'm sure everyone around here wants to cooperate," Aric offered. "We don't want people to be frightened away from what this area has to offer. It will be bad for tourism and business. The summer months are when we make most of our money off tourism, so I believe everyone will want to cooperate."

"Just like that?" Jack was clearly dubious. "You're going to agree to it even though you clearly don't like me?"

"I didn't say I didn't like you. I said I understood why you insisted on visiting. Charlie is the main reason. Your questions are secondary. That doesn't mean you'll let them go."

"So, I can just question your workers and you don't care?" Jack was clearly baffled. "That's ... very generous of you."

"I'm a generous guy. Just ask my wife." Aric winked at me before standing. "As for me, I can guarantee I haven't seen any strange animals running through the woods. I have no idea what happened to that couple. I hope you find out, though. That's all I have to offer you."

Jack was resigned. "Then I guess I'll have to take it ... and say thank you."

"I think that would be best for us all."

TWO HOURS LATER we were done questioning Aric's workers. We'd made absolutely no headway on the investigation. Jack waited until we were in the Jeep, the air conditioning blasting at our faces, to speak.

"What did you think?"

I shrugged. "They seemed surprised by the questions and didn't act as if they were holding anything back. None of them have seen anything. Did you expect them to say anything different?"

"I don't know." Jack chewed his bottom lip. "They all seemed honest and forthright."

"So, what's the problem?"

"The problem is that there's almost always one kook in every bunch. There's always one guy who has a fantastical story to tell, especially once that guy finds out what we do for a living. We didn't get that today."

I stilled, surprised. "You're basically saying you're suspicious because Aric Winters didn't have one nutjob working for him."

"I know it sounds ridiculous."

"It does," I agreed, although secretly I couldn't help but wonder if he was right. "Maybe there's nothing to the story."

"Or maybe everyone at the lumberyard was warned ahead of time to keep those stories to themselves."

"But ... why?"

"I don't know, but I have every intention of finding out."

That didn't sound good. If Jack pressed the issue I had no doubt Aric would push back. Then, once Zoe got involved, we would be looking at a righteous cluster of crap.

No, that didn't sound good at all.

TWELVE

*W*e checked another business before hitting a diner for lunch. Jack wasn't saying much – his thoughtful nature forcing him to turn introspective – and I was decidedly uncomfortable with how taciturn he had become. I opted to force the issue.

"I know you're angry …."

Jack cocked an eyebrow as he sipped his iced tea. "What makes you think I'm angry?"

"You're not talking to me."

"I believe we're talking right now."

I scowled. "You know what I mean."

"And I don't believe I said I was angry." Jack kicked back in his chair and regarded me with an expression I had trouble processing. "Why do you think I was so furious last night?"

"Because you were worried we would ding the Jeep – or lose it in the woods – and you didn't want to be held responsible for it." That seemed the most practical answer. "Oh, and you're a bit anal retentive and you like control, so it bothered you when we didn't announce our intention to leave."

Jack's eyebrows migrated north, his handsome face reflecting … something. There was a time I didn't think he was all that expressive.

That was a mistake. He simply expressed things in his own way. Right now, for example, I believed that his expression indicated he was debating leaving me in the diner to find my own way back to the inn because he'd had enough "together" time. I was fairly certain he regretted his insistence on forcing me to be his partner in crime for the day.

"You're an idiot if you think that's actually true," Jack muttered, shaking his head. "I just ... you are unfreaking-believable sometimes. Do you really think that's why I was worked up?"

"I ... ." His reaction caught me off guard and forced me to change course. "I don't know what to think. You're starting to make me wonder if I accidentally dropped my brain while we were running around last night."

"I often think you might have dropped your brain." Jack grunted as he rubbed his chin. "Charlie, I'm not trying to be the downer on your otherwise upbeat day. That's not who I want to be."

"I didn't say that's who you wanted to be."

"But you think it," Jack countered. "What do you see when you look at me?"

Uh-oh. That sounded like a loaded question. "Um ... I see a loyal guy who would die to keep his co-workers safe." That seemed like a safe answer.

"What else?"

Oh, now he was putting me on the spot. "I don't know what you want me to say, Jack." I squirmed in my chair. "If you want me to say something specific ... ." I trailed off, uncertain.

"I want you to tell me the truth." Jack rested his palms on the tabletop and stared hard. "Tell me what you see when you look at me."

It was obvious he wasn't going to let this go. I considered lying, perhaps to spare his feelings, but more to save myself. Ultimately I couldn't give in to that urge. I had to tell the truth.

"Fine." I blew out a sigh. "You're a bit intense. The first day I met you I thought you hated me on sight. I couldn't figure out why because I hadn't done anything – at least not yet – but you really seemed to dislike me."

Jack made a face. "Charlie."

I held up a hand to quiet him. "You started this game. Let me finish before you blow up."

"Fine." Jack folded his arms over his chest. "Continue."

"I was pretty sure you wanted to kill me after that first night Millie and I took off for the golf course while we were in Hemlock Cove," I supplied. "I thought you might actually shake me for a second, and I was a little afraid of you."

Something I couldn't identify flashed in the depths of Jack's eyes, but he remained quiet.

"Then, after spending a bit more time with you, I realized you weren't as gruff as you pretended to be." I offered a wan smile. "You started occasionally talking to me like a person instead of the newbie you were forced to take on. It didn't happen often, but there were times when – I don't know – you almost seemed able to tolerate me.

"Then the day at the mining town happened," I continued. "Everything is kind of jumbled in my mind about that because I was so afraid. I do remember thinking that everything was going to be okay because I knew you were close. That kind of settled me."

"You saved yourself that day, Charlie," Jack pointed out. "You saved yourself ... and Chris ... and Millie. You did that."

"But knowing you were close gave me the strength to remain calm," I explained. "I know it doesn't exactly make sense, but ... for some reason I knew you'd come. That allowed me to think. I figured that even if I died in the process, if I could lead Zach and Naomi away that you would get to Chris and Millie, and it would all be worth it."

"It would be worth it to die?"

I shrugged. "It would be worth it to save them."

"Ugh." Jack's expression was sour. "You terrify me sometimes. You're so gung-ho."

"I think that's one of the reasons you don't like me. I get it. You don't have to like me. What I did last night wasn't smart and you don't understand it. I don't blame you. But it's private. I don't want to talk about it."

Jack stared at me so hard and for so long I thought he'd forgotten what we were talking about. When he finally did find his voice, I was surprised by the words he offered.

"You're wrong about me not liking you," he said. "I like you fine. You make me laugh, even though sometimes I wait until I'm alone and behind closed doors to laugh because I don't want to encourage you. You're bright, funny and engaging."

I was flabbergasted. "Oh, well … ." My cheeks burned with pleasure.

"You're also impulsive, you think before you speak and you drive me absolutely batty," Jack added, causing my smile to slip. "I don't dislike you. I'm sorry if I gave you that impression. I'm really sorry if I made you think I'd harm you. That's not who I want to be."

I balked. "I didn't think you'd hit me or anything. You were just so angry … I thought there might be some shaking involved."

"That will never happen." Jack was firm. "I might yell, but I would never hurt you. I'm a little … annoyed … that you would think that."

"I didn't really think that." My answer was perfunctory, but I realized I meant it. "I'm sorry that I even said that. It wasn't fair."

"If you thought it, then it was fair." Jack tapped his fingers on the table. "I don't yell at you to be a hardass. I know that's difficult to believe, but it's true. I want you to be safe. If something happens to the people in this group under my watch I will never forgive myself."

"I know. I didn't mean to hurt your feelings." In truth, I didn't know I was capable of hurting his feelings. It was a sobering thought. "I'm self-involved sometimes." That was hard to admit, but true. "I only see how things affect me. That doesn't seem fair to you … or anyone else, for that matter. I promise to work on it, because that's not the person I want to be."

"I think the person you are is fine." Jack turned earnest. "You're loyal and mostly trustworthy."

I didn't like that qualifier. "Mostly?"

"Charlie, you're hiding something." Jack refused to back down. "Do you think I don't see that? Do you think I'm going to let it go? Heck, you had a stranger lying for you in his place of business today."

It took me a moment to realize he was referring to Aric Winters. "I didn't ask him to lie for me."

"No, I'm sure you didn't," Jack agreed. "I saw the look on your face in the Jeep before we went inside. You were afraid of what he might say. It made me feel a little bad for you."

"That didn't stop you from forcing me to go with you."

"I didn't feel that bad." Jack offered a mirthful smirk. "He lied to cover up whatever you were doing at his house."

"I didn't spend more than a few minutes with him. That wasn't a lie."

"No, but he knows what you talked about with his wife because that's the sort of person he is," Jack noted. "It's very clear he loves his wife and will do whatever it takes to protect his family. He protected you, too. He had no intention of throwing you to the werewolves, so to speak. I find that interesting."

"It's not that interesting." Especially because his wife had no answers and couldn't offer help, I silently added. "We weren't there for very long."

"And you're not going to tell me what you discussed, are you?"

I opened my mouth even though I had no idea what I was going to say. Ultimately, I merely shook my head. "It's not important. It really is private. I swear it doesn't have anything to do with this investigation."

Jack sighed, resigned. "Then I guess it's none of my business. I have no choice but to step back."

He didn't seem happy about that. "I'm sorry. I just ... it's private."

"Then I hope one day you feel you can trust me with private stuff so you don't feel so uncomfortable where I'm concerned." Jack scratched the side of his nose. "Until then ... I'll do my best to refrain from frightening you."

I was sheepish. "You didn't really frighten me. I mean ... you kind of did because I was sure I was going to lose my job that night, but I knew you wouldn't really hurt me. I shouldn't have said that. It was mean and thoughtless."

"No, it was impulsive and you honestly felt it in the moment so you said it. That's what you do."

"Because I have a big mouth," I grumbled, shaking my head. I felt bad because he felt so bad. "I'm not afraid of you, Jack. You have a hair-trigger temper and sometimes you suck the fun out of life, but I meant what I said. The knowledge that you were out there and looking for me is what kept me sane in Texas. I'll never forget that."

Jack managed a wan smile. "I don't think I'll ever forget it either."

"That's good, right?'

Jack shrugged. "I guess it depends on how you define good. I was terrified that you were going to die before I could get to you."

"But I didn't."

"Because you saved yourself. I guess I should be happy about it, but it still haunts me a bit. Ah, well, it does no good to focus on it. What do you say we get through lunch and then hit the last business on the strip? After that, I'm not sure where we should look."

I forced a smile because I thought he needed it. "Sounds like a plan."

THE LAST BUSINESS ON our list was a riverside water enthusiast place that offered kayak, canoe and inner tube rentals for trips down the waterway. There were only a handful of employees, and because it was the middle of the day, the workers were free to talk to us as long as necessary.

"You always hear strange stories about this area," Brian King offered, his hipster hair pulled back in a man bun that I could tell irritated Jack to no end. "I mean ... what kind of rumors are you looking for? We have all kinds."

"We'll take anything," Jack said. "Do you ever hear weird animal stories?"

"Well, everyone is afraid of the Dog Man," Brian replied. "No one ever goes out alone at night. And if you're going to party in the woods you have to make sure that you do it in a group ... and that you build a fire. The Dog Man is afraid of fire."

"Is that so?" Jack managed to keep his face relaxed, but I was certain it was a struggle. "Have you seen the Dog Man?"

Brian nodded, his face stone cold sober. "I was coming home from a party one night and he was in my backyard. I swear he was there and wanted to do me harm." Brian made the sign of the cross and kissed his fingertips before lifting them to the sky. "I think he wanted to warn me about my life choices."

"I see." Jack flicked me a quick glance but looked away before I could burst out laughing. "And what do you think the Dog Man wanted to tell you about your life choices?"

"That I should stop drinking in fields and come up with a career plan," Brian answered without hesitation. "That's why I'm here."

"Because you want to rent kayaks for the rest of your life?" The question was out of my mouth before I realized how rude it sounded. Thankfully, Brian was not the type to pick up on sarcasm.

"I want to be a river guide," Brian explained. "That's a real thing, by the way. I didn't know it was until I talked to a guy. There are these people from the city who pay people from the country to show them good fishing spots and everything. I want to do that."

"Oh, well, that sounds … neat." I had no idea what to say to that, so I allowed Jack to take over the conversation.

"What about other rumors?" Jack prodded. "Have you ever heard about the Dog Man attacking people?"

"The Dog Man likes to keep to himself and just run around the woods unless you're making poor life decisions," Brian supplied. "He's not a killer. If you believe some people, there's a different sort of killer in the woods and he only comes out under the full moon."

Ah, now we were getting somewhere. "A lycanthrope?"

"No, man." Brian was deathly serious as he leaned forward. "People say it's a werewolf."

I licked my lips before responding. "That is a lycanthrope."

"A werewolf is a lycanthrope?" Brian puzzled it out. "I guess that's okay. I prefer the term werewolf. It's more scientific."

"Yes, well, as long as it's scientific." I shifted my eyes to the pathway that had been busy only moments before and realized that one of the workers – I believe the boy introduced himself as Ty before losing interest in the conversation and wandering away – was speaking to an animated-looking man who wore a wide-brimmed hat and carried fishing gear. "What's going on?"

Brian shrugged and stepped toward Ty. "I don't know. I can ask." He cleared his throat. "Hey, Ty, what are you going on about?"

It took a moment before Ty realized anyone was talking to him. When he turned in our direction, the look on his face told me he'd managed to trip over something more than idle gossip.

"It's all anybody is talking about, Brian," Ty enthused. "They found that woman who went missing. I mean ... they actually found her."

My heart seized. "Where did they find her?"

"And how did she die?" Jack asked, moving closer to me.

Ty furrowed his brow. "Die? She's not dead, man. They found her alive in the woods. They're taking her to the hospital. Kelsey Porter actually saw her as she was being loaded into the ambulance. Said she looked like a wild animal. I guess that doesn't matter as long as she's alive, right?"

Jack and I exchanged dumbfounded looks.

"Right," Jack said finally. "Hey, um, where is this hospital?"

THIRTEEN

*J*ack placed a call to Chris before we drove to the hospital. To my utter surprise, he instructed me to drive while he worked on his phone. I couldn't figure out what he was doing until we hit the parking lot.

"The police details are sketchy so far," he announced as we hopped out of the Jeep. "From what I can tell, a search team found her. She was a decent distance from the campsite."

I arched an eyebrow. "Oh, is that what you were doing?"

"What did you think I was doing?"

I shrugged. "I thought maybe you were overcome with the desperate need to text … or maybe play *Pokémon Go*."

Jack snorted. "I only play *Pokémon Go* when I'm done with my work for the day."

I choked on a laugh. That was as close as he ever came to a silly joke. "Well, we'll have to play together one day. I'll show you how a proper raid battle is won."

"Oh, I think I'll be the one doing the teaching." Jack put his hand to the small of my back and prodded me through the front door, taking a moment to glance around the lobby before pointing toward a row of chairs and couches. "We should get comfortable over there."

I balked. "Why aren't we trying to see her?"

"Because we're not family and she'll be inundated with police officers, family, friends and medical personnel for the next few hours."

"But ...."

"No." Jack shook his head. "We need to wait for Chris and the others. That's standard operating procedure."

"I'm not sure I like standard operating procedure," I groused as I scuffed my shoes against the linoleum floor and resignedly made my way to the couch Jack indicated.

"Oh, tell me about it." Jack chuckled as he sat next to me – something I'm sure was a proactive move in case I decided to wander – and returned his attention to his phone. "You have to be patient, Charlie. That's your biggest fault. You never look at the best way to tackle something. You're more interested in the immediate way."

"And why is that wrong?"

Jack managed to contain his temper as he lowered the phone and met my gaze. "That woman has been through a lot. She's been missing in the woods for days. Her husband is still missing. We have no idea what she saw out there. Do you really think our needs take precedence over hers?"

That was so not what I was getting at. "I didn't mean to imply that our needs – and by 'our' I know you really mean 'my' needs – trump hers. We require answers, and her husband is still out there. Perhaps if she gives us something good to go on we'll be able to find him alive too."

"I get that's your natural inclination, but we're not police officers." Jack was firm. "We're a separate investigative branch. We're pretty low on the food chain when it comes to an emergent situation like this."

"Fine." I blew out a sigh. He made sense, which was irritating. "I guess I just want to know where she's been and what happened."

"We all want to know," Jack said, his attention back on his phone. "The police aren't reporting much yet. That could mean that she was so far gone they couldn't question her before transport or it could be that they simply haven't had time to update their files."

I knit my eyebrows. "How do you know what they're putting in files?"

Jack shrugged, noncommittal. "I might have a way to read their files."

Oh, well, that was interesting. "You hacked their computer system?"

Jack growled as he shifted to study the people behind us and make sure my voice – which was prone to carrying – wasn't so loud that we drew unnecessary attention. "Why don't you say that a little louder?" he suggested. "I haven't spent any time behind bars in a good year or so. I find I miss it, and illegal tampering with police files is a great way to get back to my roots."

The statement was so odd I could do nothing but stare. "You've been in jail?"

Jack rolled his eyes. "It was a long time ago; part of my misspent youth. The military basically beat my wild ways out of me. Don't worry about it. I won't do anything that puts you at risk."

I didn't care about that. "I want to know how you do it. Can you teach me?"

Jack's lips curved. "That would be unethical."

"So?"

"It's also illegal."

"I can live with that."

Jack heaved out a sigh. "I don't want you getting in trouble."

Ugh. And here I thought he was turning adventurous. "Why must you always be so practical? Maybe I want to learn to be a bad girl. Have you ever thought of that? I can be more than one thing."

"I know you can." Jack's expression was somber. "But I like you the way you are. For now, we'll keep the hacking to me. It's a difficult skill to teach anyway, and we don't have time now."

I wasn't sure I believed his reasoning. "I think you just don't want to teach me because you're worried I'd start hacking everyone because I'm a busybody."

"You're definitely a menace when you want to be." Jack's lips curved as I smacked his arm. "We don't have time right now, and

I'm pretty sure Chris wouldn't like it if I shared this little trick. For now, you'll have to live with disappointment. This is my private thing."

Hmm. "Are you just saying that because I won't tell you what I was doing last night?"

"No. I'm saying it because it's true. If you want to start trading secrets, that will have to wait for another day. We really don't have time. I wasn't lying about that." Jack shifted his eyes to the automatic doors as they whooshed open to allow Chris and Hannah entrance. They appeared to be alone, although I had no idea if that was a good or bad thing. "You guys made it."

"Of course we made it." Chris's eyes sparked with interest. "Did you think we wouldn't? Lisa Savage survived a lycanthrope attack. This is unprecedented. How soon do you think we can get in to see her?"

Jack blinked several times in rapid succession, his eyes reflecting dumbfounded disbelief as he studied our boss. "I can't believe you just said that. You're as bad as Charlie."

"Hey!" I had no idea why I was offended. It simply seemed like I should be given Jack's tone.

Jack ignored my outrage. "We're not getting in to see that woman anytime soon. You know that, right, Chris?"

"I most certainly don't know that," Chris shot back. "I'm not leaving this hospital until we talk to her. She's our one link to a lycanthrope. Do you think I'm simply going to forget that?"

Jack made an exaggerated face as he shook his head. "I guess I should be glad you're not screaming the word 'werewolf,' but I can't quite force myself to that way of thinking. Could you please calm down just a bit?"

Chris sucked in a deep breath and let it out, repeating the procedure three times before flashing a condescending smile. "Happy?"

"Not even a little." Jack tipped his phone screen so Chris couldn't see it and adopted a serious expression. "That woman was discovered in rough shape. I don't know much, but I do know that. You can't force the hospital to let you see her before local law enforcement and her family gets a chance to talk to her. It's simply not going to happen."

Chris refused to back down. "Yes, but we're the group in the best position to find the lycanthrope."

"You don't know it was a lycanthrope." Jack made a face. "Right now, we simply have a woman who went missing days ago. We have no idea about her condition – whether she's even conscious – and the hospital staff needs time to treat her."

"Do you think I wouldn't give them time?"

Jack shrugged. "I have no idea. You seem a little out of sorts."

"He's just excited," Hannah interjected, unsurprisingly taking our boss's side. "I don't blame him. This is a big deal. You guys are over-looking one little thing, though."

"And what's that?" Jack queried blankly.

"I have a medical background that allows me clearance at a lot of places," Hannah replied. "I can't guarantee that they'll allow me to see Lisa Savage, but I might be able to get some information on her condition."

"Oh." Jack straightened. "I didn't even think of that. It's a good idea. You should definitely go."

"I'll go with you," Chris offered, a shy smile playing at the corners of his mouth.

"Oh, that's sweet." Hannah's cheeks turned pink. "It's just ... um ... I don't think the medical personnel will talk to me if I have a civilian in tow. I ... oh ... no offense."

"None taken." Chris was resigned as he took the open chair to the right of the couch. "Hurry back if you get information."

Hannah bobbed her head, gracing the back of Chris's head with a longing look. "I definitely will. I'll try not to be gone too long."

"That would be best for all of us," Jack said. "Chris might implode if you disappear for an extended period."

"I heard that," Chris muttered.

"I didn't whisper."

"You said it with derision."

"I'll work on it." Jack cast me a sidelong look. "That seems to be the promise of the day."

ONCE HANNAH WAS GONE there was nothing to do but wait. Jack seemed perfectly happy with that, his phone garnering most of his attention. Chris and I were another story. We were more restless, prone to pacing, and the occasional sigh managed to eke out.

"You guys should talk about something to distract yourselves," Jack suggested. "You'll go crazy otherwise … or drive me crazy."

"Yes, and nobody wants that," I said dryly. "Do you have an idea for a topic?"

"I'm sure you'll come up with something."

I pursed my lips as I considered his dismissive statement. In truth, there was something we could talk about, and now that Jack suggested a conversation I couldn't shake the idea, even though it was probably one of the more terrible ones I'd had in recent memory.

"Fine. We'll talk about something." Chris flashed an easy smile as he rocked back and forth in his chair. "How are you finding your work at The Legacy Foundation, Charlie? Are you enjoying yourself?"

I nodded. "Yes. I'm having a great time and learning a lot."

"Good."

We lapsed into silence.

"Oh, geez," Jack muttered. "That wasn't much of an effort."

"It's all I've got," Chris snapped.

"Then let Charlie think of something to talk about," Jack instructed. "She loves to talk. In fact, I'd dare say there's nothing she loves more."

He meant it as an insult, but I couldn't be bothered to care. He wasn't wrong, though. Talking was one of my favorite activities, and now that the spotlight was on me I couldn't shut my mouth. "So, um, when are you going to ask Hannah out?"

The question was out of my mouth before my inner editor could gag me. Ah, well, there was no going back now.

Chris was so surprised by the question he practically choked. "W-w-what?" His face turned a deep shade of red. "I ... what?"

"Good grief." Jack rubbed his forehead. "You just went for it, didn't you?"

I saw no reason to lie. "You said we should talk. That's the only thing I could think of to talk about."

"You think I like Hannah?" Chris was so perturbed he hopped to his feet, sat back down, and then hopped up again before circling the chair and looking anywhere but at me. "I can't believe you think that."

I slid a glance to Jack and found him watching Chris with outright mirth.

"Not that I want to encourage Charlie or anything, but I don't think you're as suave when it comes to hiding your feelings as you think," Jack prodded gently. "Anyone in a room with you and Hannah for more than five minutes can tell you're interested in one another."

"Really?" Instead of denying the charge, Chris flopped in the chair and pressed his hand to his eyes. "That's so not what I wanted to hear."

"Why not?" I asked. "If you both like each other, why not ask her out and move things forward?"

"Because I don't want to pressure her. I mean ... I'm her boss. What if she thinks I'm a sexual harasser or something? Oh, good lord, you don't think she believes I'm a sexual harasser, do you?"

"Have you grabbed her butt or commented on her boobs?"

Chris was scandalized. "Absolutely not!"

"Then I think you're safe." I couldn't contain my grin. "I think you should ask her out. It would be good for both of you ... and relieve some of the pressure I'm sure you're both feeling."

"I can't ask her out." Chris turned whiny as he looked to Jack for backup. "Tell her. Asking out someone you work with is a bad idea, right? Actually, it's a terrible idea."

"It wouldn't be my first choice," Jack agreed. "I mean ... what happens if you break up? That's on top of the pressure both sides would feel because everyone will be watching. In a situation like ours, it kind of feels like a pressure cooker at times – or even a meat grinder under the right circumstances – and the entire dynamic of the group could be thrown off by a breakup."

I pinned him with a dark look. "What if they don't break up?"

"What are the odds of that?"

"People get together and stay that way until one of them dies all the time," I argued. "That's what happens with soulmates. Maybe Chris and Hannah are soulmates. Have you ever considered that?"

"I can't say it's anything I've spent a lot of time pondering," Jack replied, blasé. "The simple fact of the matter is that people break up all the time. I'm not saying it would happen to Hannah and Chris, but it could, and then where will we be?"

He didn't give me a chance to answer before barreling on. "I'll tell you exactly where we'd be. We'd be stuck in a painful situation with two hurt people who can't get past feelings they probably shouldn't have had for each other in the first place. How can that ever be considered good?"

My temper ratcheted up a notch. "You're looking at it from the male perspective. Try looking at it as a human being instead of a droid. Chris obviously cares a great deal about Hannah."

"And not dating her will allow him to keep caring without putting himself or this group at risk," Jack fired back.

"The group isn't everything. Beyond all of this, people are allowed to have lives. How do you know Chris and Hannah won't find exactly what they're looking for on an emotional level, pop out a few ridiculously smart and urban legend-crazy kids, and live happily ever after?"

Jack shrugged. "How often does that happen? It's not the norm. I say you're smart to play it safe, Chris. Don't risk the group because your hormones are out of whack."

"Ugh." I wanted to punch him in the face. "Don't listen to him, Chris. The group is great. It could be so much more, though. It could be everything you've ever dreamed about."

Chris looked torn. "I'm afraid."

I understood that. "I'm sure she is too. Just ... give it some thought."

Chris nodded, reticent. "Yeah. Maybe."

I slapped Jack upside the head with the meanest glare in my repertoire. "And you need to stop being such a killjoy. Some people are okay with falling in love. Just because you're cold hearted doesn't mean everybody is."

"Whatever." Jack avoided my gaze. "I wasn't trying to be difficult."

"Well, if that's true you failed miserably at whatever you were trying to do," I argued. "Maybe you should try working on that."

"Yeah, yeah, yeah."

This time the silence that settled over us was uncomfortable. I was grateful when Hannah appeared and headed in our direction. She looked serious, which I thought was probably a bad omen.

"I didn't get anything," Hannah announced as Chris scrambled to his feet. "The doctor is being tightlipped. He looks concerned, maybe even a little overly worried. He wouldn't share information, but suggested I stop by later – maybe tomorrow – for an update."

"That's disappointing," Chris grumbled. "I thought for sure you'd get something."

"I did my best."

"Yeah." Chris exhaled heavily. "I guess there's no reason to hang around if we can't see her."

"No," Hannah agreed. "We can try again later. What about you guys? What did I miss down here? Was it anything good?"

Now that was a loaded question if ever I'd heard one.

FOURTEEN

$\mathcal{W}$e headed back to the inn, Chris and Hannah in one vehicle and Jack and me in another. The drive was uncomfortable – at least for me – and I considered letting the conversation die.

Sadly, that's not how I'm built.

"Did you really mean what you said?"

Jack stirred, briefly tearing his eyes from the road long enough to grace me with an unreadable glance. "You'll have to be more specific."

"What you said to Chris," I prodded. "The thing about love never being worth the effort."

"Oh, geez." Jack made a clucking sound with his tongue. "I'm pretty sure that's not what I said."

"That's what I heard."

"That's because your mind is a terrifying place to visit."

"Yeah, well, it's basically what you said." I wasn't in the mood to let it go. "I don't understand how you can believe something like that."

"You heard what you wanted to hear because that's not what I said," Jack shot back. "Still, I happen to believe that it's a bad idea to mix work and personal relationships. There's a lot of room for things to go wrong when that happens."

"There's also a lot of room for it to go right."

"Maybe, but that doesn't outweigh the bad."

Ugh. He was such a Grinch sometimes. "So, you think there's no hope for Chris and Hannah. That's what you're saying, right? Even though it's almost painful to watch them pine for one another, you think it's better they pretend they don't have feelings for each other."

"I didn't say that." Jack's effect was flat. "In fact, as far as Chris and Hannah are concerned, I think they're the type to beat the odds."

The change in his stance threw me. "Now, all of a sudden, you're for their relationship?"

"I think that Hannah and Chris are both socially awkward individuals who are unlikely to find love outside of a work environment." Jack chose his words carefully. "They both thrive on the science and enthusiasm of this job. That makes them different."

"If you think they're the exception to the rule, why did you try to dissuade Chris from asking her out?"

"I want him to be sure. I really do think Chris and Hannah could make it work. They're both easygoing and rarely cause drama in the workplace. I see them going on one date, realizing they're hopelessly in love, and showing up married the next day. It will be simple and easy with them because that's who they are."

"Oh, so it's everyone else you have a problem with," I muttered. "I'm guessing that's why you've spent the better part of the last few days hiding from Laura. You know any relationship you have with her is bound to end in drama."

"That is not why I've been dodging Laura. I want nothing to do with Laura because she's Laura."

"But you dated her before."

"We've already talked about this," Jack growled. "We didn't date. She showed interest, I turned her down. She decided that was the same as me declaring war. She then spent what felt like forever trying to torture me. I have no idea why she's back to playing the innocent ingénue."

I had an idea. "She was thrown by what happened with Zach. She thought she was a good judge of character, but it turned out she isn't.

That made her re-think everything else, including the bad feelings she was harboring about you.

"I wouldn't worry about it," I continued. "She's easily distracted, as you witnessed when she saw the photograph of Aric Winters. She doesn't really want you. She just doesn't want to be alone."

"I figured that out myself."

"I wish she would figure it out so I wouldn't have to put up with another conversation in which she threatens to make me pay for spending time with you," I groused.

Jack's hands tightened on the steering wheel. "What?"

It was too late to take it back, like always. "I just meant … um … she wants to make sure I don't try to throw myself at you because she's ready to make her move. She's worried that your protective nature and my propensity for trouble will ruin things."

"Laura ruins things on her own," Jack pointed out. "As for the rest … you do you and don't worry about Laura. She's not your boss. If she gives you grief, tell me and I'll handle it."

His reaction was surprising. "You'll handle it?"

Jack bobbed his head. "She's obviously not ready to pick up on hints, so I have no choice but to handle it. She doesn't do subtle, which means I'll have to be overt."

"Are you going to be mean to her?"

"If it becomes necessary."

"Can I watch?"

Jack cracked a grin. "I'll text you before it happens."

"That's the best offer I've had all day."

I SPENT SOME TIME in my room screwing around on my computer. That was expected, although the information I searched for had nothing to do with mid-Michigan lycanthropes and everything to do with Zoe Lake-Winters.

She wouldn't answer the question about dying, so that meant there might be something to what I saw in our shared visions. I didn't grasp everything – I mean, how could I, right? – but that didn't mean I couldn't put pieces of the puzzle together. She mentioned Covenant College, so that's what I searched. What I found was ... unbelievable. I mean absolutely unbelievable.

A knock on my door jolted me so that I was irritated enough to open it with a scowl. When I found Millie standing there, my agitation evaporated and I jerked her into the room. "You're never going to guess what I found."

"Well, hello to you too." Millie looked me up and down, taking in my messy hair and rumpled clothing. "Were you napping?"

"No. I was researching the school that Zoe used to attend. It's quite the story."

"Oh, well, do tell." Millie settled at the small chair in the corner of the room and watched as I planted myself on the bed and reclaimed my laptop. "So, up until last year, Covenant College was a relatively small university that boasted students from all across the state."

"Okay, I'll bite. What happened last year?"

"Every building on the campus burned to the ground. It's all very vague how it happened – or why – but it's no longer there. The university board decided not to rebuild. Now it's just a piece of flat land, and you can't tell anything ever stood on it."

Millie furrowed her brow. "How is that possible?"

"How indeed."

"There has to be more than you're telling me," Millie prodded. "I mean ... a college campus is more than one building."

"According to what I can find, Covenant College was more than fifty buildings. We're talking dorms, library, the university center, the book store, classroom buildings, a sports activity center and even a football stadium."

Millie merely sat there, her mouth open. Finally, all she could come up with was "Huh."

"I have a theory, if you're interested."

"Oh, well, I love a good theory." Millie smirked. "Something tells me your theory is going to involve a certain mouthy blonde and her absolutely beautiful husband."

I thought about the image I saw, the one in which I was certain

Zoe was dying. "I think that Zoe Lake-Winters died on that campus and was somehow brought back to life."

"Oh, I can't even." Millie slapped her hand to her forehead. "Kid, I like you a lot and love your enthusiasm, but I think you're going a bit nutty here. I know what you think you saw, but there's a very good chance that Zoe was badly hurt. Her husband seemed awfully protective of her, after all. Maybe he almost lost her and that's why he wants to stay close."

"I think he almost lost her a number of times – and maybe she's almost lost him too – but this was different. I swear she was dead."

"And yet she's alive and running around," Millie argued. "I'm not saying you're full of crap or anything."

"Good."

"But you are full of crap." Millie made a face when I glared. "What? That woman is alive. She might very well have been hurt. I can see that. She's alive now. She didn't die."

"That doesn't explain what happened at Covenant College," I persisted. "All remnants of those buildings are gone. There aren't even burned-out husks left behind. From what I can find, no cleanup crew ever went in there. It simply turned into a field."

"I don't see how that's possible. Just because the news stories don't mention cleanup efforts, that doesn't mean they didn't happen. Construction crews aren't the stuff of titillating journalism."

She had a point ... which I hated. "Well ... ."

"You need to stop obsessing about this." Millie raised a finger to still me. "I get that you're all geeked about this woman because you linked minds or whatever – and that truly must be freaky and fantastical because you're different – but I don't think she is what you think she is."

"And what do you think I believe her to be?"

"I think you're looking at her as some sort of messiah. She's just a woman. Sure, she might be a woman with powers, but she's still a woman. She's a woman with the hottest husband I've ever seen and a mouthy kid who acts just like her. Did I tell you what happened with the kid when I was upstairs?"

I shook my head.

"She was whining about the batteries and Aric finally got irritated and found some and switched them out for her. Then he kissed the top of her head, told her she was just like her mother and then he left her and the dog to watch television."

"What kind of dog?"

Millie was taken aback. "What does that matter?"

"I'm just curious. Does it look like a wolf? Like maybe a wolf shifter or something? Maybe they have more than one kid and hide it as a dog."

"Oh, good grief! It was a German shepherd. Its name was Trouble and it sat on the floor with the kid and waited for her to drop potato chips. He licked her face, listened when Aric told him to sit and basically acted like a dog."

"That doesn't mean it wasn't an act."

Millie practically exploded with frustration. "They're a simple family."

"There's something different about Zoe." I couldn't let it go. "I need to know what that is."

"Why?"

"Because I hate being alone." I wanted to draw back the words the instant they escaped. The sympathetic look on Millie's face made me realize I should've kept my mouth shut and quit while I was ahead.

"You're not alone, Charlie." Millie lowered her voice. "You have us. You have me … and Bernard … and Hannah … and Chris. You have Jack."

"I drive Jack nuts."

Millie's lips curved. "You do. I can't wait to see how that plays out."

What was that supposed to mean? "I don't understand."

"You will." Millie slowly got to her feet and shuffled to the side of the bed. "Kid, you're not alone. I know it has to feel that way because you're different, but you're not. You can't chase around Zoe because you think you're the same. I think you'll find nothing but heartbreak if you continue down that path."

"We joined for a reason."

"You did. I think you're both powerful, and it was probably an accident or something."

Zoe said the same thing. I never told Millie about that part of the conversation. I didn't want to say it aloud. "I still think there's something there."

"Then chase it." Millie's smile was kind. "Don't chase it so hard you lose sight of everything else, though."

"I won't."

"Let's hope not."

WE HAD DINNER IN THE inn's dining room for the second night in a row. Even though I wasn't keen on the animal heads staring at me while I ate my steak and potatoes, I had to admit the ease of eating on the premises far outweighed the discomfort.

"I'm going to call the hospital again," Hannah announced as she wadded her napkin and left it on top of her plate. "I'm not ready to give up on an update just yet."

"We'll be waiting here," Chris offered, his smile so wide it looked almost painful.

Hannah also found the smile a bit deranged, because she had an odd expression on her face when she walked away from the table. Chris didn't relax his mouth until he was sure she was out of sight, and then exhaled heavily and slouched in his chair.

Laura clearly wasn't in the mood to watch true love play out. She rolled her eyes and focused on Jack. "So, what is our next move?"

"I honestly don't know." Jack wiped the corners of his mouth with his napkin and reached for his glass of wine. "We need information from the wife. We have no idea if she's even conscious. We don't know if she knows what happened. We don't know if her memory is intact. Heck, we don't know if she's so traumatized she can't speak."

"You'd think she'd want to help the husband if she could," Bernard pointed out. "Won't the police put information like that in their files?"

"Yes, and I keep checking. There are small updates, but nothing substantial."

"So, what should we do, Chris?" Laura's eyes were expectant as she turned to our boss. "Should we head back out to the woods tomorrow? Maybe we should adjust our search grid and move closer to where the wife was found."

"That's an idea, but I don't know if it's a good idea," Chris replied, his eyes focused on the distant hallway that Hannah disappeared down to use her phone. His mind was obviously elsewhere, which was impressive because he almost always fixated on the case above all else. "The police are bound to be taking over that area. They probably won't like it if we tromp all over their evidence. We have clearance for the campsite and the surrounding area. I think we should stick close to there."

"We've already been over it twice," Laura complained. "It was a waste of time … and ridiculously hot."

"And yet somehow you survived," Jack noted.

"I wouldn't get too full of yourself," Laura sneered. "While you and Charlie were out doing … whatever it was you were doing … the rest of us were working hard."

"We were working hard too." Jack refused to be drawn into a fight. "We questioned a good thirty people. I can't help it if you were stuck doing something you disliked."

"You could've taken me with you."

"I thought Charlie would be more help." Jack kept his eyes averted and followed Chris's gaze, I'm sure to give himself a focal point. He watched as Hannah appeared at the end of the hallway, her phone in hand. She appeared to be talking to someone but it was impossible to make out what she said. "It turns out Charlie was a great deal of help, so it all worked out."

"Hannah looks like she's getting somewhere," Millie said.

"I'll ask her." Chris hopped to his feet, throwing down his napkin as he pushed out his chair. "I'll talk to her and … just talk to her."

The second part of the statement seemed to be uttered more to himself than us, and I couldn't help but watch, curiosity crawling along my neck, as he hurried toward Hannah. There was something heavy about the way he carried himself, as if he had a purpose that was different from what he said to us.

"Well, I still think that I should've gone with you," Laura lamented, ignoring what was about to happen in the hallway. "It's ridiculous that I was left behind while you took her. I have more seniority."

"Shh," I admonished, lifting a finger to my lips and staring at Chris. I sensed something was about to happen.

"Don't shush me!"

"Just … watch." I bit the inside of my cheek as Chris reached the end of the hallway. Hannah's face registered surprise as she lowered her phone and looked at him. She said something – I had no idea what – and the next thing I knew Chris was cupping her chin in his hands and his lips were on hers.

I felt like a voyeur, my cheeks burning, and even though I knew I should look away I couldn't make myself do it. I watched Chris make a move I never expected, and Hannah reciprocate … once she got over her shock.

I finally dragged my eyes from the new couple to Jack and found him grinning as he watched. He shook his head, pressed the heel of his hand to his forehead, and then grabbed his glass of wine. As if sensing me watching him, he flicked his eyes to me and didn't move them until he'd drained the glass.

"I guess you were right, huh?"

"Stranger things have happened."

"They have. Let's hope this works out."

"I think it will."

"I want to argue with you, but I think it will too. Just don't let being right about this one thing go to your head."

I smirked. "I'll do my best."

FIFTEEN

*C*hris and Hannah's kiss was the talk of dinner, even though they were both so red-faced when they joined the rest of the group it was obvious they wanted to talk about something else – anything else, really – but Chris was a good sport despite his embarrassment.

"And what brought that about?" Millie asked, her lips curving into a smirk as she took her seat between Bernard and me at the large round table in the center of the inn's dining room.

Chris shrugged. "I just thought it was time."

That was an interesting response. I didn't disagree with it, but it was odd all the same. "I thought you were going to take Jack's earlier advice," I admitted, dropping my napkin into my lap. "That's the way it seemed."

"What was Jack's advice?" Hannah asked, recovering quickly from the surprise and focusing on me. She was a practical sort, so once Chris changed the rules of the game she was quick to adjust to her new reality. That's simply the way she operated.

"He doesn't think workplace romances are a good idea," I replied.

"That's not exactly what I said," Jack hedged when Hannah gave him a thoughtful look.

"I'm curious why you would say that," Hannah said. "Why don't you approve of work romances?"

"Because if there's a breakup things become uncomfortable," Chris supplied. "I thought about what he said – I don't disagree with it – but then I decided to do it anyway."

"Why?" Hannah's eyes were contemplative as she searched Chris's face.

"Because what Jack didn't take into account was that I couldn't not do it." Chris beamed at Hannah as her cheeks flushed. "My heart wouldn't let me. I don't know why I didn't wait until we were alone – it was as if I was overcome by some magical force pushing me to do it right here and now – but Charlie said we should talk about it so I decided I couldn't wait to talk about it. Once it was in my head it was as if that was all I could think about."

"Charlie said, huh?" Hannah smirked. "It seems Charlie has advice for everybody on this front."

"Yeah, she's very wise," Chris agreed, bobbing his head and clearly missing the weighted look Hannah shared with me. He wasn't aware that I'd had a similar conversation with Hannah before talking to him. I figured that was probably a good thing. "She said I should talk to you, but I realized I'm not very good at talking – unless it's about work – so I decided to kiss you instead. I think it was probably the better choice despite everyone staring at us."

Chris sounded so clinical – and yet so hopeful at the same time – it took everything I had not to burst out laughing.

"I think it was definitely a good idea," Millie enthused, smiling fondly at her nephew. "We've all been waiting for this since ... well, pretty much the beginning."

Hannah tucked a strand of her pale hair behind her shoulder and focused on Millie. "Since the beginning?"

Millie grinned. "Oh, honey, we've been waiting for this since you joined. I was starting to worry it wouldn't happen. Of course, in my heart I knew it absolutely would if I stayed out of the way and let you go at your own pace. Some things are just meant to be."

"And you think we're meant to be?" Hannah slid a sidelong look to

Chris, her unease obvious even as the potential for joy swamped her pretty features. "How can you know that?"

Millie shrugged. "It's just a feeling I get."

"I get it, too," I added, grabbing the menu from the center of the table. "I think it's weird that you two are essentially sharing your first date with us. I mean ... I'd think you'd want to be alone and talk things out by yourselves, but Millie is right. You need to do what feels natural."

"Huh, I didn't even think about that." Chris stroked his chin as he gave Hannah a thoughtful look. "Do you think we should eat alone and talk?"

Hannah nodded without hesitation. "That's a fine idea."

I widened my eyes, surprised. "I didn't mean you had to do it now."

Hannah and Chris ignored me, remaining focused solely on each other.

"There's a table in the corner." Chris pointed. "It's tucked away and we can be alone."

Hannah beamed. "I like what you're suggesting."

Chris held out his hand to her. "Shall we?"

"Yes. Absolutely."

My mouth dropped open as I watched them go, my eyes refusing to look away until they sat at their table and started gazing into one another's eyes. "This is like the weirdest courtship ever."

"It definitely is," Millie agreed. She stared at the couple for a long moment and then shook her head, chuckling as she turned back to us. "I can't believe one of them finally made a move. I swear I thought the polar ice caps would finish melting before this happened."

"I think it's nice," Bernard offered. "I think they're both sweet and made for each other. I love when people are made for each other." He cast Millie a sly look before reaching for his wine. "There's nothing better than young love. Er, older love is okay, too. Well ... I guess it's fair to say I'm fine with all love."

Jack cocked an eyebrow as he shook his head. I had my suspicions about Millie and Bernard's relationship – something they refused to talk about – but I was under the impression Jack knew the truth. He wasn't sharing what he knew.

When people refuse to gossip it drives me nuts, just for the record.

"I think workplace romance is a good idea," Laura announced, taking advantage of Chris's departure to switch chairs and nab the one closest to Jack. "It makes things easier and you don't have to worry about someone being upset if you keep strange hours because you're out chasing non-existent werewolves."

I narrowed my eyes as Laura rubbed her finger over Jack's wrist, causing him to shift in his chair.

"I think we should have more romances in the workplace," Laura added. "We don't have nearly enough now."

Millie rolled her eyes. "Honey, I think you might just get your wish … only not in the way you think."

Laura's face was blank. "What does that mean?"

"Don't worry about it." Millie pursed her lips as Jack cleared his throat and jerked his arm from Laura. His discomfort was evident – something that amused me – but Laura either didn't catch on to the signs or purposely ignored them. I was leaning toward the latter.

"Charlie, how was your day?" Millie asked, purposely changing the subject. "Did you go anywhere interesting? Your day had to be better than our day."

"What was wrong with your day?" I was legitimately curious.

"I was stuck in the woods with a whining woman who doesn't see the world for what it really is," Millie answered without hesitation, glowering at Laura. "What about you?"

"Well, we visited area businesses asking if any of the workers had seen anything weird in the woods," I replied. "It wasn't exactly what I'd call a thrilling outing."

"That's why you should've taken me, Jack," Laura prodded. "It would've been thrilling with me."

"Oh, geez." Jack rolled his neck and stared at the ceiling. "I don't even know what to say to any of this. How is this even part of the conversation?"

"Don't say anything," Bernard suggested. "If you pretend she's not there maybe she'll go away. It works with ghosts."

"It doesn't work with ghosts," Millie argued. "It doesn't work with oversexed tarts either. Jack's been employing that tactic for days, but his shadow has yet to notice he's in pain whenever she throws herself at him."

"Who's his shadow?" Laura asked, finally picking up on the conversation. "You're talking about Charlie, aren't you?"

I balked. "I'm not his shadow. He made me go. He wanted to gauge how I reacted to seeing Aric Winters." In my rush to defend myself, I realized too late that I probably should've left his name out of things.

Millie's eyebrows flew up her forehead. "You saw Aric Winters without me?"

"I don't like hearing about Aric Winters," Bernard grumbled, rubbing his forehead. For some reason his reaction warmed my heart.

"Don't worry about it." I leaned closer and patted his forearm. "He's completely in love with his wife."

"Of course he's in love with his wife," Millie barked. "Did I say otherwise? That doesn't mean he isn't the finest specimen of a man I've ever seen. I mean ... he's so hot he looks as if he could do porn."

"Oh, good grief." Jack smacked his forehead. "I don't want to hear this."

"You should've thought about that before you dragged Charlie off to see Aric," Millie shot back. "That was clearly a job that I should've been assigned."

"Wait, are we talking about the same Aric Winters from the photographs?" Laura was lagging behind in the conversation. For some reason, that made me inexplicably happy. I was more of an insider than her for a change. It was a petty thrill, but I never pretended to be above pettiness.

"Yes, and you're not part of this conversation," Jack said, keeping his eyes on me. "Don't turn this into a thing. We've already talked about why we had to visit Mr. Winters. Everything worked out in the end. Why do you have to make it a thing?"

That was a good question for which I didn't have a serviceable answer. "I don't know. I just do."

"What did he say?" Millie probed, focusing the conversation on something she was interested to hear. "Did he remember me?"

I smirked. "He said spending time with you was the highlight of his evening."

"Did he really?" Millie was clearly tickled because she leaned back in her chair and beamed. "Did I tell you how he looked with his shirt off? His abs looked drawn on." She wasn't talking to anyone in particular and she took on a far-off expression. "I kind of wanted to trace them ... with my tongue."

Despite the fact that I often found Millie entertaining, even I was uncomfortable with her words. "I definitely should've kept my mouth shut."

Jack cast me an irritated look. "Live and learn, huh?"

"Definitely."

I WAITED UNTIL I WAS certain everyone had retired to their rooms for the evening to sneak out again. It was a calculated risk – something that could easily blow up in my face – but I thought ahead this time and arranged for an Uber so I didn't have to take one of the Jeeps. I figured that Jack couldn't complain about me wasting my own time if I didn't steal one of the rentals.

I was on the main floor and heading toward the front door when Millie stepped into my path. Her expression was hard to read, but she seemed somber.

"You scared the crap out of me." I lightly slapped her arm as I waited for my heart to stop racing and my breathing to return to normal. "You need to stop sneaking up on people. It's undignified ... and it makes me nervous."

Millie made a dubious face. "You're nervous because you're about to sneak out again. Don't blame that on me."

"But ... how did you know?"

"Because you're you and I could practically see your mind working throughout dinner. I'm not an idiot."

No, she could never be confused for an idiot. "I have something I need to do. It can't be helped. I'm not taking one of the rentals. I called an Uber. It should be fine."

Millie didn't look convinced. "I don't know if you should head back to the Winters house alone. I know you're intrigued by her – and barely look at him, which I don't get – but she doesn't seem keen to give you the answers you're looking for."

She wasn't wrong. Zoe Lake-Winters was guarded and secretive. I wasn't sure I could blame her. She didn't know me, and her family was her first priority. "I do want answers." Pretending otherwise would be a waste of time. "I'm not going to the Winters house, though."

Surprise lit Millie's features. "You're not?"

I shook my head. "I'm going to the hospital."

"Why?"

"Because sneaking into Lisa Savage's room will be easier at night," I explained. "I want to see her for myself."

"What if you get caught?"

"Then I'll lie and find a way out."

"What if you get caught by Lisa Savage?" Millie persisted. "She could call the police and have you arrested."

"She could," I agreed, "but I'm guessing they'll have her sedated for the night."

"And why do you think that?"

"That's how it usually works." This wasn't the first time I'd planned an excursion to a hospital to talk to a victim. I didn't think admitting that now would do much good. "I just want to touch her and see if I can get a reading."

"Can you do that?" Millie was understandably intrigued. "Can you touch her and see what she went through while she was out there?"

I didn't have an easy answer. "Maybe. It doesn't always work. It depends on how traumatized she is, what images embedded in her mind. It's kind of a crapshoot, but I want to see if I can find out anything of interest. Her husband is still out there, after all."

"I understand." Millie was thoughtful. "Even though you're not taking a rental, Jack will melt down when he finds out."

I knew that was true. "I can't live my life by what Jack wants."

Millie's expression softened. "He only wants to keep you safe."

"I know. I'm not angry with him. I also can't tell him the truth. He won't understand."

"I don't necessarily think that's true, but it's a conversation for another time." Millie turned serious as she studied the empty lobby. "Part of me wants to go with you because I'm curious, but the other part knows it's a mistake. I need to stay here and cover your retreat."

Uh-oh. That sounded possibly dangerous. "What do you mean by that?"

"Simply that I need to be close in case Jack decides to search for you." Millie rubbed her hands together as she warmed to her topic. "He'll stop at your room first and then come down here to check on the keys. I need to plant myself on the couch and pretend I'm reading so I'll already be down here when he shows up."

"And then what?"

"And then I'll tell him you're in the bathroom or something." Millie waved off the question as if it didn't matter. "Don't worry. I've got everything under control. I've got your back." She flashed an enthusiastic thumbs-up. "Go and psychically invade her mind until we have the answers we need."

I really wished she hadn't phrased it that way. "Um ... yeah. That's not generally how it works. Basically I just touch her and see what's on the surface of her brain – like if there are snarling teeth or animal claws – but I rarely get everything."

"I don't need to know the nitty-gritty." Millie made a face. "Go. I've got everything covered here."

I had my doubts, but I didn't have a lot of options. "Be careful ... and text me if something comes up."

"I'm on it."

She seemed so sure of herself I could do nothing but walk away ... and continue to fret. Why did I believe the exact opposite was true?

16

SIXTEEN

*T*he driver dropped me near the front door. I considered asking him to stay in case I needed to make a hasty getaway, but I didn't think that was proper Uber etiquette, so instead I paid and waved as he buzzed out of the parking lot. I would have to find a way back to the inn on my own, whether that involved calling for a second Uber or hitching a ride. That was a problem for future me, though. Present me had other things on her mind.

The lobby was mostly empty. I knew which room Lisa was in thanks to Hannah, so I pretended to have an agenda and headed straight for the elevator. I learned a long time ago that most people will not question your reason for being where you shouldn't be as long as you put on a good show – if you look like you belong there then people will believe it.

The sixth floor was quiet when I stepped off the elevator and the woman behind the nurse's station desk didn't as much look up. I left her to play whatever computer game she was playing – something with a mutant teddy bear wearing a hat briefly popped into my mind – and turned to my right. I studied the hospital's floorplan online before leaving the hotel, and that proved to be beneficial now.

I slowed my pace as I approached Lisa's room, making sure to keep my footsteps quiet. If a cop was stationed outside her room I'd have to come up with a way to distract him so I could get inside. My mind was busy with possibilities when a hand shot out of the vending machine alcove to the right and grabbed my arm.

I was so surprised I opened my mouth to scream but Zoe Lake-Winters, her blue eyes flashing with warning, clamped her hand over my mouth. She dragged me into the alcove and immediately started shaking her head.

"If you scream, I'll punch you in the boob," she warned, serious. "I might not be big, but I can punch like a dude. You've seen my husband. He taught me."

I stared at her for a long moment, taking a moment to allow my heartbeat to return to normal, and then I nudged her hand away from my mouth. "Please tell me you washed your hands. You're in a hospital and you strike me as the sort who likes to touch things and then carry the germs around forever."

Zoe snorted, amusement lighting her pretty features. "I like you. I can't help it. You remind me a lot of me, like, ten years ago."

That was kind of insulting. "Aren't you forty?"

"So?"

"I'm only twenty-three. That's closer to two decades."

Now it was Zoe's turn to be offended. "Not in my head."

"And yet simple math makes it true."

"We'll compromise at a decade and a half." Zoe slowly lowered her hand and gave me a once over. "I'm glad to see you didn't dress all in black for this excursion. You wouldn't have made it past the front desk if you had."

"This isn't my first time."

Zoe licked her lips and nodded. "No, probably not. Stay here a second." She held up her finger and moved to the hallway, looking left and right before returning. "You're trying to visit Lisa Savage."

I saw no reason to lie. It was the same reason she was here. "We can't get any information on her prognosis ... or even what's wrong with her. I thought if I could touch her ... well, you know what I thought. That's the same reason you're here."

"Not exactly," Zoe hedged, shifting from one foot to the other. "I was going to try something else."

"What?"

Zoe opened her mouth, furrowed her brow, moved her mouth, wrinkled her forehead and then exhaled heavily. "I think we need to talk."

That sounded promising. "Where?"

"There's a coffee shop right around the corner. It's less than two minutes if you drive."

"I took an Uber."

Zoe made a face. "Of course you did. Come on. You can ride with me."

"What about Lisa?" I vaguely gestured toward the hallway.

"There's a police officer sitting in her room. I mean ... right inside. I was trying to think of a way around him, but then I saw you. I think our conversation is more important ... at least for right now."

"You might not believe that if you were Ethan Savage and still missing."

"Good point." Zoe gave my shoulder a soft shove. "But I'm not Ethan Savage, and we definitely need to talk."

ZOE PICKED A CORNER table that was far removed from the rest of the coffee shop patrons. It was a bit late for a caffeine buzz, but the shop was bustling with hipsters and what looked to be a few mothers desperate for solitude.

"There's nothing to do in this area if you're a certain age," Zoe explained as she sat in a chair and sipped her cappuccino. "We're concerned about the trouble Sami will manage to find when she hits her teenage years because of the dearth of options."

"I think Sami is the sort of kid who will find trouble no matter where she is, so worrying about where you live is probably a waste of time," I said as I stripped my straw of its wrapper. I opted for a blender drink with a lot of ice and strawberry flavoring. I had no doubt I'd be riding a sugar high when it was time to head back to the hotel.

"I think you're probably right," Zoe agreed. "That's the kind of kid I was. Is that the kind of kid you were?"

It was hard to describe the kind of kid I was. "Not really. I tried to be good because I was always so worried about my parents. We figured out pretty quickly that I could ... um ... see things that other people couldn't. I had a penchant for blurting out those things when I was a kid. That never went over well."

Zoe chuckled. "That must have been hard on your parents."

"It was."

"Still, you made it to adulthood and managed to survive. That has to be a relief for them."

"They died when I was a teenager." I left out the fact that they'd adopted me. My birth parents either died or abandoned me when I was four. I could remember nothing before then. Whenever I told that story it made people sad, so I decided to leave it out ... at least for the time being.

Zoe's expression fell. "I'm sorry. That must have been hard for you."

I shrugged and blinked back tears. I had no idea where the urge to cry came from, but I fought it off. "I like to think they'd be proud of where I landed. I worked hard to get here."

"Yeah." Zoe kicked back in her chair and searched my face. "We've done some intensive digging on The Legacy Foundation. It's an interesting group. We'd never heard of them until you blurted out the name. Now that we know, we can't help but be a little worried."

"Because you're magical?"

Zoe stared me down. "Because I'm different ... like you. What I find interesting is that you're hiding among a group of people who would love to study you. You're exactly what they're looking for. That's either incredibly smart or ridiculously stupid."

"I like to think of it as smart," I said. "I can control what I do and fly under the radar. Er, well, at least for the most part. I want to help others."

"And you want to find answers regarding what you are," Zoe noted. "I don't blame you. Answers are key. I struggled with the same thing when I was eighteen."

"You did?" She was finally opening up and I was eager to hear what she had to say. "Does that mean you didn't always know what you were?"

Zoe sipped her coffee and shook her head. "I had no idea until I showed up at college and everyone else seemed to know what I was. I lived in the dark, hung out with some unsavory people and didn't find out the whole truth for a very long time. In between, I muddled through and tripped over trouble at every corner."

I was intrigued. "What are you?"

"I'm a mage."

I knit my eyebrows as I ran the word through my head. "Doesn't that basically mean 'magician' for all intents and purposes? I mean ... are you really saying you're a magician? I saw inside your head and that's not the word I'd use to describe what I witnessed."

"I would deny that, but I know it's a waste of time," Zoe grumbled. "You're like a Kardashian at a shoe sale. You won't let it go until you conquer everyone."

I snorted. "I don't know how I feel about being compared to a Kardashian, but I get what you're saying."

"Insulted. You're supposed to feel insulted about being likened to a Kardashian."

"Duly noted."

Zoe rolled her eyes at my smirk. "It's a long story and I won't get into specifics, but true mages are ... different. They're selected as children, removed from their homes and trained to keep both sides of magic – we're talking good and bad here – from getting too strong of a foothold. They're not supposed to get involved in the battles but make sure nobody gets out of control."

"Like security guards at the mall."

"Basically." Zoe rubbed the back of her neck. "My parents were both true mages. They spent a very long time doing their jobs. Then they met, fell in love, and fled."

"Why?" The story was beyond fascinating. "I mean ... why did they have to run?"

"Mages aren't supposed to fall in love with one another. They're most certainly not allowed to breed. Mine did, though, and they somehow managed to stay off the mage police radar. They raised me in private and never told me what I was."

"So ... you're like a super-duper mage, right? If you have double the powers you're something special."

"I guess that's one way to look at it. Another way is that my powers are coveted and every low-life magic thief on this side of the equator wants what I have ... and they've come for me."

The reality of Zoe's situation was like a kick in the gut. "I didn't think about that. I guess I should have. I saw some of the things you've gone through, and when I was inside your head it was as if I was living your life."

"Then you know I've had a great life." Zoe sipped again. "I'm not sorry about what I am or where I ended up. In general, I'm happy. Things have been much better the past year."

I put a few of the puzzle pieces together. "Since Covenant College was wiped off the map."

Zoe arched an eyebrow. "I'm impressed. How did you tie me to Covenant College?"

"It wasn't all that difficult. Whoever you paid to wipe your information from the student database was good, but I know somebody better."

"Your good buddy Jack?"

I refused to answer the question. "What happened at Covenant College?"

Zoe stared long and hard into my eyes. "I could make you answer. You probably don't believe that, but it's true."

On the contrary, I had no doubt she could. I felt her power in the brief time we were connected and recognized she was fully capable of taking me down. It was humbling ... and also a relief. Knowing that I wasn't the most powerful person on the block made me feel better, more human even.

"What happened at Covenant College?" I repeated.

Zoe sighed. "I won't hurt Jack. I saw his heart and mind while we were in the woods, and he seems a genuinely nice guy, if a bit strict and sometimes morose. He's not a bad man, so you don't have to worry about me hurting him."

I balked. "I'm not worried about you hurting him. I can see what kind of person you are. You only go after the bad guys."

"Yes, I'm like Batman." Zoe pressed the heel of her hand to her forehead. "I don't know how much I can tell you about Covenant College. The entire thing is weird. I mean ... like, so weird. I thought for sure that the college burning down would be the top story on the news for months. Instead, people talked about it for days and then let it go."

Hmm. That was mighty interesting. "I guess a little magic was involved in that, too, huh?"

"You wouldn't believe me if I told you ... and, no, I'm not going to tell you. It's not important and it's not entirely my story. Suffice it to say that Covenant College was built upon a vortex of evil and needed to be taken down."

"I'm fine with that." I had figured it was something like that. The way the college was eradicated and forgotten so quickly was truly dumbfounding. Magic had to be involved. "Because you're a mage, does that mean Sami is a mage? Is your husband a mage, too?"

Zoe immediately started shaking her head. "I'm not here to talk about Sami and Aric. Don't push me on them. You won't like what happens if you do." Her voice was chilling and I believed she meant what she said. "I've decided to tell you about me because ... well ... you won't let it go. As for everyone else, it's really none of your concern."

"Except I'm here investigating a potential paranormal murder," I pointed out.

"I thought you were here looking for werewolves."

"I don't like it when you use that derisive tone. You just told me about a school burning to the ground and no one noticing. Werewolves aren't out of the realm of possibility."

"They're definitely not," Zoe agreed, taking me by surprise. "Werewolves are real. I have no doubt about that. So are witches, vampires, sphinxes and any number of other creatures that I don't have time to list. They're all real."

I sucked in a breath. "Have you run across all of them?"

"A time or two. That's not really important either. What's important is Ethan Savage. He's out there somewhere."

"You've met werewolves." I adopted a rational tone. "Do they eat people?"

"No."

"What do they eat?"

"Chocolate cake." Zoe made a face that warned me to back off from my line of questioning.

"Fine." I held up my hands. "I'm sorry for sticking my nose in your business. You have to understand, though, I've rarely run across anyone like me. And, yes, I know you're really not like me. I know you're something else, but you're closer than most."

Sympathy flitted across Zoe's features, and that almost made me feel worse. "I get it. I'm sorry you're in the position you are. I really am. It doesn't seem fair. Didn't your parents tell you what you were?"

"They didn't seem to know." I pictured my poor, worried, beaten-down parents not long before they died. They spent their lives trying to protect me, but I frightened them beyond belief. "I asked. They researched. No one knew."

"That makes things worse." Zoe shook her head. "Tell me exactly what you can do. I know a few people. I can ask questions, maybe come up with some answers for you."

"Really?" I couldn't keep the hope from my voice. "Are you serious?"

Zoe nodded. "I even have one of them on speed-dial. She has a cranky toddler at home, but she'll answer. She always does."

I chewed my bottom lip. I wasn't sure now was the time for a deviation of this sort. On the flip side, when would I get another chance to tap the resources of a mage? I mean ... it was just so fantastical.

"Okay." I made my decision on the spot. "What do I have to lose?"

Zoe turned serious. "You need to be careful. You could lose everything. I know that seems rich coming from me, but you have to consider your personal safety when it comes to sharing your secret. You don't know me. I know it feels like you do because you were in my head, but you really don't. You just happen to be lucky because I'm a bleeding heart and overall good person ... unless you talk to my mother-in-law, of course. Then I show traces of being related to the Devil."

"Is the Devil real?"

"I have no idea. I've seen numerous devils in human form, though. You need to be careful. You can trust Millie."

"I do, but she only knows because of an accident."

"Yeah. That was the thing in the abandoned old west town, right?" I widened my eyes, causing Zoe to smirk. "I saw in your head too," she reminded me. "Now tell me what you can do. I can't promise that we'll come up with answers, but I might be able to point you in a different direction."

"That sounds great." I let out a shaky breath. "So, basically, I have psychic flashes and I'm telekinetic. Oh, and I've seen a ghost or two. I also saw the Chupacabra, but it was after a fall down the stairs and Jack is convinced I imagined it. Oh, and I met some witches and they think I might have witch in me. That's basically everything."

Zoe smiled. "Well, then let's see what we can find out."

SEVENTEEN

"Try it again."

Zoe lifted her hand in the air, her fingers glowing purple, and nodded.

I was exhausted. Our conversation in the coffee shop led to Zoe insisting we head to the woods to test my powers (something that felt as if it lasted for years rather than hours). So I nodded and concentrated, waiting for the blow to come.

This time when Zoe tossed a zinger of magic in my direction it harmlessly bounced off and fell to the side, catching both of us by surprise.

"That was much better." Zoe beamed as she moved closer, taking a moment to look me over under the muted moonlight. The temperature remained high even though darkness fell hours before, and my skin was sticky because of the humidity. "Does anything hurt?"

I shrugged. Everything hurt. I didn't want to come across as a baby, though. "I'm fine. What did you just throw at me?"

"Not much," Zoe admitted, dragging a hand through her curling hair. It seemed she wasn't immune to the humidity either. "It was just a little something that wouldn't have hurt you. That wasn't the aim, though. I wanted to see if you could block, which you did."

I felt triumphant because of that, even though it seemed a small win compared to the fifteen times she'd smacked me upside with magic that I couldn't block. "So, what do you think that means?"

Zoe shrugged. "I have no idea. I told you, my friend is doing research. She has a lot of books. She says that your powers don't necessarily mean you're anything. You could be a witch ... or something else ... or you could simply be a powerful individual with few powers. We simply don't know."

That definitely wasn't the answer I was looking for. "So what should I do?"

"Keep doing what you're doing." Zoe ordered. "Hide who you are. Don't tell the people you work with unless you're sure you can trust them. You haven't been there long enough to be sure, although Millie seems fine."

"She's great. She's kind of like a grandmother, but a fun one who always wants to go out drinking. She's obsessed with your husband, by the way. She can't stop talking about seeing him shirtless."

"Yes, well, it's a marvelous sight." Zoe grinned as she bent over and rooted around in a bag, coming back with two bottles of water and handing me one. "I heard you stopped to see Aric this afternoon. He said Jack was a little intense and he felt sorry for you."

"Jack isn't so bad." I had no idea why I felt the need to stand up for him. "He's a good guy. He's just ... regimented. He thinks people should act a certain way, follow the rules to the letter and never act out of sorts. He can't help himself."

Zoe snorted as she swigged from the bottle. "Aric was kind of like that when we first met. We had a lot going on and there was a time I thought he didn't put me first. I was wrong. He did put me first, and we worked things out. He turned out to be completely trustworthy."

I couldn't figure out what she was trying to say. "Does that mean you think Jack is trustworthy?"

"I don't think he's after you because of what you are or anything." Zoe tilted her head to the side, considering. "I think he's a good man with a lot on his mind."

"Like what?"

Zoe made a tsking sound as she wagged her finger in front of my face. "I'm not telling you that. It's an invasion."

"I could look for myself."

"You could, but you're not great at controlling it yet, and Jack isn't the sort of person I'd test your powers on."

She had a point. "I guess I should get going. I need to walk back to the inn. It will probably take me half an hour. We're fairly close, right?"

Zoe nodded and pointed. "It's that way. I'll take you. You shouldn't be walking around in the woods alone at night."

"I don't want to impose."

"You're not. It will take five minutes. And then I won't have to feel guilty about leaving you to walk home alone. Speaking of home, we need to get going." Zoe checked her phone screen. "Aric expected me home almost two hours ago. He's probably freaking out."

"Probably?" The new voice was a low rumble as a dark figure cut through the trees next to the clearing and approached Zoe. He towered over her, although she didn't appear afraid, and the look on his face displayed a lifetime of agitation. "Why didn't you call?"

"I forgot." Zoe took another drink of her water. "How did you even find me? I have no bars on my phone out, so you didn't track me that way. Besides, you know you're in deep trouble if you ever put a tracer app on my phone again. We talked about that."

"We did," Aric agreed, his tone congenial, even though I could sense he was edgy. "We agreed that you're my wife and I love you. If that means tracking your phone, I'll do it. That's not what I did tonight, though."

"So how did you find me?"

"Sami." Aric's answer was simple and caused me to search the darkness behind him for the youngest Winters family member.

"I guess I should've seen that coming," Zoe muttered, shaking her head. "Where is she?"

"Locked in the truck with Trouble and a bad case of the 'I can't believe you're making me do this' flu," Aric replied. "She wasn't happy about being dragged away from the house, but I insisted. What are you doing out here?"

"Testing Charlie's magic."

I lowered my gaze and stared at my feet.

"I see." Aric flicked his gaze to me. "And?"

"And we have no idea what she is, but I taught her to put up a shield. She needs to practice just in case."

"And that's what you've been doing?"

Zoe nodded. "What did you think I was doing?"

"Checking on Lisa Savage so we could get answers about her husband," Aric replied without hesitation. "That's the priority right now, isn't it? If something is out hunting in these woods we want to know about it."

"There was a cop in her room. I couldn't get inside. I'll try again tomorrow."

Aric sighed. "Fine. Do what you want."

"Don't I always?"

"Yes, and it drives me crazy." Aric smacked a loud kiss against Zoe's mouth before focusing on me. "Are you okay? You look a little pale."

"It's been a long night." I meant it. "I feel drained." I wanted to ask how Sami had managed to track down her mother in the middle of nowhere, but I figured that might set off Aric, and I didn't want to push things. Zoe had already gone above and beyond, after all. "I just want to head back to the inn and go to bed."

"I need to take her," Zoe added. "She took an Uber to the hospital, which is where I found her. I don't want her walking back to the inn on her own."

"Definitely not," Aric agreed. "I'll take her. Give me the keys to your car. You can take Sami back to the house in my truck."

Zoe was instantly alert. "Why? What's wrong with Sami?"

"She's a little upset," Aric said. "She didn't like not knowing where you were."

"Ah." Zoe pursed her lips. "Okay. I'll take your truck. You make sure Charlie gets back to the inn. As for you … ." Zoe swiveled to face me, her expression unreadable. "I have your cell number. I'll call if I get any information."

"Thank you very much." I meant it. "You've been much nicer than I would've probably been in your shoes."

"Don't sell yourself short." Zoe patted my shoulder. "Practice the shield. It might become important. I don't get the feeling that you've come up against many magical enemies – which is a good thing – but it's always good to be prepared." Zoe started walking toward the trees and then paused. "Before you leave town, I totally want to hear the story about the Chupacabra."

I chuckled as I nodded, flicking my eyes to Aric to see if he was irritated about having to drive me to the inn before joining his family. He seemed excited.

"You saw the Chupacabra? Tell me all about it!"

ARIC WAITED IN FRONT of the inn until he was sure I'd reached the lobby door. I offered a wave, which he returned, and then let myself inside the blessedly cool lobby. I intended to head straight to my room and pass out. Instead, the sound of raucous laughter in the nearby bar caught my attention.

I found Millie, Bernard and Jack sitting at a small table. They had a pitcher of beer between them and appeared to be having a great time.

"It's not a freaking werewolf," Jack announced. "Stop saying it is. That's just ... ridiculous."

I took a tentative step inside so I could listen.

"You don't know that," Millie challenged. "It could very well be a werewolf. The whole point right now is that we don't know what it is. You don't always have to be such a downer when it comes to this stuff. Occasionally you could be fun."

"Yeah, yeah." Jack waved off the comment. I couldn't be certain, but I was almost positive he seemed a little drunk. I'd never seen him that way before – although he'd seen me sloshed a time or two – and I couldn't help but marvel at the way his wide smile lightened his handsome face. "Because believing in werewolves is fun."

"It is. You're just being a spoilsport." Millie flicked his ear before reaching for the pitcher. "I think we should get another round."

I decided to make my presence known. I hadn't done anything wrong and it didn't appear that Jack was prostrate with worry about me. "I think you've had enough." I stepped closer to the table and smiled at the trio of flushed faces. "Have you guys been drinking all night?"

"Just for the dark part of it," Jack replied, downing the contents of his glass and fixing me with a cock-eyed look. He was definitely drunk, which I found amusing. "Where have you been?"

"What makes you think I've been anywhere?" I took the seat between Bernard and Jack and shook my head when Millie mimed pouring me a beer. There was already a headache knocking against my skull thanks to my work with Zoe. I didn't need to exacerbate things.

"I looked for you," Jack replied. "I went to your room and you weren't there."

"That doesn't mean I left."

"Which is exactly what I told him," Millie interjected, her lips curving. "I pointed out the keys to the rentals were on the pegs, but he insisted on checking the parking lot – trusting soul that he is – and then started pacing because he was convinced you were off doing something stupid."

"Which I'm sure you were," Jack added, pouring more beer. I worried he had a dilly of a hangover in his future. Of course, that could also be fun because I wouldn't be the one hungover for a change. "Where were you?"

"I was outside taking a walk." That seemed like the simplest answer. "I needed some air."

Jack furrowed his brow. "There's nothing surrounding this inn but woods. You shouldn't walk around out there because Millie's were-wolf will get you ... and no one wants that." Seemingly amused with his own words, Jack snickered. "Werewolf. What a stupid idea."

"It's almost as bad as me claiming to see the Chupacabra, right?"

I expected Jack to jump on the topic but instead he shook his head.

"You were hurt. You were in that basement alone. You were afraid. There's no telling what you saw."

I scratched the side of my neck as I regarded him. "But you said I couldn't have seen what I thought I saw."

"That's because I didn't want you freaking yourself out." Jack drained another glass of beer – thankfully they were small glasses – and reached for the pitcher. I rested my hand on top of his to still him. "I'm not done."

"You should be done." I kept my voice gentle. "In fact, why don't you let me walk you to your room? That will be a nice change."

"Fine." Jack knuckled his eye as he stood on shaky legs. "I don't remember drinking enough to get drunk."

I pinned Millie, who looked self-satisfied and smug, with a hard look. "I doubt very much that you did it yourself."

"No." Jack, wobbly, nodded his head. "Millie peer-pressured me."

He looked so earnest I couldn't stop from laughing. "Millie is evil. You should know that." I directed him toward the door and glanced back at a cackling Millie and Bernard. "You guys should call it a night too."

"Thanks, Mom, we'll get right on that," Millie drawled. "Don't worry about us. We're fine. I'm more interested in you. How was your trip?"

I spared a glance at Bernard, but he was too busy staring into his half-empty glass to look in my direction. "It took a turn. I'll talk to you about it tomorrow."

"Why not tonight?"

"Because I'm putting Jack to bed and then doing the same." I briefly rubbed my pounding forehead. "I have a headache."

"Okay. See you tomorrow." Millie waved me off. "Make sure Jack has water and aspirin handy. He'll need it tomorrow morning."

"Yeah. I figured that out myself."

It took me five full minutes to get Jack up the stairs and to his room. He led me down the wrong hallway twice before remembering his room number. Then he fumbled with his keycard so many times I almost blew my stack before grabbing it from him and helping him inside.

His room was exactly what I'd expected, military neat and sterile. I left him to grapple with his shoes while I grabbed a bottle of water from the mini-fridge and placed three aspirin tablets on the nightstand.

"Come on, big guy." I clapped my hands to get Jack's attention. "It's time for bed."

"I'm getting ready." Jack made a face as he stripped off his shirt, leaving me agog at his body. He was sculpted and lean, his shoulders broad and his chest bare of hair. He clearly liked a little manscaping with his morning shower. While he wasn't as ripped as Aric Winters, he was pretty close.

Heck, he almost took my breath away.

"What are you looking at?" Jack grumbled, unbuttoning his jeans before I could make an escape. Thankfully he wore simple black boxer shorts beneath the jeans, so I didn't see anything that would traumatize me ... or cause excessive drool.

"Just get in bed, Jack." I moved to lift the covers and cried out when his forehead smacked into mine. "Ow!"

"Sorry." Jack placed a hand on either side of my face and stared into my eyes. He was intense and somber. "Are you okay? I didn't mean to do that."

He was so serious I could do nothing but melt. "I'm fine, Jack. You just took me by surprise."

"Yeah." I thought he would release my head, but he merely stared harder. "You weren't out taking a walk, were you?"

"I was." I felt uncomfortable under his studied gaze. "It was hot and I needed time to think on my own. I'm not used to all this togetherness. Sometimes I simply need a break."

"I'm not good at the togetherness either." Jack continued staring. "You shouldn't wander around by yourself. It's dangerous."

"I'll keep that in mind."

"I don't want you to get hurt again."

"I'll do my best to make sure that doesn't happen." I forced a smile for his benefit. "You're going to be miserable tomorrow morning. You know that, right?"

"Yeah." Jack took me by surprise when he released my head and leaned forward, gently pressing his forehead against mine. It was a soft gesture, something I never expected thanks to his tough-guy persona. "You need to be careful. If you get hurt, it won't be okay. You were already hurt once, and that was more than enough."

Being so close to Jack, sharing a moment that felt intimate even though I knew he was beyond drunk, was enough to get my heart racing. "I'll be careful. You don't have to worry about me."

"I have to worry about you."

"Because I'm the newest member of the group?"

"No. Well, partly."

"What's the other part?"

"I can't live with the idea of you being hurt." Jack heaved out a sigh before running his hand down the back of my head and pressing a quick kiss to my forehead. "Now I need to go to bed. I want to pass out before I throw up."

I remained rooted to my spot, my cheeks burning in the aftermath of the kiss. It could be considered chaste, I reminded myself. It's not as if he kissed me on the lips and went for it. The kiss was tender more than anything else, almost brotherly.

And yet ... it felt different. I couldn't put a name to the emotion rushing through me, but it certainly wasn't chastity.

It took me a moment to shake myself from my reverie. "Um, I'll check on you in the morning."

"Okay, Charlie." Jack was on the verge of passing out, but he cocked one eye and stared. "Lock your door when you get back to your room. Be safe."

I chuckled. "Ever the security guru, eh, Jack?"

"Be safe." Jack pressed his eyes shut. "I'll make sure you're safe. I won't fail you again."

EIGHTEEN

I got coffee from the main floor before knocking on Jack's room door the next morning. I could hear him shuffling around inside before opening it. He looked rough when he granted me entrance, his long hair damp from a shower and his features unnaturally pale.

"How are you feeling, big guy?" I was going for levity, but the look on Jack's face told me I'd missed the mark.

"If you're here to make fun of me ... or be loud ... I suggest going someplace else." Jack's voice was low and gravelly. "I'm not in the mood."

"I'm here to bring you coffee." I handed the drink over. "It's got chocolate in it. I thought you could use the sugar."

Instead of making an offhand remark about how chocolate coffee was for girls – something he'd told me more than once – Jack wordlessly took the coffee and drank at least a quarter of it in one gulp. I sympathetically smoothed his hair without thinking, my mind briefly wandering to the near kiss the night before and the way his lips felt against my forehead. When I shook myself from the reverie, I found Jack staring at me with unveiled interest.

I cleared my throat. "So ... how are you feeling?"

"Where did your mind just go?" Jack took another sip as he narrowed his eyes. "I remember something about you from last night. What is it?"

Uh-oh. That was a loaded question. There were so many ways I could go with the answer. "Um ... you'll have to be more specific."

"I can't remember."

My heart inadvertently constricted at the admission. He didn't remember almost kissing me. Of course he didn't. He was drunk, and things that you would otherwise never consider always seem like a good idea when you're drunk. "I'm sure it's not important." I worked overtime to sound breezy. "You'll probably want to take out your hangover frustration on Millie. She's the one who got you tanked."

"I remember some of that." Jack drank his coffee. "I was doing something and she distracted me with a trip to the bar. I ... you." Jack slowly leveled his gaze on me, his expression twisting. "I was looking for you."

My heart thumped harder. "Why?"

"Because I knew you were going to take off again." Jack winced at the clink his coffee cup made when he set it down. "That's what you did. You took off, although I have no idea how since you didn't take one of the rentals. I remember checking on that."

"So you're basically saying that you checked on me because you assumed I was a thief." I knew getting self-righteous would work against me, but I couldn't stop myself. "That's real nice, Jack." I turned to leave, but he shot out a hand and gripped my elbow. "Let me go."

Jack did as I instructed, but he didn't move his eyes from my face as I tamped down my fury. "I checked on you because I was worried you'd take off and do something stupid. You did take off. I know you did."

"I was getting some air."

"You seem to need a lot of air."

"We all do. We need oxygen to survive."

"Charlie ... ." Jack must have realized he sounded petulant because he adjusted his tone. "I'm allowed to worry about you. You're my responsibility. I'm not going to apologize for that."

"You're not my father."

Jack chuckled, the sound harsh. "Trust me. I don't want to be your father. That's the last thing on my mind."

"What do you want?"

"What do you mean?"

I realized pushing him was the wrong thing to do and decided to back off. "It doesn't matter. I didn't take the rental car and I was on my own time. Why does it matter where I was?"

"Because I want to know."

He seemed so sincere I couldn't leave him with nothing. "I went to the hospital hoping I could sneak into Lisa Savage's room and talk to her."

Whatever he was expecting, that wasn't it. Jack was flabbergasted. "You what?"

"Don't worry." I waved off what I'm sure was about to be a righteous diatribe. "I didn't get close to her. She had a police officer in her room. After that I went to a coffee shop and then came back here." That wasn't technically a lie. I did all those things. I simply left out the part where I spent two hours in the woods practicing magical tricks with Zoe. I didn't think that would go over well so I simply omitted it.

"I can't believe you did that." Jack turned gruff as he shook his head. Despite the change in his demeanor, I sensed a cloud of calm descending over him. He was relieved that I went the stupid route and visited the hospital. I couldn't help but wonder what he was thinking about my actions before that. "You need to be more careful."

"I just wanted to be helpful." That was true. "I thought if I could get some information we would know where to start this morning. I came up empty-handed. I'm sorry."

"Well, it's not the end of the world." Jack dragged a hand through his hair. "I don't think it was exactly smart, but it certainly wasn't the end of the world."

"That's good to know. I would hate to be the cause of the apocalypse."

"Ha, ha." Jack finished downing his coffee and tossed the empty cup in the trash receptacle by the door before holding it open. "Let's get some breakfast and then we'll talk about what we're doing today. We need to come up with a plan."

"Okay." I was agreeable to the suggestion because I was out of ideas.

When I stepped into the hallway, I noticed Laura stood about ten feet away, and the look she shot me when she realized I was walking out of Jack's room overflowed with venom.

"Well, well, well. What do we have here?"

It took Jack a moment to grasp what Laura was insinuating. He glanced between her and me and then at his door before finding words. "We're going down for breakfast. We want to divide everyone up for the day, you know, disperse the work evenly."

"Let me guess; you're going to spend the day with Charlie." Laura's tone was so icy it caused chills to cascade down my spine. "That's on top of the time you two have already spent together."

"Oh, it's not what you think," I protested hurriedly. "I was just bringing him coffee."

Jack held up his hand to silence me. "It's none of her business what we were doing."

His reaction surprised me. "It's not?"

"No." Jack held Laura's gaze for an extended beat, a challenge of sorts flowing between them. "We're going downstairs for breakfast. That's all you need to know, Laura."

Laura slanted her eyes to me. "I believe you and I are going to need to have a talk later."

That didn't sound good. "I ...."

"Leave her alone," Jack ordered, his bossy nature on full display, the hangover casting a pall over his features only moments before completely eradicated. "She hasn't done anything to you and it's not your business what she does with her private time. Stay out of her way."

"Or what?" Laura folded her arms over her chest. "What happens if I don't follow your rules, Jack?"

"You don't want to find out." Jack put his hand to the small of my back and prodded me in front of him. "Let's get breakfast, Charlie. It's going to be a long day and we need the fuel."

I risked one more glance over my shoulder and cringed as Laura scorched me with a glare. "Okay." I waited until I was sure we were out of Laura's earshot to speak again. "She'll make me pay for that. You know that, right?"

"You'll be fine." Jack flashed his first smile of the day. "The good news is that she thinks I'm doing stuff with you, so she probably won't be hitting on me any longer. This is best for everybody."

Of course he'd think that. "Or it's simply going to cause her to double her efforts because it's even more fun to take something from me while trying to snag you."

Jack's smile slipped. "Huh. I hadn't thought of that."

"That's because you don't think like a girl."

"I consider that a compliment."

"It won't be a compliment when she unleashes her fury," I pointed out. "She'll come after me."

"Don't worry. I'll protect you."

For some reason, Jack's response made me feel light and giddy. Ugh! That was such a girl response. I hated myself for it. "What if you're not around when she comes after me?"

"I'll stick close. It will be fine."

It was only after I gave it some real thought that I realized Jack sticking close would cut down on visits with Zoe. Hmm. I couldn't help but wonder if that was on purpose.

JACK AND I WERE tasked with returning to the hospital when Hannah was told in no uncertain terms that she wouldn't be allowed to visit Lisa Savage. In addition to that, the doctor in charge of Lisa's case informed Hannah that her obsessive calls were starting to become intrusive. From a neutral standpoint, I understood that. Chris and Hannah took it as a personal affront, though. They insisted Jack and I take over hospital duty while they adopted another plan of attack. I had a feeling that plan involved spending the day making out

– something I would never say out loud – but it was really none of my business.

"What do you think we should do?"

Jack and I sat in the Jeep and stared at the hospital, opting to remain in the parking lot until we made our decision.

"I have no idea." Jack rubbed his forehead and leaned close enough to the vent that the freezing blast from the air conditioning hit him smack in the face. "I can't decide if Chris assigned this to us because he didn't want to do it himself or he really thought we might have a better shot of getting answers."

"I think he just wanted to spend quality time with Hannah. To do that, he needed to get rid of us."

"Quality time with Hannah, huh?" Jack smirked. "You're probably right. I have no problem with that ... other than the fact that he expects us to somehow talk to Lisa Savage even though she's being protected from all angles."

"Yeah." I instinctively reached over and pushed Jack's hair from his forehead. "How are you feeling?"

He cast me a cock-eyed look. "I'm fine. It's just a hangover. It will be gone ... well, it will be gone when it's gone. I can somehow manage to function despite the headache."

"I'm sure you can." I pulled my hand away and forced my eyes to the hospital. Being in close proximity to Jack was starting to do weird things to my hormones. I couldn't remember being this off-kilter around a man since college ... and that was only because I was too stupid to know better.

I could feel Jack's eyes on me as I stared at the large building, my mind working through possible scenarios. We needed to talk to Lisa Savage. There was no getting around that. We were operating in the dark, and the police didn't seem keen to share information.

"What are you thinking?" Jack asked after several moments of silence.

I shrugged, noncommittal. "I don't know."

"No, I saw something pass through your eyes." Jack straightened.

"You had an idea. You simply can't decide if it's a good or bad one. I know you."

"You barely know me," I corrected. "You don't know what I was thinking."

"I do." Jack was so self-assured it was grating. "I can recognize some of your facial expressions now. You just had an idea. You're afraid to share it with me."

"That's because you'll think it's a bad idea."

"You don't know that. Try me."

"Well ... ." I pressed my lips together and gathered my courage. If Jack thought it was a juvenile idea, so be it. It was the only idea I had and if I didn't tell him we very well could be stuck at the hospital the entire day. "They don't monitor candy stripers."

"Okay." Jack waited for me to continue.

"When I was here last night, I noticed the candy stripers have their own lounge of sorts," I continued hurriedly. "They keep their uniforms inside. So, if I were to walk in there and pretend I belonged, I could steal a uniform. I'm the right age to pretend I'm a candy striper."

When Jack didn't immediately respond I forced my eyes to him and found him tapping his lip, a thoughtful expression on his face.

"Wait ... you don't think this is a terrible idea?"

Jack smiled, catching me off guard. "I don't know if it's the hangover talking, but I don't hate the idea. What happens if you get caught?"

"Then I make a break for it and run into the woods. They're not going to chase a candy striper. They don't even question candy stripers."

"How do you know that?"

"Because I watched the candy stripers yesterday afternoon and last night. They don't watch them. They're almost invisible."

"Huh." Jack made a tsking sound with his tongue as he shook his head. "You've been thinking about this a little longer than you let on, haven't you?"

I held my hands out and shrugged. "Maybe. It's our best option. You know it and I do, too."

"I can't go up there with you." Jack turned serious. "This is something you'll have to do on your own."

"I'm fine with that."

"And you're not afraid?"

In truth, I liked the idea of an adrenaline rush. "I'm not afraid."

Jack threw up his hands in defeat. "Okay. Let's do it. Good luck ... and I'll bail you out if you get arrested."

That was comforting. Kind of.

SNEAKING INTO THE CANDY striper lounge was easier than I thought. No one questioned me, and the room was quiet and empty. I found a rack of uniforms that looked to be for temporary volunteers and grabbed one close to my size (although a tad small), frowning in the mirror when I saw the way my boobs popped. There was no way that would be conducive to patients remaining calm.

I did my best to pretend I knew exactly where I was going and headed toward Lisa Savage's room. I remembered its location from the night before. The hallway in front of her room was empty, and I was relieved to see that she appeared to be alone. Of course, the woman was awake and on the phone – which was simply bad luck all around – so there was no way I could approach her without looking out of sorts.

Instead, I made a big show of dusting the chairs in the hallway and crouched low so I could listen through the cracked door. I should've felt guilty about eavesdropping, but really I didn't. I lost all sense of guilt when I heard the first sentence.

"They're never going to find Ethan, Mom!" Lisa sounded as if she was close to teetering over the edge, her voice shrill and cracking. "He's gone. He's not coming back!"

I swallowed hard as I wrapped my head around the information. Had Lisa Savage seen her husband die? Did a lycanthrope do it? Was there something else tearing through the woods and torturing people?

"Mom, I'm not being a defeatist." Lisa turned weepy, and I had to tamp down the feelings of guilt rolling through me. This was a private moment. This woman was mourning her dead husband. I shouldn't be intruding. "Oh, I'm not being dramatic either, Mom!" Lisa practically exploded. "I don't know what else there is to tell you. I've told this story fifty times now and it's not going to change. The forest came alive and swallowed Ethan whole! That's it. There's no more. He's gone and he's not coming back!"

NINETEEN

*J*ack was waiting in the Jeep. I never did get up the courage to invade Lisa Savage's privacy and question her about what happened. Instead, I listened to the rest of the conversation with her mother, tried my best not to cry when she burst into hysterical tears during the conversation and then hurried back to the candy striper lounge to change back into my clothes.

Jack looked concerned when I climbed into the vehicle. "Do I need to burn rubber and get out of here because the cops are coming?"

It was a lame joke, but I wanted to give him credit for the effort. "That's not necessary. I wasn't caught."

"Okay." Jack gently brushed my hair from my face to study me. "You're pale, Charlie. I'm hungover, but you're the one who looks sick. What happened?"

"I ... ." How could I explain what I overheard? More importantly, how could I justify how I felt about what I heard?

"You're starting to worry me." Jack grabbed my hand and gave it a hard squeeze. "Look at me. There you go. Just tell me what happened and we'll figure it out. Something bad clearly happened." Jack jolted as something occurred to him. "Did Lisa Savage die? I wasn't under the impression that her injuries were that severe."

"She's not dead." I found my voice, although it was raspy. "She actually looks pretty good for a woman who was missing in the woods for several days. Maybe a little pale and bruised, but otherwise fine. I mean … well, fine physically."

"Okay." Jack kept his gaze even. "Then tell me what happened. Did your candy striper plan not work?"

"Oh, that worked like a charm." I perked up a bit. I loved being right. "They had a whole rack of uniforms. I grabbed one that was close to my size – although it was a little small – and I caught four doctors staring at my boobs while heading to the sixth floor."

Jack made a face. "Did one of them touch you? Give me a name and I'll take care of it."

I snorted. "They just stared. I took it as a compliment because most guys don't stare at my rack since there's not much to look at."

Jack shook his head. "Your rack is fine. It's nice. I mean … it's fine. I … don't look at me like that." His cheeks flooded with color. "I don't understand how we got turned to this topic. Get to the important stuff."

"Did you hear that, girls?" I looked down and talked to my chest. "He doesn't think you're important."

"Don't make me start yelling," Jack warned. "I'm very close to losing it. My patience isn't what it normally is."

I smirked, his reaction serving to lighten my mood. "The candy striper thing went fine. There wasn't a cop guarding her room. We lucked out there."

"So you got to talk to her." Jack leaned closer, his fingers still wrapped around my wrist. "What did she say? What happened? If you tell me it was a werewolf I'll lock you in the back and never let you out."

I rolled my eyes. "You're getting ahead of yourself. There was no cop, but I didn't go in her room. She was on the phone with her mother, and I didn't want to invade her personal space. The door was cracked, so I listened in while dusting furniture."

"Oh." Jack straightened. "That was actually pretty smart."

"I'm capable of having a smart thought now and then, no matter what you think."

"Yes, well, let's not get snarky." Jack licked his lips. "What did you hear?"

"She's an emotional wreck and seems to be all over the place."

"I would think that's normal for someone who has been through what she's been through." Jack turned pragmatic. "She's probably still in shock. Did she mention the husband?"

I nodded. "She said some weird stuff, Jack. That's another reason I didn't go in and try to question her. I don't think she's properly addressing what happened to her. I think she's like one of those people who believe they've been abducted by aliens or something."

Jack narrowed his eyes. "Please tell me she didn't describe a flying saucer or little green men."

"She didn't. She did say that the forest came alive and swallowed Ethan whole. That's exactly how she phrased it. Then she turned hysterical and started crying. I could only hear her end of the conversation, but it sounded to me as if the mother was trying to calm her down."

"I want to know why the mother isn't at her daughter's bedside," Jack mused, releasing my wrist and leaning back in his seat. "I mean, I'm no expert on parental concern, but wouldn't most mothers do just about anything to make sure their child wasn't alone during a trying time like this?"

I hadn't even thought of that. "I don't know. I might say the mother hasn't had time to make travel arrangements, but Lisa Savage has been missing for days. Most mothers would book the first flight to a location for a missing child, even if that child is an adult."

"Exactly." Jack absently stared at the hospital as he ran the conundrum through his head. "I don't get why the mother isn't here. She should've been here before her daughter was found."

"I'm not sure how important that really is," I said. "Maybe the mother is in another country or something. Maybe she is in town and had to run an errand and Lisa merely melted down and needed to talk to her while she was away from the room. Or, maybe it's something else. Maybe Lisa and her mother aren't that close."

"I guess." Jack didn't look convinced. "I still find it odd. That's something to check on later. What about Lisa herself? Did she say anything else about the camping trip and what happened to Ethan?"

"She was all over the place," I replied. "I don't think she's processed what happened. Maybe whatever did happen was so terrible she made up the story about the forest swallowing him because that's what she thinks she really saw.

"I know you don't want to hear it, but maybe she did see an animal," I continued. "Maybe it was a very big animal, and maybe it did some terrible things, and maybe her mind can't comprehend it so she's blocking it out."

"There are all kinds of trauma. She might be blocking it out. That doesn't mean a werewolf attacked."

"That doesn't mean a werewolf didn't attack." I refused to back down. "You're a nonbeliever, Jack, but I know there are things out there that we can't explain. Not everything can be pigeonholed into neat little boxes."

"Did I say that they could?"

"No, but … you don't want to believe. It's simply the way you're wired."

"And you do want to believe," Jack shot back. "That makes you see things that might not be there."

"Like the Chupacabra."

Jack let loose a weary groan. "Why must you always bring it back to that? I mean … why?"

"Because I saw it."

"Honey, you fell down a flight of stairs and hit your head. Hard." He didn't realize he'd called me "honey," and even though I kind of liked it I managed to keep my anger and irritation at the forefront of my brain. "You don't know what you saw. You were lucky to survive at all."

"I know what I saw."

"Ugh." Jack slapped his hand to his forehead. "If I agree that you might have seen the Chupacabra, do you agree to stop bringing it up every time we argue? You use it as a weapon to insinuate I don't have faith in you, and that's not true."

His vehemence caught me off guard. "Oh, well, I guess I can agree to that," I said. "I just don't like it that you don't believe me."

"It's not as if I think you're lying. It's that ... you were hurt, and badly. I'm not even sure you know what you saw." He held up his hands to quiet me when I opened my mouth to push things further. "I'm done with this argument. You might have seen the Chupacabra. I'm fine with that."

He was offering an olive branch, and I knew I should take it. "Okay. Then I'm sorry for jumping on you all the time when you say I didn't see the Chupacabra."

"Great." Jack exhaled heavily and stared at the Jeep's ceiling. "What do you think we should do now? I'm not sure where to look."

"I want to go back to the scene." The words were out of my mouth before I realized it. Once I had time to reflect, I understood that was probably our best move. "I want to look around again when there aren't so many people trampling around."

"And what is it you think you'll find?"

"I don't know. Probably nothing."

"But you need to do it."

I bobbed my head. "We don't have anything else pressing tying up our day. We can take a look, right?"

"I don't see why not."

THE WOODS WERE QUIET, almost stuffy and overbearing in the heat and humidity. The police tape remained up, although it sagged in places. The tent still stood, tattered and leaning, and the other remnants of a simple camping trip remained scattered around the site.

"What do you think it was like?" I prowled close to the tent, dragging my fingers over the shredded material in the hope I would be hit with a psychic flash.

"What do I think what was like?" Jack knelt next to the abandoned campfire pit and used a stick to dig in the ashes.

"The scene here that night." I wanted to get a picture, and Jack was good at exploring crime scenes. "How do you think it happened?"

"I don't know. I wasn't here."

"You can read things."

Jack exhaled heavily as he lifted his head. "I've been following the footprints and paying close attention to the way things are scattered. I think I have an idea."

"Tell me."

"It's not fact."

"I still want to know."

"Fine." Jack licked his lips and snagged my gaze. It was almost as if he was about to tell a ghost story by the campfire and wanted to make sure he had my full attention before he started. "I think they were in the tent. From the looks of it, they had two sleeping bags zipped together."

"So they could get it on," I mused, nodding. "They were newly-weds. That makes sense."

Jack snorted. "I like how you immediately went there. But that's true. I have no way of knowing if they were awake or asleep, but they obviously heard something. Someone ... or some thing ... came in from that direction." He pointed to the east. "He stopped by the camp-fire long enough to leave prints, and then he went to the side of the tent."

"They were animal prints, right?" I didn't want to box Jack into a corner, but I needed clarification. "Whatever walked by the campfire and approached the tent was an animal."

"There was an animal here, but that doesn't mean an animal did this. There were human prints, too."

"But only two sets."

Jack shook his head. "Three. There were three sets of shoe prints here. One was for a woman, size eight shoe. One was for a man, size eleven shoe. The other was for a man, size thirteen shoe. I isolated all three prints. I'm positive about that."

My mouth dropped open. "You haven't mentioned that before." It seemed a little convenient that he would bring it up now. "Why is that?"

"Because I can't be sure where the third footprint came from." Jack groaned as he stood. Apparently his hangover was still slowing him. I'd almost forgotten about it because he bounced back so quickly. "It might've come from someone the night of the attack. It also might have come from someone tromping through the campsite after they disappeared. And yet still, it most likely came from a cop or rescuer who walked through an area he shouldn't have walked through."

"Oh." Realization dawned. What he said made sense. I hated that. "So you think an animal could've been here but maybe it was just a wolf or something, and that I'm a spaz for no good reason."

"I find you amusing when you're a spaz." Jack winked before sobering. "There are paw prints. The thing is, I don't know what to make of them. There shouldn't be wolves in this area, but there has been a resurgence of wolves in northern Michigan in recent years. It's possible one migrated this far south."

"Or it could be a werewolf."

Jack's smile slipped. "You're trying to drive me crazy, aren't you?"

I shrugged. "It doesn't take that much effort. In fact … ." My hand brushed against the tent flap as I stood, and an image of a woman screaming in terror as she fled the tent filled my senses. I almost toppled over as I tried to comprehend the vision.

And then I began to fall.

As I fell, images flashed in quick succession.

Lisa Savage waking to a noise.

Her sleepy husband telling her she's imagining things and to go back to sleep.

A ripping sound as the tent wall gives way.

Screaming.

Lisa scrambling against the cold ground to make her way through the tent opening.

More screaming.

Ethan yelling for his wife to run as he prepared to fight ... something.

Cold yellow eyes in the darkness.

Snarling.

More screaming.

I heard Lisa wailing as she disappeared into the forest and it wasn't a sound I was likely to forget anytime soon.

Jack caught my arm and jerked me up before I hit the ground. I widened my eyes as my downward momentum ceased and I was harshly yanked out of the visions. "What the ... ?"

"That was about to be my reaction." Jack's face flooded with worry as he cupped my chin and forced my eyes to him. "Did you faint?"

Hmm. That would probably be better to claim instead of owning up to a psychic vision. Of course, it also would make me look weak. I hated looking weak. "I'm not sure." I moved to shove away Jack's hands, but he refused to budge. "I just felt lightheaded. I didn't faint."

"You came freaking close." Jack's expression was pained. "Charlie, what just happened?"

"I ... it's hot." It was a lame excuse, but I didn't know what else to offer.

"It is hot," Jack agreed. "But you've been in hot places before. This was something else. What?"

"I ..."

"Tell me." Jack looked almost desperate. "Whatever it is, you can trust me."

My heart ached at his pained expression. I realized part of me wanted to tell him. It would make things easier if he could accept it. Then I heard Zoe's words in my memory, warning me not to tell anyone and to be extremely careful about whom I trusted with my secret. She was a powerful mage who could burn down a college and get away with it. If she was that strong and lived in fear, what hope did I have?

"I'm just hot." I felt guilty upon uttering the words, especially given the way Jack pulled back. He released my chin and planted his hands on his hips as he regarded me. I felt exposed – something I really hated – and went on the offensive before I gave it much thought. "I'm allowed to faint. That doesn't mean I'm weak. Don't look at me that way."

"I didn't say you were weak." Jack's voice was chilly, remote. "I don't care if you almost fainted. Well, I care. I don't care that you somehow think that makes you a weak female. I care about why it happened."

I smoothed the front of my shirt and averted my gaze. "It's hot."

"Right. It's hot." Jack's voice was distant. I was afraid to look up, so I kept staring at my shoes. "Charlie, I know you have a secret. I don't want to push you, but something weird is going on. You had the same look on your face when I came upon you and Zoe Lake-Winters the other day. The exact same look."

I opened my mouth to argue, but he cut me off.

"Don't. I'm going to finish this." He squared his shoulders. "Something is bothering you. I really wish you trusted me enough to tell the truth, but I'm starting to think it's my fault you don't. Why would you tell me when I gave you so much crap after the Chupacabra thing?

"I don't want to force you into a situation in which you feel you have to tell me," he continued. "That doesn't seem fair. You don't have to keep everything a secret, though. You don't have to go to strangers for help. I'm right here."

Tears pricked the back of my eyes. "Jack … ."

"Don't." He pressed the heel of his hand to his forehead. "Just take a moment and rest. Once you're feeling better we'll head back to the Jeep. Think about what I said. You can trust me."

I wanted to trust him. I realized I wanted that more than just about anything. If he couldn't believe in Bigfoot … the Chupacabra … or a lycanthrope, though, how could he possibly believe in me?

TWENTY

"*A*re you ready?"

Jack spent the next twenty minutes ignoring me as he made his way around the campsite. I watched him, a mixture of dread and worry taking over my nerves, but remained silent because I didn't want to set him off. Still, the way he carried himself made me think he'd discovered something while making a big show of pretending I wasn't sharing oxygen with him in the clearing. I couldn't just let it go.

"What do you see?"

Jack finally lifted his eyes and met my gaze. Instead of anger lurking in the dark depths I thought I saw sadness. It threw me for a loop. "What makes you think I saw anything?"

I was determined as I stood, brushing off the seat of my pants and adopting a smile that I was certain didn't make it to my eyes. "I saw the way you were studying the ground. You may think you know me best – and you very well might because you're observant – but I've come to know you, too. What did you see?"

Jack swiped at the side of his face as he regarded me. "I'm almost afraid to tell you this, because I think we should head back to the inn so you can rest."

"I'm not tired."

"You almost fainted ... because of the heat."

It was a direct challenge I couldn't ignore. "I'm sorry if I hurt your feelings. It wasn't my intent. I ... I can't explain why I almost fainted. You'll think less of me, and I don't want that."

"What is that supposed to mean?"

"Nothing. I ... ."

"No, you meant something very specific, but you're afraid to tell me." Jack planted his hands on his hips. "Are you pregnant? Is that it? If so, it's not the end of the world. We'll figure a way to work through it. If you have to do office work then we can leave you behind on trips."

I was flabbergasted. "Pregnant?"

"Pregnant women faint a lot."

"What soap operas have you been watching?"

Jack wrinkled his brow. "I think I'm confused. I'm trying to give you a way out, be supportive, and you're giving me nothing but grief."

"You're trying to saddle me with office work," I shot back, hopping to my feet. I was beyond livid now. "First of all, I'm not pregnant. Why you would even think that is beyond me. Apparently I need to go on a diet or something."

"That's not what I said," Jack protested. "You look fine, great even. I mean ... you don't look fat."

"Not that there's anything wrong with that," I grumbled, rolling my neck. "I'm not pregnant. I am insulted you think that, and I might have to lock myself in a room to cry later because it's upsetting in a way that makes me want to pretend it's not upsetting and then break down later."

"Oh, don't cry." Jack gripped the top of his hair so tightly I worried he might give it a tug and yank some of it out. "I didn't mean it the way you're taking it."

"Whatever." I sucked in a breath. What were we supposed to be talking about again? Oh, right. "Secondly, even if I were pregnant, that doesn't mean you can just lock me in a room and cut me from the action. That's sexist, misogynistic and altogether boneheaded thinking. I could totally continue kicking butt with a baby on my hip. That's how rocking I am."

Jack's expression turned dark. "You just said you weren't pregnant."

"I'm not. You need to have sex to have a baby. I've been living like a nun since joining this outfit. I don't have time for sex."

Jack straightened. "That's a little sad ... and something of an over-share. I didn't need to know that."

"Oh, what does it matter?" I was fed up with him and his attitude. I couldn't take one more second of his passive aggressive Neanderthal man shtick. "We're all up in each other's business. You want to know the secret I'm keeping. I want to know what happened between you and Laura, although I have no idea why because it's seriously none of my business. But I can't stop thinking about it."

Jack extended a warning finger. "I told you what happened with her. Nothing happened. She's a psycho. She believes something happened, but it didn't. I can't fix that."

"And it's none of my business." I meant it. "You're still a bullying butthead when you want to be, and that is my business. You're right. I do have a secret. That means I don't spread it around. That secret is not that I'm pregnant, though."

"Well, great." Jack threw up his hands. I could practically feel the fury rolling off him. "I was trying to be sensitive."

"By telling me I look fat?"

"You don't look fat. I never said that."

"You insinuated it."

"I did not." Jack took three long steps and planted himself in front of me. "You are turning this into something it doesn't need to be. I didn't mean to hurt your feelings – and you're certainly not fat – but you are hiding something."

"And it just kills you that you don't know what it is, doesn't it?"

"You have no idea."

The simple declaration took my breath away. "I ... ."

"No, I'm talking now. You need to stop flapping your lips." Jack's eyes were filled with fire and he squeezed my lips shut when I tried to respond. "I'm talking. You talk enough for the rest of the team combined. I'm talking now."

Oh, well, this was simply undignified.

"You're right about it not being any of my business. It's not. But I can't help myself from worrying about you. If you expect me to explain why, I can't. You scare the crap out of me and I simply can't explain why I feel the need to poke my nose in your business. It's like an urge I can't fight."

I was dumbfounded and gently nudged his fingers from my lips. "Can I talk now?" I kept my voice low.

Jack nodded.

"I'm not trying to hurt you, and as much as it should irritate me that you think you're the king of the world and that means you get to watch my every move I'm absurdly touched, and I can't explain that." I let out a pent-up breath. "I need time to think about things. I'm not keeping secrets to be mean. I'm also not pregnant. I swear it's not that."

"I … well … ." Jack uncomfortably shifted from one foot to the other.

"I just need time." My voice was more plaintive and whiny than I would've liked, but I couldn't stop that. "I'm dealing with stuff that I can't explain, and I don't think I should feel guilty for it."

"No, I don't think so either." Jack was morose. "Is it girl stuff?"

"You mean like menstruation and hair braiding?"

Jack cracked a smile. "Yeah."

"I guess … kind of. But I'm not pregnant." I was still aggravated that he thought that. "Are we okay here?"

Jack nodded. "We are."

"Good. Now I want to know what you were looking at."

Jack stilled and for a moment I thought he'd insist we return to the Jeep. Instead, he merely shrugged. "There's a fresh set of tracks … and they look like animal tracks."

I couldn't contain my excitement. "Do you think the lycanthrope came back?"

Jack sighed. "I think something was out here. I have no idea what.

I'm not an animal expert. I'm going to guess it's not a werewolf because the print is really small."

"Maybe it's a baby lycanthrope."

"Or maybe it's a coyote."

I made a face. "Jack ... ."

"I'm done arguing. I meant that." He lifted his hands to signify defeat. "If you want to believe it was a werewolf, that's certainly your prerogative. I think it was a coyote ... or maybe a bear cub ... or maybe even a domesticated dog."

Hmm. That hadn't occurred to me. "Do you think we can follow it? Just for a bit, I mean. Maybe it will lead us to something."

"Like Ethan Savage?"

"Like anything. I just want answers at this point."

Jack sighed. "Okay, but if you feel faint I want you to tell me. I don't want to wander around the woods forever. This isn't my area. I'm afraid we'll get lost if we go too far."

"I'm sure we'll be fine." I wholeheartedly believed that. "You should lead the way."

"Yes, that sounds wonderful," Jack muttered as she shook his head. "I'll lead the way to the werewolf."

"Just don't ask if it's pregnant when we find it," I called out.

"Ha, ha."

WE WALKED FOR WHAT FELT like a long time, Jack's gaze intent on the ground as I followed and pretended to see the indentations that he claimed belonged to an animal. It wasn't until we were well into our trip that I realized something was off about his demeanor.

I waited another hour to question him on it. He swore everything was fine.

An hour after that, I gave voice to the fear that had been growing in the pit of my stomach throughout the afternoon.

"We're lost, aren't we?"

Jack's hair was a matted mess thanks to the heat and humidity.

When he turned, I could see the resignation and shame on his face. "It's going to be okay."

Holy crap! We really were lost. I thought I was being dramatic and whiny. Clearly that wasn't true. Son of a … ! "How long have we been lost?" I managed to keep a cap on my emotions, but just barely.

"About two hours, maybe a little longer."

I didn't like that one bit. "We have no idea where we are and we've been lost for more than two hours?" I turned shrill, like a crying teenager who just found out she can't afford to purchase her favorite pair of skinny jeans. "How is this even possible?"

Jack absorbed the verbal assault without blinking. "The prints just stopped, and when I tried to find them – you know, pick up another trail – I couldn't. By then the trail back was gone and I couldn't find it."

I was agog. "I know how we got lost, but … how could this happen?"

Jack held his hands out and shrugged. "I don't know. But we have another problem."

Oh, well, this was just great. "And what would that be?"

"My phone has zero service. Check yours."

No service? I should've seen that coming. We were in the middle of nowhere, after all. I dug in my pocket and retrieved my phone, internally cursing the cellular gods when no bars showed on the display screen. I tried placing a call anyway, getting nothing but that annoying bell sound to tell me it wouldn't go through.

"Nothing?" Jack grabbed the phone and stared at it. "Crap. We really are lost."

I couldn't stop from exploding. "Are you freaking kidding me? You're supposed to be some sort of survival expert. How could you possibly get us lost?"

Jack didn't cringe, instead taking it on the chin. "I need you to remain calm. It's not as if we're going to die."

That was rich coming from him. "Really? Ethan Savage probably thought the same thing when he took his wife for a simple camping trip."

"Charlie ... ."

"No. No. I'm resigned to my fate. We're lost in woods where were-wolves hunt. This won't end badly or anything."

"Oh, geez." Jack slapped his hand to his forehead. "You're going to make this intolerable, aren't you?"

I borrowed his phrase from earlier. "Oh, you have no idea. Me and my made-up baby are totally going to dog you until we die, which probably won't be long after the sun sets."

"We have hours before that happens."

"Oh, well, that makes me feel better," I drawled. "The anticipation won't kill me or anything. Of course, that's because the werewolf will."

"I thought you called it a lycanthrope."

"I will kill you if you don't fix this."

"I'm on it."

I TRUSTED JACK WITH MY LIFE. No, seriously. He was a skilled guy who wouldn't quit unless he had no other option. When darkness fell and Jack insisted we make camp for the night, I wanted to believe we still had options. Jack calmly argued that wasn't the case, and set about making a campfire even as I ratcheted up my whining.

By the time he was done and settled on the ground, I had a choice. I could remain pouty and sit on the other side of the fire or stick close to him in case a werewolf attacked. Despite my frustration and anger, I chose to sit next to him.

"Don't worry, Charlie." Jack kept his voice low as he poked a stick in the fire and kept a wary set of eyes on the trees. "They'll have real-ized we're missing by now. The Jeep has GPS. They'll have figured out where we were heading and put together a search party."

That perked me up. "Do you think they're looking for us right now?"

Jack shook his head. "They're not going to send searchers when it's dark, especially because we're not missing children. We're on our own until morning."

That was so not what I wanted to hear. "Do you think it will come for us?"

Jack slipped his arm around my back, a move I was sure was meant to bolster my courage or at least soothe my frazzled nerves, and tucked me in at his side. Unfortunately for him, I felt neither soothed nor courageous. I did feel a little hot and bothered. Jack's proximity made my heart pound and my stomach turn liquid.

"No one will come for us." Jack sounded certain. "I'll stay up all night. You'll be safe. I promise."

I wanted to believe him. "I think Ethan Savage probably thought the same thing about his wife."

"And she survived."

"I'm not willing to sacrifice you for myself," I countered. "I won't run into the woods screaming and leave you behind. You should know that."

Jack's expression turned quizzical. "Is that what you think Lisa did?"

I realized too late that I'd tipped my hand. "I ... don't know." Crap! How was I supposed to cover for that? "She seemed like a woman swimming in guilt at the hospital. Maybe I'm reading too much into things, but ... I just can't shake the feeling that something like that happened.

"It doesn't matter," I continued. "I won't leave you. If something comes, we'll face it together."

"No." Jack shook his head. "You'll run. That's what I want."

"I won't run."

"Charlie ... ."

"Jack, it won't happen. Save your breath."

Jack exhaled heavily, his mouth so close to my face I could feel his warm breath as it lightly caressed my cheek. "You'll be the death of me ... and not just for the reasons you think."

The sentiment was heartfelt. "I don't mean to be difficult."

"No, but ... ."

My heart started racing when Jack lowered his mouth. I wanted to ask what he was doing, but knew that would break the spell. I wanted to remind him this was the absolute worst time for him to be doing this. It would be better with a shower and a breath lozenge. Of course, he probably wouldn't even consider succumbing to the mood under normal circumstances.

I didn't say any of the things racing through my head. Instead, I waited ... and let my heart pound away in anticipation.

When Jack's lips touched mine I felt as if a wildfire raced through my veins. The kiss was soft, sweet and airy. It turned manic within seconds, though, and before I realized what was happening Jack had me pressed tightly against him as he turned the sweet interaction into a sweaty explosion.

I liked both versions of the kiss, and fireworks were detonating in my brain before I realized that something else might be exploding a little closer. Even when I saw the light and heard the crash I didn't pull away. I couldn't.

I was too lost. It was Jack who ended the kiss ... and then immediately sprang into action.

"What the holy hell?"

TWENTY-ONE

*M*y ears were still buzzing from the kiss when Jack turned aggressive.

"What is that?"

"What?" I felt drunk, lost in a sea of emotions I couldn't put a name to. Jack, however, was completely focused on something.

"That." Jack inclined his chin toward what looked to be a ball of light peeking through the heavy foliage.

"I ... what?" My mind refused to cooperate, and when Jack lowered his eyes to mine he looked more agitated than besotted.

"That!" He grabbed my chin and forcefully pointed my attention away from him, causing me to frown when I saw the ball of light and finally registered that it wasn't a product of my imagination.

I couldn't be sure – I'd never seen anything remotely like it, of course – but it seemed to be watching us. Inherently I knew the sphere didn't have emotions or even a brain, but it seemed to vibrate with laughter as it surveyed the situation. I couldn't hear that laughter anywhere but inside my brain, but I knew exactly who sent the light ... and why.

"Stay here." I pulled away from Jack and scrambled to my feet, eagerness to learn more about the light propelling me forward. Jack, however, was not amused by the idea.

"Where do you think you're going?" He moved to grab me around the waist, but I managed to evade him, although I stumbled a bit and lurched sideways for three long steps before I recovered. By the time I straightened, I was staring directly into the ball.

I was mesmerized. I heard Jack cursing behind me, but I couldn't look anywhere but directly into the ball of light. It seemed to be laughing – and maybe waving – and then it started whispering.

"Come. Walk that way."

It didn't point, but I instinctively knew which way it wanted me to go. "Come on." I was resigned to Jack following. There was no way he wouldn't.

"Where are we going?" Jack's frustration was palpable as he started kicking dirt to douse the fire. Hmm. I had to give him credit. I was so enamored with the ball of light I would have wandered away from the fire, which wasn't a very responsible thing to do.

"We're about to get out of here," I answered, immediately moving around the light and heading toward the trees behind it. "I don't think we're all that far from safety."

"And did the glowing ball of ... whatever that is ... tell you that?" Jack was incredulous. "Do you know what that thing is?"

"I have no idea."

"Did it speak to you?"

That was an odd question. "Did you hear it speak?"

"No, but ... you seem to suddenly know where we should go."

"Just follow me. I think we're close."

Jack cursed, but I heard his feet as he stomped behind me. I focused on the path ahead and left behind the emotions of the immediate past. Now was so not the time to dissect every little thing regarding the kiss.

We didn't walk far. It couldn't have been more than an eighth of a mile or so. I knew before I pushed through the wall of trees that we were at our destination, and when I stumbled into the small clearing I found two figures watching me with amusement.

The ball of light – when did that even return? – danced a bit before blinking out of existence. When that happened, only the full moon remained to illuminate Aric and Zoe's faces.

"What are you doing in the middle of the woods?" I blurted out.

Zoe snorted, genuinely amused. "I was going to ask you the same question. What are you doing out here?"

"I … well, we're lost." I risked a glance at Jack and found him glowering at Aric and Zoe. He clearly wasn't happy. "Look, Jack, we're saved." I was going for levity, but his only response was to move closer to me. The unspoken warning his body broadcast was for Aric and Zoe … and he clearly meant business.

"You're lost, huh?" Zoe pursed her lips. "How long have you been lost?"

"All day." I tentatively wrapped my fingers around Jack's wrist to make sure he didn't go all alpha and start throwing punches. Aric looked amused more than anything – in fact, I was surprised he didn't burst out laughing and make matters worse – but he also looked the sort of man who enjoyed a good brawl. Jack was strong and trained, but there was something about the way Aric carried himself that told me he shouldn't be trifled with. "Jack … it's okay."

"It's not okay," Jack snapped back, finally shifting his eyes to me. They were on fire. "We're lost in the middle of the woods and these two just happened to appear out of nowhere and you don't find that suspicious? For the love of all that's holy, Charlie, something happened to Lisa and Ethan Savage, and these two are wandering the woods as if it's nothing. Doesn't that make you question their motives?"

I shrank back in the face of his vehemence. "I feel lucky that we found them so we can get out of here."

"Then you're an idiot," Jack barked.

Hey!" Zoe's temper was on display as she took a step forward and glared at Jack. "Don't yell at her. It's not her fault you got lost. I'll bet you were leading the way and it's your fault you got lost. Don't take it out on her."

"And how do you know that?" Jack challenged.

Zoe shrugged. "Men never ask for directions. It's a known fact."

"Zoe, don't turn this into a war," Aric pleaded, his eyes kind as he held up his hands and stepped forward. "No one wants a fight here. As for being lost, if you'd kept going a bit you would've ended up at our house." He pointed through the trees and I saw the lights emanating from the upper windows of the now-familiar abode when I peered hard through the leaves. "You're not really lost. You're very close to the road."

"Oh." I exhaled heavily, relief washing over me. "That's good to know." I poked Jack's side, desperate for him to relax. "See, Jack. You didn't really get us lost at all. There's no reason to be upset."

Although somewhat placated by the sight of the house, Jack refused to lower his guard. "How did you know we were out here?"

"We didn't," Zoe answered. "Although, we did have a guest about an hour ago."

"Who?"

"Millie." Zoe smirked. "She was looking for you two. Apparently your group is worked up. Millie volunteered to check our house … and ask Aric to strip out of his shirt again to give her strength to continue the search."

I couldn't hold back my chuckle. "That sounds just like her."

"She's a trip," Zoe agreed. "She makes me laugh. She was seriously worried about you two, though. No one has heard from you since this afternoon, and they've called out the cavalry for a search. They found one of your rentals close to the original campsite. I figured you guys were out here and perhaps got turned around."

"So you came out to find us?" Jack was back to being suspicious. "How did you know you would find us? How did you even know it was safe to look? Heck, the thing that dragged off the Savages could still be out here. I have trouble believing that you'd risk your lives for strangers."

"And I have trouble believing you're such a tool," Zoe shot back. "Shut your hole, and thank your lucky stars anyone bothered to look for you."

Jack's eyes turned black, a clear sign that he was about to lose his temper. "You listen here ... ." He took a step forward, his finger extended, and found his path blocked by a furious Aric Winters.

"Don't wag your finger at my wife," Aric growled. He seemed to grow in stature as he vibrated with anger. "Don't get close to her either. And don't even think about threatening her. I'll rip your head off and use it to play catch if you're not careful."

As far as threats go, it was impressive. Even though I knew him to be the amiable sort, I kind of believed him. Jack looked embarrassed. "I wasn't going to hurt her."

Aric didn't back down. "No, you weren't."

"I don't hurt women."

"Maybe not, but you've got a temper." Aric folded his arms over his chest and stared down Jack. "What is your deal anyway? You've been nothing but a pill since you arrived. I understand you have a job to do – and it's not always an easy job – but there's no reason to be as insufferable as you seem to insist on being."

Jack was taken aback. "What are you saying?"

"He's telling you to stop being an ass." Zoe pushed past Aric, ignoring the look he shot her and stopping in front of me. She almost smiled as she looked me over but I could tell she was as tense as I felt. "We were a little worried. We decided to check the property behind the house. I guess we lucked out."

I could read between the lines and understood what she wasn't saying. She created the ball of light to search for me. She cared enough to make sure I was okay. I couldn't help being profoundly thankful.

"I'm glad you did." I smiled. "I was afraid of staying in the woods all night alone."

"I was there to protect you," Jack protested.

"You got her lost," Zoe shot back. "It's your fault this happened."

"You don't know that." Jack had officially reached his limit and I knew he was spoiling for a fight. "She could've been the one who got us lost. It's not as if I wouldn't have followed her into the woods to keep her safe."

To my utter surprise, Zoe's expression softened. "No. That's true. I see it in you. Loyalty, I mean. But you still got her lost."

"How can you possibly know that?" Jack protested.

"I know everything."

Jack cocked a challenging eyebrow. "Everything?"

Zoe nodded without hesitation. "Everything. I know all and see all. Just ask my daughter, who swears up and down I spy on her and that's how I know about her secret cookie stash and her crush on the Mason boy down the street."

Aric stilled. "Mason boy? Trevor Mason?"

Zoe nodded. "The blond one who fancies himself a teen model."

"Why didn't I know about this?" Aric sounded legitimately irritated. "Why does no one ever tell me the things that happen under my own roof?"

Instead of reacting with an apology – or even a sympathetic cluck – Zoe merely rolled her eyes. "No one tells you about Sami's crushes because you freak out about them. She's thirteen years old. She's allowed to have a crush on a boy … even if that boy is a sniveling little weasel who thinks he belongs in a boy band."

Aric wasn't convinced. "No, we talked about this. She's not allowed to like boys until she's thirty."

"Yeah, yeah." Zoe waved off Aric's righteous indignation. "You guys are probably hungry and thirsty. We can handle both problems at the house. Aric will call Millie and tell her you're all right. Of course, something tells me that means Millie will show up again so she can pet Aric, but I think he likes the attention so it's all good."

Aric groaned. "I don't like it when she asks me to flex. I'm too old to constantly flex."

Zoe absently patted his arm. "You'll live. Come on, we need to get these two back."

I immediately moved to follow, but Jack grabbed my arm before I could take a step. "What?"

"Just one thing," Jack called out, licking his lips.

Zoe arched an eyebrow as she slowly turned. "Yes."

"What's with the ball of light?"

Zoe's expression didn't as much as twitch. "What ball of light?"

"The one we saw in the woods right before Charlie announced she knew where to go and took off, leaving me no choice but to follow her."

"I have no idea what you're talking about," Zoe replied, her face immovable. If I didn't know she was lying I would totally believe her. "I didn't see a ball of light."

Jack's mouth dropped open. "I saw it zipping through the woods right before we found you guys. It was definitely out here."

Zoe slid her eyes to Aric. "I think he's delirious from lack of water. It was hot today, so he's probably dehydrated. We should get him back to the house."

Aric nodded. "That sounds like a good idea. In fact ... ." He trailed off when another ball of light, this one blue instead of a warm yellow, careened through the trees and barreled directly toward Zoe. "Uh-oh."

Uh-oh was right. The glowing sphere didn't seem to care that it had an audience. It zipped into the small circle, made a buzzing that suspiciously sounded like chatter, and then winked out of existence.

For her part – and I have to give her credit, because her only reaction was to briefly press her eyes shut while regrouping – Zoe refused to act as if the ball of light was something that should be discussed. "So ... what were we talking about again?"

Jack made an incredulous face. "Seriously? We were talking about the ball of light that just disappeared."

"I didn't see a ball of light." Zoe was adamant. "You must have imagined it. Charlie, did you see anything?"

She was really putting me on the spot. When I looked to Jack I saw such frustration and worry that I couldn't deny him support. "Zoe, don't do this to him."

"She's just being a pain on my behalf," Aric supplied, smoothly stepping forward. "She doesn't want you guys to know about the security system my father's company is developing. It's top secret and we're not supposed to talk about it. We're also not supposed to let anyone see it. Zoe was so worried about Charlie that she begged me to use it.

189

"I'm not sorry I did," he continued, not breaking stride. "It led you guys to us, and that's important. Still, I have to ask you to keep what you saw to yourselves. If word gets out before the security system hits the market a competitor could steal it."

Jack opened his mouth to say something – and I had a feeling it wasn't anything that could be considered nice – but he didn't have a chance to barrel forward because Zoe tightly gripped Aric's arm and forced his eyes to her. She clearly had something else on her mind.

"What, baby?" Aric was instantly alert.

"Didn't you hear what it was saying?" Zoe queried, her eyes earnest.

Aric shook his head. "The voice commands on that thing are terrible. I can never understand what it says."

What he really meant was that Zoe used her magic to conjure it, she was the only one who could understand, and whatever information she was processing would have to be explained to him despite the fact that he deemed the lights a security system under his control.

"I didn't understand what it was saying at first, but now I do." Zoe licked her lips. "'Man.' It said 'man.'"

"Maybe it was talking about Jack," I suggested.

Zoe shook her head. "It also said 'water.' I thought it meant Jack needed water, but now I think it was something else."

I had no idea what she was thinking, what she believed, but it was obvious our adventure wasn't over yet. "What are you saying?"

"It said 'man' and 'water.'" Zoe dragged a hand through her hair before shifting so she faced to the south. "There's a river not very far away."

"So what?" Jack challenged. "What does that have to do with anything?"

I'd already caught up with Zoe's train of thought and couldn't contain myself as I scurried to chase after her. "It said 'man' and 'water,'" I called over my shoulder. "There's a river close by ... and there's a man in it."

Jack instantly understood what I was saying. "Ethan Savage."

"It can't hurt to look." Aric fell into step with Jack. "Everyone stick together. I don't want to risk anyone getting lost."

"You don't have to worry about that." Zoe's voice filtered through the darkness. "I'm in the lead, and I never get lost."

"Says the woman who drives into the ditch whenever a bee happens to fly into the truck cab," Aric muttered, shaking his head. "Hey, maybe I should lead the way."

"Don't even think about it."

TWENTY-TWO

*Z*oe was fleet footed as she raced toward the river. She seemed to know exactly where she was going. I struggled to keep up and was so focused on not tripping I almost slammed into her back when she pulled up short in front of the slow-moving river.

"Holy crap," I gasped, trying to catch my breath. "I didn't even know this was here. I've been dying for something to drink for hours."

"I come out here when I want time alone." Zoe narrowed her eyes as she scanned the length of the river bend. "It's peaceful ... with no whining child or flexing husband."

"I heard that," Aric grumbled as he caught up with us, Jack close on his heels. "I don't walk around flexing."

"If you didn't walk around flexing we wouldn't have the kid in the first place," Zoe pointed out. "In fact ... there!" She narrowed her eyes as she caught sight of something next to the far bank. "Come on."

Zoe was in the water before Aric could stop her, and because I didn't want to miss out on the action I stuck close to her. I heard Jack muttering behind me – something about me being the death of him and living life with a constant migraine since I popped into his life. Aric found his complaints amusing.

"You'll get used to it. You might even grow to like it."

"You think I'll grow to like migraines?" Jack was understandably dubious. "I'm guessing not."

"You'll be surprised what you grow to like – and even love – in the long haul. Trust me. The things you find important now will fall by the wayside when something more important comes along."

"That's exactly what I'm afraid of."

I tuned Jack out – forcing the memory of our kiss to the back of my brain – and followed Zoe to the crumpled figure on the ground. It was a man, his clothes ragged and tattered. His skin was so pale I was convinced he was dead.

"Ethan Savage," Jack said on a breathy exhale. "It really is him."

"It is," Zoe agreed, dropping to her knees and moving her hands to Ethan's neck. "I feel a pulse, but it's faint." She snagged gazes with Aric, and I could practically sense a silent conversation between the two of them. "We need to call for an ambulance right now. He won't make it much longer."

"I'm on it." Aric yanked his phone from his pocket.

"You don't get service out here," Jack said. "That's one of the reasons we were lost."

"That's why you get satellite phones if you want to live in the country." Aric pressed in a number. "We'll need to move him to the house. Waiting for emergency personnel to find this place is a bad idea."

"Are you sure we should move him?" That seemed like a bad idea to me. "I saw on television that you shouldn't move someone with unknown injuries."

"It's either that or let him die here," Zoe countered. "I have no intention of doing that. Make the call, Aric. Then we have to get him to the house ... and fast."

WHO IS THAT?" Sami hopped to her feet, her German shepherd barking like crazy as Zoe threw open the sliding glass door and led the way for Aric and Jack to carry Ethan Savage's limp body to the couch.

"He's the missing man," Zoe replied, making a face when the dog barked so loudly it echoed throughout the great room. "Knock that off, Trouble." She raised a finger, which instantly quieted the dog. "We don't need you adding to this insanity."

I was impressed. "You're like a dog whisperer. Why did you name him Trouble?"

"We named him after Mom," Sami replied, her eyes keen as she moved toward Ethan. "Where did you find him?"

"By the river."

"I thought you were looking for those two." Sami vaguely gestured toward Jack and me. "Were they all together?"

"No, but they were close," Zoe replied. "The paramedics are on their way, Sami. I think you should take Trouble and go to your room."

Sami balked, her black hair flying as she straightened. "You can't cut me out of this. This is the most exciting thing to happen since … well, you know when."

"And that's why we want you in your room." Aric was stern. "It will be easier if you go there, kid. We're not trying to be mean, but there are going to be a lot of people in here."

Sami narrowed her eyes, and I was certain she was about to say something her parents wouldn't like. She must have thought better of it, though, because she ultimately wrinkled her nose and sashayed her hips as she stormed out of the room.

"Come on, Trouble!" The dog obediently followed, his tail wagging. "They don't want us to be part of the action. That's typical. They're all up in my business when they're bored, but now that something is actually happening it's as if I don't exist. I'm used to it. I'll sit in a corner in my room and pretend to be invisible!"

Jack's eyebrows flew up his forehead as Sami slammed her door and Aric and Zoe looked at each other.

"She gets that from you," they uttered in unison, causing me to smile.

"She seems … energetic," I supplied as I knelt next to Ethan. "You must have your hands full with her."

"She's not too bad," Zoe countered. "According to my mother, I expect her to turn into a demon when she hits sixteen. My mother says that's a karma thing and that I have it coming."

"I don't know what I did to deserve that," Aric complained. "I was a good teenager."

"You were not," Zoe scoffed. "I've heard the stories your mother tells."

"Since when do you listen to my mother?"

"Only when she says something I want to hear." Zoe licked her lips as she studied Ethan's sallow complexion. His breathing was shallow, and I worried each breath he took would be his last. "Jack, can you do me a favor and wait on the front porch for the paramedics? Show them directly in. He doesn't have much time."

I thought Jack would argue with the directive, but he merely nodded. "I'll also call our team while I'm out there, Charlie," he said. "They should know we're okay so they can call off the search."

"Okay." I held his gaze for a long beat, my heart twitching at his expression. We'd yet to talk about the kiss – the kiss to end all kisses, really – and the night had taken a turn neither of us expected. I wasn't sure when we would get a chance to talk things over. I also wasn't sure if I wanted that to happen. I didn't know what he would say, and I was terrified he'd pretend it never occurred, although I had no idea why I felt that way.

Okay, that's not true. For some reason I wanted him to fall at my feet, declare his love and then continue that kiss. I may be a badass monster hunter, but I'm still a woman, and he makes my heart go pitter-patter. Sue me.

"I'll be right back, Charlie," Jack promised, as if reading my mind. "We'll get through this."

I bit my lower lip as I watched him go, my mind jumbled. When I finally looked back at Ethan I almost fell over from surprise. Zoe, her hands glowing blue, was leaning close and whispering.

"What the hell is that?" I almost shrieked.

Zoe made a face. "Shh!"

"But ... ."

"Be quiet," Aric ordered, his tone forcing me to snap my mouth shut. "We don't want Jack running back in here because he thinks we're doing something to you."

I was flabbergasted. "Jack wouldn't think that."

"Jack's mind is all tangled," Zoe argued. "Whatever happened in the woods – and, yes, I saw that freaking hot kiss thanks to the sentry I sent out – has him all messed up. Is that the first time you guys did that?"

Mortification climbed my cheeks. "I ... you ... he ... you saw that?"

Zoe chuckled as she pulled back her hands and extinguished the blue flame. "I did. It looked fun. I was going to let you guys continue and see where things led, but you sensed the sentry so I couldn't continue watching without alerting you to my presence."

I had no idea what to make of that. "Do you think he liked it?" The question was out of my mouth before I realized how ridiculous it sounded.

Zoe burst out laughing, amusement practically dripping from her tongue. "Oh, Charlie, you make me smile. You remind me of me."

"She kind of reminds me of you too," Aric admitted, his smile fond. "She doesn't think before she speaks and she knows how to drive a man crazy without even trying. Poor Jack doesn't stand a chance."

That didn't sound particularly good to me. "I think he's re-thinking what happened."

"He probably is." Zoe was calm. "Don't worry about it. Things will work out."

"How can you be sure?"

"I already told you. I know all and see all." Zoe straightened and turned her head to the open front door. "The emergency personnel are here."

I swallowed hard and focused on Ethan. "Do you think he'll make it?"

Zoe's lips curved. "He should be okay. I did enough to head off the major damage, but left a little something for the doctors. It would be too hard to explain otherwise."

"Is that what you were doing? I mean ... you healed him, right?"

Zoe's smile never slipped. "I have no idea what you're talking about."

I wasn't about to be deterred. "Is that how you cheated death? Is that how you're still here?"

Zoe didn't answer, instead striding toward the door. "He's this way," she called out.

I turned to Aric for confirmation, but his expression was impossible to read. "I'm so confused."

"You'll be okay, Charlie." He sounded sure of himself and grinned a little when Jack hurried through the door after the paramedics and immediately looked to make sure I was okay. "Both of you will be. Trust me."

I WAS EXHAUSTED BY the time we made it back to the inn. All I wanted to do was tumble into bed. Unfortunately, that wasn't a possibility, because the members of our group demanded answers.

So, instead of showering and shutting my eyes so I could think about everything that happened during the day, I was forced to eat sandwiches and listen to Laura fawn over Jack.

"You poor thing." She petted his arm and poured him a glass of iced tea. She made sure to take the spot to his right so we couldn't sit together – she was obvious when carrying out the maneuver – but I was too tired and edgy to worry about that now.

"I'm fine." Jack shrugged off Laura's intense attention and focused on his plate. "It wasn't so bad. I was worried, don't get me wrong, but it's not as if we were lost in the Andes during a blizzard or anything. We didn't have to resort to cannibalism. We were fine."

"It sounds like you had a long day, though," Millie noted, her eyes on me as I shoveled in huge mouthfuls of potato salad. "Did your life flash before your eyes, Charlie? Did you think you would never eat again?"

"She's obviously starving to death," Laura answered with a derisive snort. "All those carbs are going to end up on your hips, and that's not going to work out well for you when your metabolism starts slowing in a few years."

"Leave her alone," Jack ordered, his face full of fury. "And stop doing that!" He jerked away from Laura ... hard. "In fact ... go over there." Jack pointed to the opposite side of the table.

Laura's expression twisted. "Excuse me?"

"I don't want you hanging all over me." Jack was adamant. "You make me uncomfortable on a normal day, and this day has been pretty freaking far from normal."

"Yes, Laura," Millie drawled. "Stop sexually harassing Jack. The brass back at the main office won't like it if a complaint is filed."

"Jack would never file a complaint." Laura sounded sure of herself, but I didn't miss the hint of worry that flashed across her features.

"I might," Jack muttered.

"And I definitely will, because you're making me uncomfortable," Millie added. "I shouldn't have to watch you ply that poor boy with unwanted sexual overtures. It's pure torture for all of us."

Laura scowled but wisely vacated the chair between Jack and me, scuffing her feet against the ceramic tile as she moved to the chair across from Jack. She clearly wasn't about to let things go, but she needed time to regroup.

"What happened out there?" Chris asked, his eyes dancing with interest. "How did you find Ethan Savage? I mean ... I'm sorry that you were stuck out there all day, but you found him when everyone else failed. How did it happen?"

"We didn't find him," Jack replied, sparing me a conflicted glance. "Zoe and Aric Winters found us and led us to Ethan."

"But how did they know?"

"That's a very good question." Jack's gaze was weighted, and for a moment I worried he'd announce Zoe's secret to the world. Instead, he merely shrugged. "I don't know. They were helping us and there was talk of the river. We checked it because it seemed like a natural water source, and he was there.

"Things moved quickly after that," he continued. "We had to carry Ethan back to their house because the location was too isolated for paramedics to find. Ethan didn't look very good. We carried him to the house, I directed traffic from the front, and that's basically it."

"Well, I couldn't get much information out of them, but the paramedic I talked to at the hospital after Ethan arrived said that he thought Ethan was in much better shape than he would've expected after being exposed to the elements for so long," Hannah volunteered. "They're very hopeful he'll make a full recovery. And they did say it didn't look like he'd been gnawed on or anything, so maybe an animal didn't get him after all."

I thought of Zoe's glowing blue hands. She said she'd fixed Ethan enough to make sure he survived but not so much it would tip off the paramedics. It seemed she did exactly what she'd said. The mere idea that she could fight off death was exhilarating to think about. "I'm glad he'll be okay. Maybe we'll be able to get a chance to talk to him tomorrow."

"I don't know about him, but we will get a chance to talk to Lisa," Chris said. "She contacted us shortly before you guys returned. She wants to meet the people who rescued her husband. I mentioned we had questions about what happened, and she said she'd be willing to answer them if she got a chance to talk to her two heroes."

I shifted uncomfortably on my chair. "We're not the heroes. Zoe and Aric are the real heroes."

"And yet she wants to talk to you." Chris smiled widely. "This is just the best thing that could've possibly happened. It's as if you guys getting lost in the woods was destiny or something."

I swallowed a mouthful of potato salad – which suddenly tasted dry and pasty – and nodded. "Yeah. Destiny."

"We'll talk about the interview tomorrow," Jack instructed. "For now, it's late. Charlie and I are both exhausted. We need some sleep."

"And you should definitely get it." Chris hopped to his feet. "I don't want anything to get between you guys and that interview tomorrow. You should go to bed right now."

Even though part of me wanted to question Jack about what had happened, press him on the issue, I knew now was not the time. We'd been through too much to process everything, and pushing him before he was ready was a surefire way to get an answer I didn't want to hear.

Instead, I offered Chris a wan smile that I hoped he took as genuine. "That sounds like a plan. All I can think about is sleep."

"Me too." Jack wiped the corners of his mouth with a napkin and cast me a brief look. "Sleep is definitely our number one priority. The rest can wait until tomorrow."

I read between the lines and knew what he meant. He didn't want to talk about it either. He was probably as confused as me ... or worse.

"Yeah. Sleep. I can't wait to close my eyes and put this day behind me."

"That makes two of us."

23

TWENTY-THREE

I expected Jack to be waiting for me when I woke the next morning. I fell asleep hard and fast, but he haunted my dreams ... in a really hot and steamy way. I assumed things would be the same for him, so I was up and showered early.

The hallway outside of my bedroom was empty, though.

I tamped down my disappointment and headed toward the restaurant. I wasn't surprised to find everyone already assembled – even Millie, who hated early mornings – and Chris and Jack were deep in conversation when I took the open chair between Bernard and Hannah.

"Good morning." Millie beamed at me, a hint of mischief lurking behind her eyes. "How did you sleep?"

"Fine." I poured myself some coffee and ordered without looking at the menu when the waitress approached. Once she was gone, I focused on Chris because it somehow seemed easier than making eye contact with Jack. "So, are we still on for the interview?"

Chris straightened in his chair, nodding as he abandoned his quiet conversation with Jack. "Lisa Savage is expecting you in an hour and a half. She's looking forward to meeting the people who saved her husband."

"And what about Ethan? How is he doing?"

"He's still unconscious as far as we know. I'm not sure what the doctors are saying."

"Well, hopefully we'll get some news on that, too." For lack of anything better to do, I poured myself a glass of juice and downed half of it before continuing. Even though I was properly hydrated after our adventure, I couldn't shake the feeling of thirst that plagued me for much of the preceding day. "What do you want us to focus on when we interview her?"

"Well, she'll probably ask questions of you first." Chris was all business, even though I noticed his hand appeared to be leaning Hannah's way under the table. I wanted to look and confirm that it was on her knee, but there was no way I could manage it without being obvious, so I fought the effort. "Answer her, tell her whatever she wants to know, and then get the lowdown about what happened that night at the campsite. We need to know exactly what she saw."

"And what if she saw nothing?"

"Then we need to know that." Chris was pragmatic. "She might have blocked out what happened. I'm hopeful, though."

"Are you going to the hospital with us?"

Chris shook his head. "The rest of us are going to the river where you found Ethan. We want to take a look around to see if we can find prints or anything. Just you and Jack are going to the hospital."

"Imagine that," Laura muttered, a petulant frown clouding her features. She was clearly annoyed, which tickled me to no end.

"You guys need a day to recover anyway," Chris added, ignoring Laura. "When you're done at the hospital, head back here. We'll meet you when we're finished in the woods."

"Sounds like a plan," Jack said, leaning back in his chair when the waitress arrived with his breakfast. "A nice, quiet day. I think that's exactly what the doctor ordered."

I WAS A BALL OF NERVES by the time we landed at the hospital. Jack did his best to avoid being alone with me until the rest of the group departed. After that, he kept the conversation focused on Lisa Savage and our approach to questioning her. He didn't offer anything close to an opening to discuss personal matters.

"Let me do most of the talking," Jack instructed as we exited the elevator on the sixth floor and headed toward Lisa's room. "If she questions you, answer her, but otherwise I'm in charge."

I bit back a hot retort. "I've got it."

"Don't be rude or anything. Just be calm and quiet."

"I've got it."

"Don't be so quiet that she thinks you're weird, though. That might backfire on us."

I wanted to throttle him ... and then maybe try another kiss. Instead I shook my head and sighed. "I've got it, Jack. I'll try not to embarrass you."

Jack was taken aback. "That's not what I meant."

"It doesn't matter." I paused in front of Lisa's open door. "Let's do this."

"Charlie, wait ... ."

I ignored him and knocked on the door, pasting a pleasant smile on my face as Lisa looked up. She gestured for us to enter and shifted on the bed so she could prop herself. She looked unnaturally pale, exhausted even. I had a feeling her evening was one for the records thanks to the realization that her husband was actually alive. It was good news, but she'd already braced herself for his death. It wasn't something that could be easily absorbed.

"Come in. Come in." Lisa forced a bright smile as she looked between us. "You must be Charlotte Rhodes and Jack Hanson. I was told you were coming."

"Charlie," I automatically corrected, immediately wishing I would've had the foresight to stop myself from sticking my foot in my mouth right off the bat. "Most people call me Charlie. I forget my real name is actually Charlotte sometimes."

"Of course." Lisa's smile was benign as Jack and I took the open chairs at her bedside. "So ... um ... this is weird, huh?"

"It's definitely weird," I agreed, ignoring the way Jack shifted next to me. If he wanted me to be quiet he should've locked me in the Jeep. There was no way I wasn't going to be part of this conversation. "How are you feeling?"

"Tired. Drained. I don't know what to feel. They won't allow me to see Ethan because he's still unconscious in the intensive care unit. I saw him through the window, but it's not the same."

"Why won't they let you sit with him?"

"I'm not sure." Lisa shrugged her diminutive shoulders. "They've given multiple reasons. One is that they're not quite sure what's wrong with him and they have to run a lot of tests. They don't want to upset me by drawing blood."

"Oh, well … ."

"I think that's a bunch of crap." Lisa's eyes fired. "I don't know why they're trying to keep me from my own husband, but I don't like it one bit. My doctor said that it wasn't good for me to be up walking around and that I should try to relax, but I'm not sure I can."

"I don't think I'd be able to if I were in your shoes," I admitted. "If someone I loved was sick in the hospital, nothing could keep me from staying at his or her side." I thought of the way Jack sat by my side after I was almost killed in Texas. "I'm sure it will work out."

"I hope so." Lisa played with the nubs on the blanket covering her legs. "I understand you guys found Ethan. I was hoping you could tell me a bit about that. I mean … I just want something, even if it's a very brief explanation, so I can picture how it happened."

"I'm afraid that's not a very exciting story." I licked my lips and looked to Jack.

"Oh, no." He sounded irritated. "Why don't you handle all the questions, just like we talked about?" His message was clear. I hadn't listened and he was angry.

I decided to ignore his bad mood. "We arrived before you were found. We're with The Legacy Foundation. We're often called in when there are unanswered questions regarding a disappearance or death. We were investigating when we got word that you'd been found.

"After that we were hopeful we'd be able to find Ethan," I continued. "As part of our investigation, Jack and I returned to your campsite yesterday to look around. It's essentially exactly how you left it."

Lisa shuddered. "I don't care if I ever see it again. Actually, that's not true. I know I never want to see it again."

I couldn't blame her. "We kind of got ahead of ourselves while we were searching and wandered away from your campsite and got turned around. We were lost when we ran into a couple who live nearby – they're just off the main road – and by then everyone realized we were missing and went out searching. They decided to help and found us first."

"Wow." Lisa's eyes were wide. "So, you guys were lost, too."

"We just happened to stumble across your husband," I explained. "The woman who found us mentioned there was a river that wasn't far away, so we headed in that direction just to look around and that's when we found Ethan. It really was a fluke. She's the one who put everything together and decided to search there. She's kind of amazing for even thinking of it, if you ask me."

"It sounds like it." Lisa's face took on a far-off expression. "It might not have happened if you guys hadn't gotten lost."

"While we weren't happy about being lost at the time, it turned out for the best, so I think we'll both be able to laugh about it in a few weeks," I offered. "No one wants to be the person who gets lost, but I'm glad we were able to be part of the team that found your husband."

"Did he say anything when you found him?" Lisa's eyes were glassy. "Did he mention me? Did he say anything?"

"He wasn't awake, ma'am," Jack replied, obviously getting over his desire to stick me with the conversation after I ignored his instructions. "He was unconscious. Because of his location we knew it would be difficult for the paramedics to find us – even though we weren't that far from the road it was still kind of the middle of nowhere – so we carried him back to the Winters' house and waited for the paramedics there."

"And how long did it take for them to arrive?"

"Not long. A few minutes. They started working on your husband immediately. That's the last we saw of him."

"And now he's fighting for his life two floors down," Lisa mused. "I mean ... what are the odds? You only found him by chance."

"We still found him." I smiled. "As for Ethan fighting for his life, the paramedics were hopeful that he'd make a full recovery. That's what they said when they transported him here. One of our colleagues has a medical background, and she talked to them. They said your husband was in surprisingly good shape given how long he'd been out there."

That was clearly news to Lisa, and I couldn't help but wonder why the hospital staff was keeping her in the dark. Of course, for all we knew, Ethan could've taken a turn for the worse during the night. We had no idea what was wrong with him, or what needed to be done to save him. Why Lisa wouldn't be privy to all of her husband's medical information was a mystery.

"I hope your information is true," Lisa supplied, her lips a thin line rather than a smile. "I don't know what I'd do without Ethan. The thing is, I thought for sure he was gone. Hearing he was alive was like receiving a gift I didn't even know I could wish for. When I woke up this morning I was certain it was a dream."

"It's the best dream ever, right?" I flashed a bright smile. "I'd be so excited in your position. It must be terrible to not be able to see him."

"It's ... torturous," Lisa agreed. "Still, he's alive. That's the most important thing." She took a moment to collect herself and then pushed forward. "So, I understand you have some things you want to talk to me about, questions and the like. What are they?"

"Oh, well ... ." I shifted on my chair.

Jack smoothly stepped in to handle the next bit of conversation. "We're interested in knowing what happened the night you were separated from your husband. We know it's difficult to think about, but we need to know in case our investigation needs to dig deeper into exactly what is living in those woods."

"I don't know how much I can tell you." Lisa's expression turned stark. "It's all so jumbled in my head. I try to remember and yet ... it's not all there."

"Just tell us what you do remember," Jack prodded. "We understand it might not be a complete picture."

"Well … we were in the tent. I'm not sure how long we'd been inside because I'd fallen asleep. It was hot, and I remember wishing we could get some air to circulate – like maybe we should've packed a battery-operated fan or something – but I fell asleep anyway."

Lisa looked determined as she focused. "So, I woke up to a noise I didn't recognize. At first, I thought it was an owl or something, and then I remembered thinking that was ridiculous because I had no idea what an owl sounded like. I was quiet, Ethan was still asleep. He hadn't stirred.

"Then I saw this weird shadow against the tent wall. I couldn't figure out what it was because we'd doused the fire before going to bed," she continued. "I figured the moon was high and bright so we had to be seeing a shadow of sorts, but there was nothing outside our tent that could've made that big of a shadow.

"I was in that spot that's kind of between sleep and wakefulness – you know the one I'm talking about – so I was kind of slow to react," she said. "The next thing I know there were claws coming through the side of the tent and I could hear an animal growling, snapping its teeth."

Lisa's voice ratcheted up a notch and turned shrill. "Ethan was awake by now, and he told me to hide in my sleeping bag while he checked it out. I didn't want to, but he was adamant. I couldn't do anything but watch, and I heard him outside the tent … I heard him make a noise like he'd been hurt. He told me to stay inside, but I couldn't. I had to see.

"So, I crawled out of the tent and it took me a second to get my bearings," she continued. "It was so dark, and I heard terrible noises. When I finally realized what I was looking at I saw Ethan … and I swear he was unconscious. He looked dead. There were these monsters – these big, hairy monsters – and they were dragging him into the woods."

She saw the woods swallow her husband. I ran the words through my head. That's probably what it seemed like in the panic-filled moments that followed her waking. She was confused and terrified, and it seemed like the forest itself was a living entity.

"What exactly did you see dragging your husband?" Jack asked gently. "Was it a bear? Maybe a man?"

"No." Lisa vehemently shook her head. "I told the doctors … and I told the police … but they all think I'm crazy. I know what I saw!"

Now we were finally getting somewhere. "What did you see?"

"They were wolves." Lisa's voice was low and trembling. "There were at least three of them – maybe four – and they had hold of Ethan, dragging him into the woods. They growled, and I was sure they were going to eat him."

Jack and I exchanged a quick look.

"What kind of wolves?" Jack prodded. "I mean … were they the sort that run on four legs or two?"

Lisa shrugged. "I don't know. I think two, but … the doctor said I was crazy for believing that. I don't want to be crazy."

"That's okay." I patted her arm. She'd really been through it. She would probably never get over the trauma. "What happened then? How did you end up wandering around the woods by yourself?"

"I don't know how long I sat there trying to grasp what I saw," Lisa replied. "It might have been five seconds. It might have been five minutes. When I snapped out if it, I knew I had to follow. I didn't give the plan much thought. I just plunged into the woods, screaming for help and calling Ethan's name, and I got lost quickly.

"No one came until the day they found me, even though I kept walking around looking for him," she continued. "I was alone. I thought I would die alone. I was okay with that because then I would've been reunited with Ethan. I assumed he was dead, and that makes me feel even worse."

I thought my heart might break for her. "He's alive. You have a chance. You're alive. I'm sure that's what he wanted more than anything when he was being dragged away."

"Yeah. That's the type of person he is." Lisa swiped at a falling tear on her cheek. "I don't ever want to go into the woods again. Not ever."

"I don't blame you." I really didn't. "It's going to be okay now. You'll be all right. You'll get through this. You just need faith."

"I just need Ethan." Lisa mustered a watery smile. "I want my husband back more than anything."

"I hope that happens." I meant it. "Don't abandon your faith. It will get you through. I know it."

TWENTY-FOUR

*J*ack was unusually quiet on the ride back to the inn. While never an open book, he seemed troubled. I figured that was because he was as moved as I was by Lisa's story. I found out that was not the case when he dragged out a laptop in the lobby and began typing.

"What are you doing?" I sat on the couch next to him and looked over his shoulder.

Jack briefly pressed his eyes shut when I brushed against him, but was all business when he spoke. "I'm researching Lisa Savage."

"Why?"

"Charlie, I need you to do me a favor."

Jack's voice was low and even, but I sensed danger. "What kind of favor?"

"I need you to move to that chair over there." He pointed to the armchair at the edge of the small entertainment area.

I followed his finger, confused. "Why?"

"Because I think it would be best for both of us if we embraced distance right now."

I instantly had a lump in my throat. It hurt to swallow as I shakily got to my feet. "Oh, right. Sorry." I felt like a complete and total idiot. He did regret the kiss. Not only that, now he felt as if I was stalking him like Laura did, and he was eager to make sure I didn't overstep my bounds.

"You don't have to apologize." Jack glanced around to make sure no one was listening. "I'm not trying to be mean."

I couldn't meet his gaze. "Of course not. You're never mean."

"Oh, don't do that." Jack sounded miserable, yet I couldn't make myself meet the steady gaze I felt on the side of my face. "I'm just trying to get a little perspective here."

Perspective? I was fairly certain that was a nice way of saying "I thought I was going to die. I made a mistake. I want to pretend it never happened. Stop talking to me." Instead of pointing that out, I merely nodded and offered a half-mumble of understanding.

"Ugh." Jack placed the computer on the table and moved to the end of the couch so he was directly next to me. That ran counter to his edict that we maintain distance, so I was understandably confused. "Look at me."

I didn't think I could.

Jack grabbed my wrist and gave it a firm squeeze. "Look at me."

I slowly shifted my eyes to him, fighting hard to maintain a calm façade. My stomach was twisting and my heart felt as if it was being shaved with a metal cheese grater, but outside I wanted to appear strong. I didn't want Jack to question that one thing because I'd never get over the shame. "What? I'm not going to chase you around and throw myself at you. I'm not going to make you uncomfortable. I mean ... I'm not Laura."

"I know you're not Laura. That's the problem."

I didn't think it was possible for my heart to hurt more than it did when he asked me to move to another chair. I was wrong. "Right. You want Laura."

"I would die before I ever touched Laura." Jack sounded so matter-of-fact I couldn't help but believe him.

"You want someone like Laura," I corrected.

"Not even a little." Jack's expression was somber enough that I knew he was dealing with his own batch of worry. Of course, that worry most likely revolved around upsetting me.

"You don't have to explain yourself." I licked my lips as I searched for the right words. "What happened was … an accident. You didn't mean it, and it only happened because we were both worked up about being lost. You don't have to apologize … or hide from me. If you want to shut me out or have me removed from the job, I promise that's not necessary.

"I mean, I know I can't do anything if you want me gone," I continued, openly blathering in an effort to tamp down my discomfort. "I hope you don't want that, because I love this job and I worked really hard to get it. I know I'm not perfect and I've ticked you off a few times – I promise never to steal a rental car again, by the way – but I won't bother you. I won't follow you around or anything. I just … won't."

"Knock that off!" Jack's voice was harsh as he shifted so his knees touched mine and he gripped my hands so tightly I thought he might cut off my circulation. "You're seriously rambling."

"I'm sorry. I won't do that either."

"Oh, please don't act like this." Jack choked up a bit. "I swear that I'm not going to get you fired. I also don't think you're stalking me. I don't know why you'd say something like that, or how you could even consider something like that, but I don't believe it."

"You said to move," I reminded him. "You almost had to yell at Laura to do the same last night."

"And you think it's for the same reason." Jack exhaled heavily and stared into my eyes. "The reasons are not the same. I dislike Laura a great deal. I hate the games she plays. I don't want to be anywhere near her. But with you … um … ."

"It's different," I finished lamely. "You don't have to explain."

"But I do. I didn't mean for this to happen. In fact, I worked hard to make sure this never happened. But I failed miserably and this is all my fault. I need you to remember that and not blame yourself."

"Right." I had no idea what he was talking about. I didn't want to know. I simply wanted to focus on something else and pretend this conversation never happened. "Not my fault. I get it."

"You don't." Jack gripped my chin and forced my eyes to him. "I asked you to move because I can't think when you sit that close to me. Not because you irritate me, but because you wear some sort of body spray that smells like coconuts and it makes my head spin."

My mouth went dry. "What?"

"Oh, that innocent and confused look on your face only makes things worse," Jack complained. "I told myself from the start that I needed to stay away from you because you could turn into a huge distraction. I didn't want a distraction. I still don't. It's just ... I couldn't stop myself from kissing you last night. It was as if everything had built up over the past few weeks and I lost control of my emotions."

Wait ... what was he saying? "You're attracted to me?" I was dumbfounded.

Jack's sigh was filled with a mixture of resignation and annoyance. "You really didn't know. I thought there was a chance you were faking being oblivious. Now I see that's not the case."

"No, I'm pretty much an idiot all the time," I admitted, chewing on the inside of my cheek. "So, you actually wanted to kiss me?"

"No. I didn't want to kiss you at all." Jack shook his head, firm. "I meant what I said the other day. Workplace romances are a very bad idea."

My mind traveled back to the conversation in question. "Right. Bad idea. They ruin things for everyone."

"I believe that's a distinct possibility and I won't pretend I don't," Jack supplied. "The thing is, I was overwhelmed with these ... urges ... last night. I simply could not fight them a second longer. I'm not stupid enough to believe they might not return."

I was lost. I honestly had no idea what he was saying. "Jack, just spit it out."

"I like you." Jack's smile was watery. "I liked you before you fell down those stairs in Texas, but it was easier to pretend otherwise when you weren't hurt. Once you fell – actually, once you went missing and I spent thirty terrifying minutes looking for you, wondering if I'd ever see you again – something inside kicked into overdrive."

The admission was agonizingly heartfelt and made me go warm all over, which infuriated me because it was such a girly way to react. "Jack ...."

Jack held up a finger to quiet me. "No, let me get this out. I feel something for you, but I don't know what it is. That's what made me kiss you last night. I've been struggling with the feelings for weeks."

"I feel something for you, too," I admitted. "I kept thinking of it as a crush, but I knew it was something more when Laura warned me away from you on the plane and I wanted to punch her."

Jack chuckled, taking me by surprise when he gently tucked a strand of hair behind my ear. "Laura is more astute than anyone wants to give her credit for. She picked up on my feelings that night we camped out in Hooper's Mill, the night Chris went missing. She gave me a little grief about the fact that I was sitting with you in the hospital, too, but I ignored her."

"And then she decided to put on the full-court press because she thought she might be running out of time," I mused.

"Pretty much," Jack agreed. "The thing is, Charlie, I believe what I said. I think us having a relationship is a really bad idea."

"You don't want to be with me."

"I don't know what I want," Jack clarified. "There are times you drive me absolutely batty, so much so that I want to shake you. There are other times you're unbelievably sweet and I want to wrap you in a blanket and protect you. There are still other times that I just want to sit and listen to you laugh because I love the sound."

I pressed my lips together and fought the urge to throw myself at him.

"Despite all of that, I can't get over the idea that this would be a mistake," he continued. "What happens if things don't work out? The odds of things working out for us aren't good. You're young and impulsive ... and I don't think you completely trust me."

The last part jarred me. "I trust you."

"Do you? The fact that you're hiding something makes me think that's not true. I don't believe I should be privy to everything in your life, but it's obvious you're not ready to trust me. That makes a relationship even harder. I've never seen one healthy relationship that wasn't built on trust."

He had a point. "It's not that I don't trust you," I clarified. "I'm just ... there's a lot going on. Sometimes I'm afraid because you yell. I'm not afraid you'll hurt me, but I am annoyed with myself because every time you smile my heart does this somersault and I feel like a sixteen-year-old girl again."

Jack snorted. "Welcome to the club."

"This is all new to me, but ... when I was fighting to survive in Hooper's Mill I had hope because I knew you were out there. If that's not trust, I don't know what it is."

Jack nodded as he smoothed the top of my hair. "That doesn't mean I think this is a good idea. But what happens when this doesn't work out?"

"If you go in expecting it to fail, it will fail. I don't know what to tell you."

"That's a fair point. I do expect this to fail. I'm older than you."

"Not by much. I mean ... you're like four years older than me."

"It's actually closer to five," Jack countered. "Those years are important ones. I did a lot of living in those five years. I'm afraid you haven't done any living, and there will come a time when you'll want to pull away and do that living without me."

Huh. He was actually worried I'd be the one to end things. I didn't know what to make of that. "There's another way to look at this."

"I'm all ears."

"We might be tortured in a different way if we don't try. If we spend all our time pining for one another, we won't focus on our jobs and it will be a different kind of torture."

Jack snickered, the sound catching me off guard. "Believe it or not,

I've considered that, too. I've spent the better part of the last few days obsessing about what you're doing, who you're talking to and where you're sneaking out to every night. I understand what you're saying."

"But it's not enough."

"I don't know." Jack licked his lips. "I need time to think. I know that's probably not what you want to hear, but I am the sort of person who needs to weigh things and come up with the best solution after a lot of contemplation."

"Are you going to make a pro-con list?"

Jack laughed so hard I felt his breath brush against my face.

"What?" I protested. "I know a lot of people who make pro-con lists. It's a real thing."

"I think it's a girl thing, but if it will make you feel better I will most definitely make a pro-con list," Jack said. "What I really want is to table this discussion until after we're finished with this case. I want to take a little time when we get home to just ... live with the idea on both sides.

"Now, I know that's not how you usually operate," he continued. "You're the type who jumps into the pool before looking to see if there's water, but this is what I need."

I studied his handsome features for a long time, my fingers rising unbidden and fluttering over his cheek before I regained control of my senses and nodded. "Okay."

"Okay?"

"Yes. That seems fair."

"Ugh." Jack made a disgusted sound in the back of his throat and grabbed my hand long enough to press it to his cheek before releasing it and shifting further down the couch. "This actually would've been easier if you'd been a baby about it. If you'd stomped your feet and cried I could've told myself I was right to worry about the age differ-ence. Instead, you had to be all mature and accepting. That's going to irritate me."

I smiled at his rant. "That was my plan."

"I don't doubt that for a second." Jack held my gaze for a long time. "It'll be okay. We'll figure it out one way or the other. I just need to be able to focus on what's going on here. It will be a relief to be able to do it without worrying about you."

"You definitely don't have to worry about me." I squared my shoulders and pushed thoughts of rolling on top of Jack and repeating our kiss out of my head. He was right. We had a job to do. "I don't even want to go back to the woods at all now that I know what happened to Lisa.

"I mean, did you hear that story?" I continued, warming to my topic. "I can't imagine seeing wolves drag off someone I cared about. She said she was in shock. I think I would've been a lot worse than that. I probably would've curled into a ball and cried until someone came and found me."

"I don't believe that for a second," Jack countered. "You're the person who searched the dark for Chris and Millie even though you knew it was dangerous. You're the person who risked yourself with killers to protect them. You wouldn't have curled into a ball."

"Well, I would've wanted to."

Jack's lips curved. "I don't believe that, but it's not important. I think Lisa Savage is lying about what happened. That's why I want to conduct some research on her past."

I stilled, surprised. "You think she's lying?"

"Yes, but I can't figure out what she's lying about." Jack's expression was contemplative when he focused on his screen. "Part of me thinks she's lying about her reaction and that she really fled into the night – like you said – and left her husband behind. It could be guilt manifesting."

"What does the other part of you believe?"

"That she possibly had something to do with him getting hurt from the start and she's panicked about seeing him because she doesn't want to talk. I will admit that's the cynical part of me."

I was flabbergasted. "Are you serious?"

Jack nodded once.

"But they're married," I reminded him.

"Not all relationships have a happy ending," Jack shot back. "Sometimes I think happy endings are the exception."

"Has anyone ever told you what a ray of sunshine you are?"

"You just did."

I sucked in a breath and steadied myself, staring at Jack's screen as he typed away. "I don't think I believe your hunch, but it's worth a shot. Where are we starting with the research?"

"The beginning. It's always best to go all the way back."

TWENTY-FIVE

"*I* found something interesting."

We'd been working in silence – I ran upstairs to grab my own laptop, even though I had no idea what I was looking for – when Jack made his announcement. I was understandably curious why he assumed Lisa was lying, but with his good instincts I was more than willing to listen.

"Okay. Shoot."

"I've been going through a number of things because I wasn't sure where I should focus my efforts," Jack explained. "My approach has been rather scattershot, but I've found two points of interest.

"The first is that even though Lisa and Ethan have been married for only six months, apparently their relationship has been on and off since they were in high school," he continued. "They went to a Catholic school about forty minutes away All of the yearbooks are available on the school's website."

Huh. That was an interesting place to start looking. "They're both in their twenties, right?"

"Yeah. I've been able to track the evolution of their relationship through announcements and news releases."

My eyebrows winged up. "News releases?"

"They're both from wealthy families. In this area, that makes them like second-tier royalty."

"That's like the generic princess dolls when compared to the Disney ones, huh?"

Jack blinked several times as he slowly shook his head. "I don't know what that means."

"It's not important." I waved off my previous train of thought. It wasn't helpful and would only serve as a distraction. "Tell me what you found."

"Lisa and Ethan are in a lot of photos in these yearbooks. I might actually have you go through them a little closer because I was skimming them. What stood out is that they broke up at some point, because he was named 'class couple' with a different girl ... and it's someone we know."

"Who?"

"She works afternoons behind the desk at this inn."

I swiveled to look at the large desk settled in the middle of the lobby, my eyes landing on the amiable woman standing there as she answered questions for a guest. "Harley?"

"Her name is Harley Macmillan, at least according to the yearbooks," Jack supplied. "She and Ethan were all over the yearbook when they were seniors." He turned his computer so I could see the screen better, but I wanted to be closer.

"Are you going to freak out if I move close enough to look at that photo?"

Jack smirked. "No. I think I can refrain from tearing your clothes off if you want to sit a little closer, but touching me is out of the question. I don't want to turn into an animal or anything."

I rolled my eyes even as my cheeks burned at mention of him tearing off my clothes, and I was careful as I sat on the cushion next to him, making sure I didn't accidentally brush against him. "So, what are looking at?"

"Here." Jack pointed at his screen. "That's Harley and Ethan as prom king and queen."

I narrowed my eyes as I leaned closer. "Hmm. They look happy.

The cutline mentions that they were voted 'class couple' a week before the photo was taken at the prom."

"Yeah. Now, it doesn't necessarily mean anything, but I do find it interesting that Lisa and Ethan apparently had a rather rocky road. They were all over their junior yearbook together, yet the senior year-book was all him and Harley."

"Hmm." I studied the image for a long beat and then pointed to a face in the background. "That's Lisa right there. It looks as if she was on the prom court but didn't win."

"Let me see." Jack leaned so close his face was practically pressed against the screen. "You're right. She doesn't look happy, does she?"

I shrugged. "That doesn't mean she's evil or anything. I'm sure you remember what it was like to be in high school. Couples got together and broke up willy-nilly all over the place."

"They did, but it's a pattern of behavior," Jack said as he minimized the high school yearbook photo. "This is from college, and seems to show something different. Here they're very clearly together and Harley is nowhere in the picture."

"Did they go to Covenant College?"

Jack shook his head. "That's the school that burned down, right?"

"Burned down and was never rebuilt," I muttered. "What college did they go to?"

"Northwood. It's a business college. That makes sense for kids like Lisa and Ethan who came from wealthy families."

"I guess it does." I studied the new snapshot. The couple standing in the center of it smiled back at the camera, but something appeared off about their pose. "Ethan doesn't look very happy, does he?"

Jack shrugged. "I don't know. He's smiling."

"Yeah, but there was a light in his eyes when he posed for that photo with Harley. He doesn't have that light here."

"A light, huh?" Jack snagged my gaze. "I guess I can see that. You have a light sometimes."

"Oh, geez. I thought we were tabling this until after we chased down our werewolves?"

Jack snorted. "I'm just messing with you."

"Of course."

"You do have a certain light in your eyes, though." Jack turned thoughtful. "You're right about Ethan's appearance being different in the photographs. They were taken three years apart. How much could've really changed for him in that amount of time?"

"We have access to someone who might be able to answer that for us," I pointed out, inclining my chin toward Harley. "We're the only people in the lobby right now. It's a perfect time to question her."

"Then maybe you should do it."

I jolted. "You want me to question her."

"I want you to try."

"What are you going to do?"

"Watch to make sure you don't screw it up."

I scowled. "I'm glad to see you have such faith in me."

"I have faith in you. You're insightful and smart."

I preened under the compliment.

"You also fly off at the lip when you're not watched," Jack added, slowly getting to his feet. "Let's see what you can get out of her."

APPROACHING HARLEY UNDER Jack's watchful eye was nerve-wracking, but I was intrigued enough with Jack's belief regarding Lisa that I couldn't turn away. Harley didn't realize we were approaching until we were already at the desk.

"Hey, guys." She smiled at us as she continued straightening up her work station. "You guys have been lost in your own little world for a while now. I'm surprised you came up for air and took a break."

"We're researching," Jack volunteered. "The Ethan Savage case took a turn last night."

"I know." Harley brightened considerably. "You guys found him in the woods. You saved him. You're regular heroes."

"I wouldn't go that far." Jack shot me a pointed look and I knew it was my turn to speak.

"We just happened to be in the right place at the right time," I explained. "It was a fluke."

"Well, it was one lucky fluke." Harley finished spiffing up her work area. "Ethan and I went to high school together, so I was really upset when he went missing. I'm happy to know that he's alive and safe."

"Yeah, well, that's kind of what we want to ask you about," I said, shifting from one foot to the other.

Harley was obviously confused. "You want to ask me about high school?"

"We want to ask what happened between you and Ethan – we know you were class couple and everything – and how he ended up back with Lisa even though he looked happier with you." I blurted it out as if my tongue was on fire. That's so not how it went in my head.

"Oh, geez." Jack slapped his hand to his forehead. "Don't you think there might have been a better way to approach her?"

I shrugged. It was over and done with. "I did it my way. You have to live with it."

"Yeah, yeah." Jack pinched the bridge of his nose. "I'm afraid to look. Is she still standing there or has she taken off?"

Harley let loose a low chuckle at Jack's reaction, shaking her head. "You two are funny. How long have you been together?"

"Oh, we're not together," I replied. "We're just co-workers."

Harley narrowed her eyes to the point where she appeared mistrustful. "You two aren't together?"

"No."

"It's up for debate," Jack clarified. "We're not talking about it until we solve this case."

I was stunned by his fortitude. "I didn't think we were telling people that."

"Yeah, well, apparently you're not the only one with a big mouth," Jack groused, dragging a hand through his dark hair. "We're really looking for some insight on Ethan and Lisa, and we know you went to high school with them. We thought you might be willing to share."

"I don't know what to tell you." Harley nervously tugged on her index finger until it cracked. "The thing is, Ethan and I were very close for a year and a half ... and then things fell apart. I try not to think about it too much because it upsets me ... and then I feel stupid for letting it upset me because it was a long time ago."

"You loved him, didn't you?" I recognized the dopey look on Harley's face when she uttered Ethan's name. If she didn't love him, she was highly enamored with him.

"I did love him." Harley visibly swallowed. "It happened the summer before senior year. Lisa had to leave town for a modeling gig. Instead of doing the long-distance thing, they both agreed to break up while she was out of town and then get back together when she returned."

"That doesn't make much sense," Jack noted. "I mean ... if you love someone, how hard is it to make it through three months of separation?"

Harley shrugged. "I can't answer that because I honestly don't know. I only know that Ethan was hanging around ... and I was hanging around. One night we hung around together at the ice cream shop. We just sort of fell together.

"I thought it would be a summer fling and nothing more," she continued. "I enjoyed spending time with him, but I was afraid to let him get too close. By that point Ethan and Lisa were kind of like high school royalty. They'd been together since middle school.

"As the summer wore on, Ethan started talking more and more," she said. "I won't betray his confidence, but I can say that our feelings were legitimate and we were pretty much in love – or at least lust – by the end of the summer."

Jack pursed his lips as he absorbed the start of the tale. "You don't have to confirm it, but I'm guessing that Ethan felt manipulated by Lisa. She's the dramatic sort, right? She made up stories to keep herself the center of attention. She wanted Ethan to fawn all over her, yet she didn't do the same for him. That summer away from her was a mistake because Ethan began to realize what a user she really was."

"I can't betray his confidence," Harley said. "I just ... can't. I wouldn't want him to talk out of turn about me."

"Fair enough." Jack said. "You guys were together for your senior year. You were together at prom. When did you break up?"

"We tried to make it work, but deep down I think I always knew it was a fairy tale that would have to end," Harley replied. "It wasn't so terrible at first. He went to Northwood and I went to the community college in Saginaw. We couldn't see each other every day, but we were together as often as possible."

Something about the way Harley's demeanor shifted told me this story was going to take an ugly turn. "Lisa did something to get him back, didn't she?" I wasn't sure when my opinion of the shattered woman I met in the hospital changed, but now I was certain she wasn't who she pretended to be. Jack's convictions were only part of it. The other was the way Ethan lost his happiness in the course of a few short years. That was somehow devastating to me and I didn't even know the man.

"I don't know that it's fair to blame what happened on Lisa," Harley hedged.

"You're trying to be nice, but I get the feeling it's really not necessary," Jack prodded. "Just tell us what happened. We can fill in the missing pieces."

"Ethan and I drifted a bit, and then one day I went to his house to see him." Harley looked uncomfortable. "He was upset ... and crying ... and apologetic. It seemed he'd gotten drunk at a party the night before and ended up with Lisa."

"With her?" I asked before full understanding washed over me. "Oh, you mean *with* her."

Harley nodded. "They got drunk and hooked up. He was really upset and apologized over and over. I thought about forgiving him, but I figured my self-esteem was worth more than that. Somehow everyone in town found out right away and people were pointing ... and laughing ... and telling me they knew it would never last because I wasn't really Cinderella."

"Cinderella?" Jack made a face. "That's the second time someone has mentioned princesses in the last hour. Why would they say something like that?"

"I was poor and Ethan was rich," Harley replied. "He was out of my league. Lisa was always more of his speed. I only went to the same school because I got a scholarship. My parents couldn't afford to pay for me to attend, and that meant I was always the one looked down on while I was there. I mean ... until Ethan started paying attention to me."

The dark pit in my stomach turned into a dull ache. "Oh, man. I bet Lisa knew that you were insecure and preyed upon you. She probably purposely went after Ethan to snag him a second time."

"I'm sure she did." Harley was stoic. "But I couldn't forgive what Ethan did. Drunk or not, trust is the most important thing in a relationship."

I spared a glance for Jack and found him watching me with unreadable eyes. "It really is," I agreed, clearing my throat. "So, what happened after that?"

Harley shrugged. "We broke up. He got back together with Lisa. They dated for a few years. Rumor has it that last summer they broke up again, but I don't think that's true because they got married six months later. If they did break up, it couldn't have been for long."

"No." I tapped my bottom lip and thought about the brief image I saw in the vision. Despite what she said about running to her husband's aid, I was certain Lisa ran in the opposite direction and left him that night. I chalked it up to fear and allowed my sympathy to take over, but now that I had time to dwell on the situation, I couldn't help but wonder if something else really terrible happened. "How is your relationship with Lisa?"

"Lisa and I don't have a relationship," Harley answered. "We never liked one another, and the competition for Ethan only made things worse."

"But she's rich, right?" Jack asked. "I mean ... she comes from a wealthy family. I don't understand why she'd put so much effort into a man who clearly has divided loyalties when she could pretty much have whatever she wants."

"You'll have to ask her about that. Rumor has it that her family has fallen on hard times," Harley said. "They had huge financial ties to Covenant College, and when it burned to the ground they got some insurance money but their portfolios took a huge hit. At least that's what I heard. Ethan's family is really rich. I'm sure she doesn't want to give up the lifestyle she's become accustomed to, so it only made sense for her to marry Ethan."

"Right." Jack absently ran his hand up and down my back, taking me by surprise. He was the one who put the "no touching" rule in place and now he was the first to break it. "This is all starting to come together."

"It is?" I was confused. "How?"

"Strangers didn't attack Ethan in the woods. Lisa did."

The vision popped into the forefront of my brain again. "I'm not sure that's true."

"She might not have done it herself, but she definitely had a hand in it." Jack was sure of himself. "Maybe she hired someone."

"But why?" Harley asked. "What would she get out of that?"

"Money. She would be a very well-to-do widow."

"But what about the werewolves?" I asked.

Jack rolled his eyes. "There are no werewolves."

"How can you be sure?"

"Because werewolves are made up."

Huh. That was a total bummer to consider.

TWENTY-SIX

*J*ack set about researching the financial woes of Lisa's family as I spent time going through the college website for more photos. I took screenshots of the photos with my phone and when I was done I'd managed to put together a rather interesting collage.

"Take a look at this."

Jack pulled his eyes from his screen and looked at my art project. "You took time to make a collage?" He was baffled. "How – and why, for that matter – did you do that?"

"I arranged them chronologically." I refused to be baited into a fight. "As for the program, it's an app. All I had to do was drag and drop the photos."

"And you did such a neat job of it." Jack poked my side, causing me to smirk despite my reticence. "There it is. I much prefer it when you smile."

I decided to put my foot down. "You can't flirt with me while you're taking time to think. That's not allowed."

"Since when is that the rule?"

"I'm making it a rule." I held firm despite the charming smile he lobbed my way. "I don't want to get my hopes up, or get more attached to you than I already am. It doesn't seem fair."

Jack's smile slipped. "No, it doesn't. You're absolutely right. I was just feeling a little lighter after our talk. I should've taken your feelings into consideration."

Oh, I wanted to smack that thoughtful expression right off his face … and then kiss him to make him feel better. I did neither. "Anyway, look at the photos."

Jack reticently forced his attention to the screen and slowly scanned each snapshot. "He's not a happy guy, is he?"

"No, he's definitely not. There's more." I minimized the collage and pulled up a search window. "This is the engagement announcement that ran in the local newspaper nine months ago."

"I'm guessing you found something in the announcement because there's nothing that stands out about the photograph."

"Other than Ethan looking miserable, the photograph is unre-markable. Read the write-up, though."

Jack did as I instructed, his shoulders stiffening when he got to the last paragraph. "Holy … ."

"You saw it, too." I was a little proud of myself for the discovery. "According to that piece, Ethan and Lisa were supposed to add to their family a few months after the article ran. I never stumbled across mention of a kid anywhere, did you?"

"No." Jack rubbed the back of his neck as he processed. "Harley said that she heard rumors that Lisa and Ethan broke up a year ago. Then a couple months later they announced their engagement. How much do you want to bet Lisa lured Ethan back by claiming she was pregnant?"

"That sounds right out of a soap opera," I pointed out. "In this day and age, who can get away with faking a pregnancy? All Ethan would have to do is transport her to a doctor's office and demand a test."

"Except Ethan seems the trusting sort. Harley said he was shaken up when he cheated on her."

"He should've been shaken up. Cheating isn't nice … or acceptable."

"Duly noted." Jack's smile was sly, but he avoided commenting on the elephant – er, werewolf – in the room. "What if he was so shaken up because he was drugged and only thought he'd cheated on Harley?"

"I ... what are you saying?"

"Ethan seems like a lovable lout who lets everyone tell him how to live his life," Jack explained. "He went into business with his father, even going so far as to attend his father's alma mater. He dated a manipulative girl who took control of him in high school. He managed to break away from her after a summer apart and seemed really happy until he went to the same school with her and coincidentally ended up in bed with her even though he doesn't really seem to love her."

"I hate to be the practical one here – mostly because I'm not used to it – but men often think with their ... you know." I pointed toward his crotch and enjoyed the way he uncomfortably shifted. "How can you be sure Ethan didn't simply get drunk and fall on top of Lisa? Things often seem like a good idea when you're drunk."

"It doesn't matter," Jack said. "When you care about someone, you don't cheat on him or her. Ethan might not be the smartest guy in the room, especially when it comes to recognizing manipulation, but he's loyal. He wouldn't have cheated on Harley. She can't see that because she's so hurt by what went down, but I see it."

He was so passionate about the subject I couldn't argue the point. "Well, let's say Lisa is guilty of all of this. Let's say she tricked him into believing they had sex, sat back and watched while Harley dumped him, managed to finagle her way back into his life and even faked a pregnancy to get him to propose ... how does that lead to her trying to kill him?"

"I don't have all the answers. The thing is, Lisa either faked a miscarriage or owned up to not being pregnant at some point. No matter how slow Ethan is on the uptake, he had to realize she was supposed to be showing at some point."

Jack was right. His hypothesis might not have been completely on the nose, but it certainly had all the hallmarks of being close. "Lisa doesn't really strike me as the type to like camping," I admitted after a beat. "Maybe she knew Ethan was going to break up with her – and sooner rather than later – and she had no choice but to kill him if she wanted his money. She probably had to sign a pre-nup before the wedding, so the only way to get her hands on that money was to inherit it."

"Now you're thinking." Jack shot me an enthusiastic thumbs-up. "So, Lisa either suggests a camping trip or agrees to go with Ethan because she knows she needs to keep up appearances. They go to a place not far from home, but where they can be isolated. She probably hired someone to come in and grab Ethan ... and somehow he got away."

I thought about the vision. No matter what, Lisa had looked terrified when she'd fled the campsite. "Is it possible that Lisa was in danger even if she did plan everything?"

"I don't see how. She created the danger."

"What about the paw prints?"

Jack sighed, sounding weary. "Charlie, those could have been planted. They could've belonged to animals simply running wild. A werewolf attack doesn't fit what we're looking at."

"No." I had no choice but to agree. "Do you think the hospital knows? I mean ... Lisa said they wouldn't allow her to see Ethan. Maybe the police know something and they're not making it public. Maybe they ordered the doctors to keep Lisa from him."

"That makes sense." Jack started typing on his laptop again. "I'll check the police files to see if they've updated the reports. You should get on the phone with Chris. Someone needs to get back to the hospital to keep an eye on Lisa."

"Here comes Chris now." I inclined my chin toward the door, widening my eyes when Chris – and the cadre of people who trailed in his wake – barreled in our direction. He was breathless when he stopped, and the look in his eyes was so wild I involuntarily leaned back. "What's going on?"

"We just got word from the hospital," Chris gasped, his hands on his knees as he struggled to regain his breath. "It seems that Ethan Savage has made a miraculous recovery. I mean ... miraculous. He's awake and talking, and the police are on their way to interrogate him."

"How do you know that?" Jack asked.

"Hannah got a tip from one of the orderlies." Chris' smile tipped down. "Apparently he has a crush on her."

Hannah didn't bother to hide her amusement. "He's been very helpful … and he's kind of cute, but in a puppy way." She patted Chris's arm in a reassuring manner. "I prefer big dogs to little puppies."

I pressed my lips together to keep from laughing at her unintended double entendre.

"Anyway, apparently Ethan Savage was drugged with something that should have killed him. It's called Nightshade. Not available locally. He should've died from the amount found in his system. It had been in his system for days and he should've been close to death. No one knows how he survived, but he woke up and he's been talking nonstop."

I knew how he woke up. A certain blonde with glowing blue hands saved him. I had to wonder if she knew what she was saving him from when she did it. Either way, she did something miraculous, and I was astounded.

"How did the poison work?" Jack asked, forcing me back to reality.

"Well, it was diluted and cut with a psychedelic," Hannah answered, perching on the arm of my chair. "I think whoever poisoned him wanted him to wander around the woods confused so that when his body was eventually found it would look like an accident. A byproduct of the poison is that he'd be ridiculously thirsty."

"Which is why he stuck close to the river," I mused.

"And probably why he survived," Hannah added. "He might have imbibed enough water to flush his system."

"That's good." That wasn't entirely true, but it was still good. "Do they know who poisoned him?"

"That's the other part of the story," Chris said, his eyes gleaming. "When word spread that Ethan woke up, someone told his wife and she disappeared from the hospital. Apparently she walked out on her own. What do you make of that?"

Jack and I shared a weighted look.

"We have some things to share with you," Jack said. "You'd better sit down."

DINNER WAS LOUD, and I didn't miss the fact that Harley positioned herself at a corner table in the dining room so she could eavesdrop. I didn't begrudge her the information – after all, other than Ethan she'd been hurt the most – but I could tell that Jack's notions regarding Lisa's machinations were something she'd never considered. Now that she could wrap her brain around everything, she was open to the idea of Lisa being the cause of everything.

"Where do you think Lisa will run to?" Millie asked, cutting into her slab of prime rib with zest. "If you guys are right and she's broke, she probably won't be able to run far."

"I'm going to guess that a woman like Lisa had an exit plan," Jack replied. He sat next to me, his presence warm, but he didn't go out of his way to look at me. I understood – mostly because I found it necessary to look away from him most of the time, too – so I decided to pin my attention on Harley. She looked somehow lost ... and also found. It was interesting.

"By exit plan, do you mean that she had money stashed with a fake passport and a plane ticket out of the country?" Laura asked. "I know that's what I'd do if I planned to murder my husband."

Jack made a face. "Of course you would. That's who you are."

"Hey, I'm not saying she was right," Laura protested. "I'm simply saying she's not an idiot."

"She's not," Jack agreed. "She's not our problem, either." He slid his eyes to my plate. "Why aren't you eating?"

"I'm watching Harley." I saw no reason to lie. "She's absorbing all the information."

"I'm sure she's interested." Jack kept his voice low so only I could hear. "Do you think she'll go to Ethan?"

I nodded without hesitation. "I think that'll be the one good thing to come of this. She'll go to Ethan. They'll talk. They'll make a go of it."

"Do you think they'll make it?"

I shrugged. "I think that the right couple can make a go of anything." Jack's expression was thoughtful when I glanced back at him. "What?"

"Nothing. I was just thinking. You should eat your dinner." He tapped the side of my plate. "You need to keep up your strength."

"Why? Our part of this is pretty much done. Lisa is in the wind, Ethan is safe, and I'm fairly certain werewolves weren't involved."

"You're very right on that front." Jack seemed pleased about that development. "That means we'll be leaving tomorrow. We're getting up early, so make sure you get a good night's sleep."

I was taken aback by the sudden shift in our travel plans. "Why are you so excited by that?"

"Because, once we're home, I can spend some time thinking, and hopefully we can come to some sort of agreement."

"Agreement?" I didn't like the sound of that. "Do you expect us to shake hands, smile and go our separate ways when you decide it's not a good risk?"

"How do you know I'll decide that?"

"I don't, but that's how it feels." For the first time since our conversation regarding the possibility of a relationship I felt real anger about allowing Jack to have all the power in the decision. "You should probably be careful. If you take too long to decide I might just find something else to entertain me."

Jack knit his eyebrows. "Is that a threat?"

"No." I wiped the corners of my mouth with my napkin and stood. "I think it's more that I don't like the idea of you getting to decide everything. Why don't I have a say in any of this?"

Jack balked. "Charlie, we talked about this." He furtively glanced around the table and scowled when he realized Laura was watching us with unveiled interest. "This is not the time to talk about it again."

I couldn't agree more. "I have no intention of talking about this." I slid around my chair and pushed it forward so it served as a barrier of sorts between Jack and me. "I'm going to go chat with Harley. I think she needs a friend. I know I do."

"Wait." Jack made a grab for my wrist, but I evaded him.

"I need some time, too, Jack. You have thinking to do and so do I. I also want to make sure Harley is okay."

Jack extended a warning finger. "We're going to have a talk about this before the night is over."

"I can't wait." I plastered a smile on my face as I crossed to Harley. She looked guilty about being caught staring, but my intention was to put her at ease. "How are you feeling?"

Harley shrugged, noncommittal. "A little confused."

"Join the club."

"What are you confused about?"

"Men ... and how stupid they are."

Harley chuckled. "I think it's funny that you're so worked up about Jack when he's clearly crazy about you."

"He's definitely crazy." I leaned back in my chair and glanced at the clock on the wall. "Aren't you usually gone by now?"

"I am, but Fred had to leave because of the Lisa situation. He got a call and the police demanded he come to the station to be questioned."

I was confused. "Why would Fred have to go to the station to answer questions about Lisa's disappearance?"

"He was Lisa's family's attorney for a really long time before he bought the inn. He kind of wanted this to be a retirement business. He thought he could run it and hunt to his heart's content."

I eyed the pitiful deer head on the wall behind Harley's head. "Yes, well, he seems content with his killing ... and stuffing."

"He still did some legal work for Lisa's family up until last year when they lost everything," Harley explained. "He was close with Lisa – kind of like an uncle – so I'm sure he's confused by what happened. He was fond of her, so he won't believe what's being said about her."

"Do you think he knows where she is?"

Harley immediately started shaking her head. "They weren't that close. But he might know about some property the family still owns –

235

hunting cabins and the like – and he might be able to share information that will help track down Lisa."

"Oh, that's a good idea." I tapped my fingers on the table as I worked overtime to let my frustration ebb. "I don't suppose you have anything to drink, do you?"

Harley's eyebrows winged up. "You want to get drunk?"

No, that wouldn't do at all. I had someplace to be when I was certain everyone had retired for the evening. But I had time to kill before then. "No, but I wouldn't mind a little something to take the edge off."

"You and me both."

"Let's do it."

27

TWENTY-SEVEN

J spent the stretch of evening after dinner and before bed doing my best to act normal. That was never something I wanted to be – even when hiding what I could do as a teenager – but I did my best to adopt that air now ... and it felt absolutely ludicrous.

"What's your plan?" Millie asked, moving next to me as I surveyed the room shortly before eight. We'd gathered in the bar to chat, compare notes and relax. I should've realized that even though everyone else seemed to be ignoring me that Millie wasn't the type to follow the crowd.

"I have no idea what you mean." I smirked when I realized I sounded like Zoe. "I'm just standing here."

"You're doing more than that." Millie folded her arms over her chest as she regarded me. "Something happened, didn't it?"

This time I wasn't faking when I responded. "I have no idea what you're talking about."

"You and Jack. Something is ... different ... about you."

I struggled to remain calm, but I could feel my cheeks burning. Given the muted lighting in the bar, I could only hope that little detail would escape Millie's keen observation skills. "I don't know what you're talking about. We did research all afternoon. You saw the research we came up with."

"I did." Millie nodded and narrowed her eyes. "I did, but I thought something was off about you two last night. I pushed it out of my head because you had such a long day. But now something is definitely going on."

Oh, geez. This was the last thing I needed. "Nothing is going on." I couldn't meet her steady gaze. I knew I would crack like an iPhone screen against pavement if I looked into her eyes.

"Yeah, well, I don't believe you." Millie leaned close and whispered so only I could hear. "I've been waiting for Jack to get out of his own way and make a move since right after you started with us. I felt the fireworks whenever you two were around one another and knew it was only a matter of time."

I was dumbfounded. "What?"

"You heard me." Millie snickered. "You two did … something. You … ." She waggled her fingers and pressed her eyes shut, as if she was using magic to somehow divine a secret. "You kissed!"

She said the words so loudly I thought there was no possible way the rest of the group didn't hear. I snapped my attention to the small table next to the bar where Chris, Hannah, Laura and Bernard sat. None of them looked in our direction, though. When I searched the room for Jack I found him leaning against the bar and watching us. He didn't appear to have heard Millie's exclamation. He gripped a bottle of water rather than beer because he'd claimed he was barely over his previous hangover, but his eyes were trained on me. He looked deep in thought.

"You need to watch what you say," I ordered Millie as I mustered a wan smile for Jack's benefit. "You're going to ruin things."

Millie snorted. "That means there's something to ruin. I was right, wasn't I? You kissed."

We did more than that. We made out … hardcore … and then he applied the brakes because he wasn't certain I was worth the effort. Sure, that's not how he worded it, but the more I thought about it, that's how I felt. "It's complicated. If you want to jump all over someone for answers, I suggest you bother Jack."

Millie's eyes were keen as she looked me up and down. Then, out of nowhere, sympathy washed over her features. "He kissed you and then backed away because ... well, he's Jack. Oh, you poor thing." She patted my shoulder as if I were a mopey teenager who needed something to brighten my day. "I swear it'll be okay. He'll come around."

"Maybe he will." I wasn't sure how I felt about waiting for Jack to make a decision. My inner feminist thought it was a very bad idea. "Maybe I won't be waiting when he does. Did you ever consider that?"

Millie immediately started shaking her head. "You're strong, but you're young. You've been head-over-heels for Jack since you laid eyes on him."

I balked. "I have not."

"You have." Millie made a clucking sound with her tongue. "It's okay. You can't help yourself. And, look on the bright side, Jack is a really good man."

A really good man who needs to think. "I'm sure he is."

Millie's snicker was grating. "Hold strong for as long as you can. It's good to make him suffer. That's likely to take longer than you want it to, so I'll have a talk with him. He might pull his head out of his behind faster if I give him a little push."

"That sounds great." I scrubbed my cheeks, making a big show of feigning sleepiness. If I was going to make my escape, now was as good a time as any. "I'll let you tackle Jack on your own. I've had a really long day and I'm tired. I think I'm going to bed."

Millie grabbed my arms before I could disappear, turning me so I had no choice but to look directly into her eyes. "Don't let Jack get you down. He'll make the right decision. He always does. Sometimes it simply takes him longer than it should."

She thought I was moping about Jack. That was ... interesting. It was also annoying. I had a feeling it had something to do with my age. I'd rather have her believe I was turning pouty over Jack rather than try to follow me to the Winters house, so this was the best outcome I could've hoped for.

"Well, I guess we'll have to wait and see." I extricated myself from Millie's grip. "I'm heading to bed. See you in the morning."

"Goodnight, Charlie." Millie's smile was kind. "I'll talk to him. You'll see. Everything will work out."

"That would be a nice change of pace."

I WENT THE UBER route again. I figured it was my best option. I headed to my room, changed into darker clothes, scheduled my ride on the app and then left through the back door. The driver picked me up in front of the hotel and we were off within two minutes. As far as I could tell, absolutely nobody saw us.

That was a good thing.

It took about ten minutes to reach the Winters house. I could tell they were home by the way the windows lit up. I tipped the driver extra, thanked him, and then scrambled toward the door. For some reason I couldn't shake the odd thing Lisa Savage had said when she thought no one was listening in the hospital. *The forest came alive and grabbed him.* Why would she say that if she thought no one was listening? I simply couldn't understand.

I knocked three times in rapid succession and uncomfortably looked over my shoulder as I watched the thick foliage to the left and right for signs of movement. Aric opened the door. He didn't seem surprised to see me.

"We figured you'd show up." He ushered me inside, making sure to lock the door before leading me to the kitchen. There we found Zoe making hot chocolate … and spraying whipped cream from a canister into her mouth.

"Hey, Charlie." She also didn't appear surprised to see me. "What's up?"

"I came to talk to you about what happened with Ethan Savage. Have you heard?"

"We've heard." Aric sidled closer to Zoe and tipped up her chin so he could kiss away the remnants of whipped cream from the corners of her mouth. "Save some of that for the kid. She'll freak if she doesn't have whipped cream for her hot chocolate."

"I bought three canisters."

"Good girl." Aric's grin was lazy as he leaned against the counter and folded his arms across his chest. "It's good that he's going to be okay."

They were so calm. I couldn't understand it. "Yes. He had a downright magical recovery."

Zoe snorted. "Imagine that."

"Especially since he was poisoned with Nightshade and shouldn't have lived. He's something of a medical miracle."

Zoe straightened at the news, surprise evident. "What?"

"Oh, you didn't know that part, did you?"

Zoe shook her head. "I assumed he was dehydrated, maybe had a head injury we didn't see or something. He was poisoned?"

"According to the doctors. The amount of Nightshade in his system should've killed him. There are several guesses going around – including that the Nightshade was laced with a psychedelic – but he could very well be studied for weeks and months to come because of his miraculous recovery."

Zoe shrugged. "Are you worried that's going to somehow come back on me?"

"Aren't you?"

"No." Zoe calmly placed the canister on the counter. "Only three of us were here when it happened. There's no way to trace it back to me. I know you won't say anything."

"Of course I won't. It's just … you saved him and the doctors are curious."

"It will be okay, Charlie." Aric awkwardly patted my shoulder. "It's nice that you're worried, but we've been through way worse than this. They won't even question us because the possibility that Zoe somehow magically healed Ethan won't ever cross their minds."

"Really?" I couldn't help being relieved. "I was so afraid this would come back to hurt you."

"It won't." Zoe was nonchalant. "But I am curious. Do they know how he was poisoned?"

"Not that I'm aware of." I ran her through everything we'd found out during the day. "So, I think it's obvious that Lisa did something – or at least hired someone to do something – but now she's in the wind.

"What's really frustrating is that I think Ethan was a good guy who simply couldn't stand up for himself," I continued. "He refused to see Lisa for what she was. It's frustrating, because Harley is great and I think they would've been happy. Ethan obviously couldn't see past his pride to go after her."

I was feeling morose when I grabbed the whipped cream canister and sprayed some in my mouth. "Men are stupid."

Zoe pressed her lips together. The look she shot Aric wasn't lost on me. She was amused ... at my expense.

"It's not funny," I snapped.

"Oh, you're so funny I want to adopt and keep you," Zoe countered, chuckling as she hopped onto a stool and grabbed a cookie from the plate at the center of the counter. "Having boy trouble?"

I balked. "I'm an adult. I don't have boy trouble."

"I had boy trouble well into my late twenties. It's not an age thing."

Aric snorted. "You did not. Your boy trouble ended when you were twenty-two."

"Really?" Zoe pinned him with a dark look. "Who took five years to propose? Who had me thinking that he didn't want to marry me? Who kept my ring from me until after I absorbed a magic book and almost ended the world?"

I was dumbfounded. "You almost ended the world?"

"Only a little," Zoe replied, her eyes never moving from Aric's face. "I believe that would constitute boy trouble."

"Oh, you're not going to get away with blaming that on me," Aric complained. "I didn't ask you to marry me because I thought you'd say no. In fact, my father told me you'd say no. It's his fault."

"Yes, because your father always makes great decisions when it comes to things like that." Zoe rolled her eyes. "That doesn't change the fact that you didn't ask me to marry you for five years."

"I wanted to ask you the day you graduated," Aric grumbled. "Dad said it was too soon, that I would be stealing your freedom. I wanted to punch him then and I still do today. Too bad he's not around."

Something about the way they bantered made me smile. "You guys are happy, aren't you?"

"For the most part," Zoe agreed. "I'd be happier if he'd kill the bees in the hive toward the back of our property, but marriage is about compromise and we've agreed to compromise on that particular point."

"What she means is I put my foot down – which I rarely do – and forbid her from going after those bees," Aric corrected. "She's been trying to massacre bees since we moved into this house. It's ridiculous."

"You're ridiculous," Zoe shot back, her eyes softening when they landed on me. "You're upset about Jack. What's going on with him?"

"Nothing." My voice turned chilly. "What makes you think something is going on with Jack?"

"Because I've seen you two together and you could start a fire with the heat," Zoe said. "You're over the full moon for one another." Clearly she thought that was a joke because she offered up a lame chuckle. "Did he do something to upset you?"

"No." I stared at my hands so I wouldn't have to meet her gaze. "He's being very practical."

"Oh, that sounds good." Aric chuckled as he reached for the same cookie Zoe was about to snag. "You've already had, like, ten of them. This one is mine."

"Fine." Zoe made a face. "See, Charlie. Compromise. I'm giving him the last cookie and not even complaining."

"You've got another package of those cookies tucked away in your desk," Aric shot back. "Don't pretend to be a martyr."

"Yeah, yeah." Zoe waved off his comment. "Tell us about Jack."

"He kissed me."

"I know. I saw through the sentry. I told you that I was going to let him keep going to see how things progressed, but you guys saw the light, so it turned out to be a ruined moment."

"We didn't talk about the kiss until this afternoon," I supplied. "I thought he was going to pretend it didn't happen, but he decided we needed to talk."

"And?"

"And he needs to think about it." Just saying it made my stomach twist. "He doesn't think co-workers should date. He needs time to think, but I already know how it's going to end."

"So do I." Zoe was fully amused. "He's going to think about it until he can't stand it anymore, and then he's going to kiss the crap out of you again. Don't worry about it. Everything will work out."

I didn't understand how she could be so blasé. "You don't know that. He could decide that he doesn't want to try."

"He won't." Aric smirked as his eyes drifted toward the sliding glass doors that led to the back of the house. "He likes you."

"I don't know that's true," I hedged.

"He does." Aric's grin widened. "Why else would he be hiding at the far end of the property and staring at the house?"

I was startled by the news and jerked my head to stare in that direction. All I saw when I looked through the window was darkness … and the hazy edges of the kitchen appliances as they reflected against the glass. "How can you possibly know that? It's dark. You can't see that far."

"I see more than you think." Aric's shoulders tensed as he stalked toward the open door. "In fact … ."

"What is it?" Zoe was instantly alert and on her feet. She read her husband's demeanor better than most and knew something had gone terribly wrong. "Is Jack doing something?"

"No, but something is about to get done to Jack." Aric briefly met my gaze. "Stay in here with Zoe."

He had to be kidding. "You can't possibly think I'm just going to let something bad happen to Jack."

"I think you're going to stay here with Zoe while I handle Jack." Aric was firm. "There's more to this situation than you know. I don't have time to explain it to you ... I have to move. Zoe, protect the house."

Zoe moved to my side and we hovered next to the door, the dimness outside proving too thick to see through.

"I can't believe he just expects us to sit here and do nothing," I complained.

"He knows what he's doing." Zoe's expression was dark. "In fact ... ." She broke off as the distinctive sound of a wolf howling filled the air, tilting her head as her hands tightened into fists at her sides. "That wasn't Aric."

"Wasn't Aric?" I was beyond confused. "What are you talking about?"

"Stand back." Zoe lifted her hands, her fingertips already glowing. "Things are about to shift in a way that you're not going to like. I can't fix that now, but just know ... I was protecting my family."

I had no idea what she meant, but it was too late to ask the obvious question. Zoe unleashed a torrent of sparkling color on the backyard. It was only then the true horror of what we faced smacked us both upside the head.

"Oh, well, that can't be good," I muttered, my heart hammering as I focused on each dim figure in turn.

"Nope." Zoe grimaced. "Not at all. I'm so going to kick some ass."

TWENTY-EIGHT

Once the yard lit up – and I had trouble understanding exactly how Zoe pulled that off – I could make out the scene. It wasn't pretty. Aric raced toward the far end of the property, his focus laser sharp. It was only after staring for several long moments that I could make out movement ... and what I saw sent a chill down my spine.

Jack lay prone and unmoving on the lawn, his face pressed into the grass, his arms spread wide. He looked dead, which caused my heart to constrict. Even more terrifying – if that was even possible – were the two figures moving on either side of him.

"Are those ... wolves?"

"Shifters." Zoe was grim as she moved her eyes to the right and left, searching the trees for unseen enemies. "There're only two of them. You don't see more than that, do you?"

"I ... no. What about Jack? You don't think he's dead?"

"I don't know." Zoe was calm as she tugged open the sliding glass door. "I'll check. You stay here with Sami."

That sounded like the last thing I wanted to do. "I have to go to Jack."

Zoe opened her mouth to argue and then snapped it shut. "Of course you do. Come with me, but I need you to do what I say."

She looked so angry, so terrible in her fury, that I could do nothing but swallow hard and nod.

"It'll be okay," Zoe reassured me. "I'll protect you."

I wasn't worried about that. Okay, truth be told, the absolutely huge wolves stalking toward Aric frightened me beyond belief. I couldn't turn away from Jack, though. "Let's do it."

"Good." Zoe strolled through the door opening as if she didn't have a care in the world, stopping only long enough to glance back inside and raise her voice. "Sami, you stay in this house!"

I hadn't seen the youngest Winters family member since I'd arrived. I was shocked when Sami popped her head into the kitchen and glared at her mother.

"What's going on?"

"What's always going on?" Zoe didn't turn shrill, which impressed me more than her cool determination. "There are wolves on the lawn. I don't know who they are, but it's clear they're not here for hot chocolate."

"What about Dad?" Sami flicked her eyes to the open door. "Where did he go?"

"To check on Jack."

"That's her boyfriend, right?" Sami jerked her head in my direction. "Is he good or evil?"

"He's just a man."

"He's a good man," I corrected.

"He's a good man we don't particularly like because he happens to be acting like a tool right now," Zoe corrected, smoothing her shirt. "We're going to fix that problem after we fix this one, so as far as you're concerned he's on our side."

"That's good." Sami's lips curved. "He's too hot to be evil."

"Yeah, I'm going to have to explain how looks have nothing to do with being good or evil at some point. For now, you stay in this house. There's only two of them. I don't care what you hear. Whatever happens, you are forbidden from rushing outside."

Sami didn't look happy at being cut out of the action. "I can help."

"We don't need you to help. We need you to stay in here and not get in the way. Don't make me use magic to force you to stay in here. We both know that never ends well."

Sami narrowed her eyes. "Don't even think of doing that."

"Then don't make me do it."

I had no idea what they were talking about, but I was at my limit. "We have to get to Jack."

"We're going." Zoe cast one more look to Sami. "You stay in this house. That's an order."

"Fine." Sami jutted out her lower lip. "I don't like you very much right now."

"You'll survive. There's whipped cream and hot chocolate in the kitchen."

Sami brightened, her previous anger forgotten. "Yay!"

BY THE TIME WE made it down the back stairs and hit the lawn my heart was thundering so loudly I almost couldn't hear the snarling animals as they circled Aric.

For his part, Aric kneeled next to Jack's prone form to check for a pulse, never moving his eyes from the silver and white animals. He didn't seem particularly perturbed – or even aggressive – but he clearly wasn't happy we'd decided to join him.

"You should have stayed in the house, Zoe," he growled. "I've got this under control."

"Well, we decided to make it a double date," Zoe drawled, eyeing the closest wolf with overt distaste. "Do you recognize these fools?"

"No." Aric moved away from Jack so I could take his spot. "He's alive, Charlie. He's just out cold. I think they hit him over the head from behind. We'll take care of him once we get rid of them."

I wasn't convinced. "He needs to go to a hospital. His brain could be bleeding or something." I felt like crying.

Zoe grabbed my wrist to get my attention. "I'll fix him. I promise. For now, we need to focus on what's going on here. Quite frankly, it's probably good that Jack is out for this part. Explaining what's about to go down would be darned near impossible."

She seemed sure of herself, but I couldn't shake my worry. "He's not moving."

"He will." Zoe turned her full attention on the nearest wolf. "As for you idiots, do you even know who you're messing with?"

I had to give her credit. She wasn't one to quake in fear of huge wolves that snarled in a manner that made me think they wanted to eat us for dinner.

The wolves didn't speak – could they speak? – and instead circled us as they growled.

"They don't look local," Aric said as he glanced between the two animals. "In fact, I'll bet they're freelancers."

It was as if he was speaking another language. "What are you talking about?"

"It's a long story." Zoe leaned over and stared the silver wolf in the eyes. "We can't understand what you want if you don't shift and speak. I have no problem killing you without an explanation, but it might be better for all of us – mostly because I hate having to hide bodies – if you just open your stupid mouths and tell us what you want. You might even be surprised and get what you're looking for without spilling blood."

I licked my lips and shook my head, my hand unconsciously moving over Jack's soft hair. "Zoe ... ."

"Shh." Zoe held up a finger to silence me. "I'm in control here."

"She likes being the boss," Aric explained, glaring at the gray lobo. "These guys are definitely freelancers. Someone hired them to come after us. I don't understand who'd be that stupid."

"Not you," a voice hissed from the bushes, causing Aric to snap his head in that direction. He instinctively stretched out his arms to cover Zoe and me as he stared into the gloom.

"Oh, we have another guest." Zoe straightened. "In fact, I think we have another two guests if I'm not mistaken." She touched her tongue to her top lip as two shadows edged out of the foliage and onto the lawn. She furrowed her brow in confusion as my heart skipped a beat.

Zoe clearly didn't recognize the newcomers, but I did. "Who the heck are you?"

"Lisa Savage and Fred Pitman," I gritted out, confusion washing over me. "Apparently they're working together. I did not see that coming."

"Fred Pitman." Aric made a face. "You're the guy who owns the inn out on the highway."

"The one with all the dead animals on the wall, right?" Zoe queried, shaking her head.

"The one with the dead animals that stare at us while we're trying to eat," Sami bellowed from the raised porch. She stood at the railing and stared at us. "No one wants to eat with dead animals judging you while you're eating their cousins."

"I told you to stay in that house!" Zoe snapped.

"You never defined if the porch was part of the house."

Aric lifted his arm and pointed. "Inside!"

"I never get to have any fun!" Sami stomped her feet as she swept into the house.

"She's adorable," Lisa drawled, disdain practically dripping from her tongue. "It's too bad we have to kill her when we're done with you. I promise it will be quick, though."

Zoe blew out a wet raspberry that was so exuberant Lisa had no choice but to wipe the side of her face.

"You'll never get past us," Aric said. "Even if you did, you're no match for Sami."

Something about the way he said it made me sit up and take notice. I already knew Aric and Zoe were more than they let on. Sure, Zoe told me a bit about her abilities, but she was purposely vague when it came to Aric and Sami. The odds of Sami being normal when her mother was extraordinary were slim. I should've realized that.

"Oh, you talk big," Lisa sneered, "but I'm in control here."

"We're in control here," Fred corrected, raising a gun I hadn't seen when he first ventured onto the property. "We're in control. You'll do what we say and that's all there is to it."

"Yes, we're quaking in our boots." Zoe bobbed her head agreeably, her tone flat. "Please don't hurt us. Please spare our child. Please don't kill the bees when you're running to escape."

"I ... what?" Fred worked his jaw. "What are you talking about."

"Try being married to her," Aric suggested. "She's right about those bees, though. If she's not allowed to kill them, neither are you."

Fred exchanged a quick look with Lisa. "Do you understand what's going on here?"

"No, and it hardly matters." Lisa shifted her eyes to me. "This is the one we want. We can kill the others and make our escape, but we need this one alive."

Me? Was she talking about me? "I'm sorry, but ... I don't understand."

"She thinks she can use you as a scapegoat or something, or maybe a bargaining chip," Zoe explained. "She knows she's in trouble for poisoning her husband and wants to trade you for a free ride out of town."

Lisa turned haughty. "That shows what you know. I don't care about that. I want information from her, like how she got involved in this and why she felt the need to save Ethan when she could've just left him to die in the woods."

"She wasn't alone when she found Ethan," Aric pointed out.

"No, you were with her." Lisa's lips curled into something grotesque. "I blame you, too. That's why you have to die. You ruined everything for me."

"I'm pretty sure you ruined it yourself," I countered, slowly getting to my feet. I positioned myself so I stood between Jack and Lisa, a barrier of sorts. I was determined to protect him. "You only married him for his money. You knew you had to kill him to get it."

Lisa shrugged. "So?"

"So why did you choose to do it with poison?" Zoe asked. "I mean, there are tons of better ways that ensure he wouldn't have a chance to recover."

"He shouldn't have recovered this time," Lisa snapped. "He was supposed to wander around aimlessly for a few hours and then die. I spent two days in a hellhole hotel off I-75 in freaking Caro – a city that doesn't even have a Starbucks – thinking he was dead, only to find he wasn't dead. How is that even possible?"

"You weren't even in the woods the entire time," I mused. I shouldn't have been surprised by the revelation, but it irritated me all the same. "You left your husband to wander around and ultimately die while you went to a hotel and ordered room service? Nice."

"Don't kid yourself. None of the hotels in Caro are exactly five-star offerings. My hotel didn't even offer continental breakfast."

I hated her. I couldn't believe I'd once felt sorry for her. "Well … that must have been hard on you."

"You have no idea."

"What I don't get is how you're involved in all of this, Fred," Zoe noted, ignoring the gun Fred pointed at her. "How does an inn owner turn into a potential murderer?"

"Don't worry about it," Fred seethed. "We're not going to engage in some Scooby-Doo moment, so you can push that right out of your head."

"He worked as the financial advisor for Lisa's family for a number of years and then he bought the inn as a retirement venture," I supplied. "I'm guessing it was more work than he'd realized. He couldn't go back to his old job because Lisa's family lost all their money when Covenant College burned down."

Zoe jerked her eyes in my direction, surprised. "Seriously?"

I nodded. "She's broke."

"What ties did you have to Covenant College?" Aric asked, a vein working in his neck as he tensed.

"We made money off construction and tuition," Lisa replied. "It was a good gig, and we had to do very little work. When the college burned down – something no one could explain – we were simply out our money with no way to get it back. We got a few insurance payouts, but were left with next to nothing."

"And I'm guessing Covenant College is the tie you used to find these guys." Aric gestured toward the bristling wolves. "You knew that Covenant College was a haven for paranormals. You probably had that knowledge in your back pocket when it came time to off your husband. I still don't understand why you thought it was a good idea to poison him."

"Because I wanted it ruled a tragic accident," Lisa said. "I figured by the time his body was found the Nightshade wouldn't matter – especially if he could've gone a few weeks without discovery – and it simply would've looked as if he got lost and died from exposure."

"And all that was ruined for you when we found him," Zoe mused. "What a bummer for you."

"It's more than a bummer," Lisa seethed, her eyes narrowing to slits. "Now I'm in a pickle. The cops are looking for me. You guys were spreading word through the inn that I was a suspect ... and mounting theories as to what happened. Don't bother denying it. Fred heard you."

"I have no reason to deny it," I offered. "You don't have a way out of this. If we figured it out, the cops have too. I guess you know the reason you weren't allowed to see Ethan. Of course, that's why you asked to see us, isn't it? You wanted to know if we had information to share."

"And it turns out you didn't." Lisa made a face. "All this work. I just don't understand how I could've done all this work merely to have it fall apart. It's your fault."

"So ... what? You're going to take me someplace else and torture me for retribution?"

"There's no money in that. I'm going to ransom you to The Legacy Foundation. Those people are rich. They'll pay to get you back. I thought about taking him, too, but he'll be too hard to control." She gestured toward Jack and shook her head. "I guess I'll just have to kill him."

"Yeah, well, I'm not letting that happen." I squared my shoulders. "You'll have to go through me first."

As if on cue, the wolves snapped and growled, practically drooling at the prospect. I didn't like their reaction one bit.

"I have no problem going through you," Lisa said. "But I do need you in one piece, so I'm willing to offer you a trade."

"And what would that be?"

"I'll let your boyfriend live if you go willingly. I have to kill these two because they've seen me, but your boyfriend didn't. Our friends knocked him out before he even knew what was happening. We'll let him live if you come with us."

It wasn't even a remotely tempting offer. Still, I had one more question. "Before I respond, I need you to answer something for me."

Lisa feigned patience. "And what's that?"

"If you had everything planned where Ethan was concerned, why did you go through all the effort to scream and run the night these guys showed up to scare him into the woods? I mean ... I get that Ethan being lost and roaming the woods was part of your plan, but why go to the effort to put on a show yourself?"

Lisa shrugged. "Why not? I needed to be sure my story would hold up. I knew the cops would check the campsite. I needed appropriate footprints to sell my story of something – some dark creature – stealing Ethan from the scene. It was best to act out everything to sell my story. It's the little details that trip people up. I didn't want to get caught on a technicality."

"Ah." I understood everything now. "I guess that makes sense."

"So, you'll come with us?"

I shook my head. "No. I just wanted to know why you went through all the trouble to crawl and scream as you fled into the woods."

Lisa furrowed her brow. "How can you possibly know that?"

"Because I'm more than I appear to be," I answered.

"So are we," Zoe added, her expression turning dark. "You should've done your research before picking this family to screw with. It's too late to turn back now, so I guess you'll have to take your medicine."

"What is that supposed to mean?"

The question was barely out of Lisa's mouth before Aric, Zoe and I reacted. I slashed out with my magic, pitching Lisa backward and slamming her into a tree. Zoe was a little more forceful when her magic burned Fred's hand, causing him to cry out and drop the gun.

She was a small and silent predator as she stalked forward and caused Fred to shrink back in fear.

As for Aric, I watched out of the corner of my eye as his body contorted. The snapping sound that accompanied it – the noise associated with contorting muscle and bone – almost made me go weak in the knees. The wolf he turned into – one that was twice the size of the others – was big and black. The lighter wolves must have realized right away that they were no match for him because they turned tail and raced into the underbrush. Aric gave chase, and the howl he let loose was something straight out of a horror movie.

That wasn't the end of the action, though. A much smaller wolf raced down the outdoor steps and followed Aric into the woods, happily yipping as it gave chase. This one was miniature – almost child-sized – and its coat was a pretty gray color.

"You're grounded when you get back!" Zoe shrieked after the small wolf.

That's when true realization washed over me. "Sami?"

Zoe shrugged. "She takes after her father no matter what he says."

I sighed as I loosened a heavy tree branch from above and let it drop on Lisa's head, releasing my hold on her as she lolled to the side and hit the ground. "I see you've been keeping something else from me."

"My family comes first." Zoe wasn't the type to apologize. "Now, come on. We need to call the police and wake Jack. We'll need a feasible story for both. Get that brain working. Explaining all this isn't going to be easy."

TWENTY-NINE

"*That's* quite the story."

Jack rubbed the back of his head thirty minutes later, watching through Zoe and Aric's kitchen window as the police loaded Lisa, Fred and two naked men who just happened to be unconscious into cruisers.

"It is quite the story," I agreed, shifting on my stool as I tried to get comfortable. "It all happened really fast. We didn't know you were outside until you were already on the ground – and that honestly scared me, for the record .We tried to get to you as fast as possible. What were you even doing here?"

"Looking for you." Jack's mood was hard to read. "You weren't in your room when I went upstairs to check. I was worried after you disappeared from the bar without telling anyone where you were going. I figured you headed here and wanted to make sure you were okay."

"That's kind of sweet." And could've caused huge problems, I added silently. "But I was fine."

"So I see. Um … why are those guys naked?"

That was a very good question. They were that way when Aric dragged them from the woods. He was, too, and it took everything I had to look away while he dressed. Sami had scampered into the house in her wolf form and I hadn't seen her since. She was probably living in fear of her mother's reaction to her insistence on helping her father with his hunt. "I have no idea."

"They're probably meth heads," Aric announced as he strolled into the kitchen. He appeared calm, as if he hadn't just shifted into a wolf and hunted down and beat the crap out of two other wolves. "They're going to the hospital to be tested before being jailed."

I wondered what the hospital staff would find. Of course, Aric's father was a senator who had ways of changing records. It probably didn't matter what was in their systems. I heard Aric on the phone with his father while Zoe was healing Jack before the cops arrived. Apparently they were coming up with a plan, one they didn't share with me.

That was probably for the best.

"What about Fred?" I asked, hoping to steer the conversation to a safer topic. I didn't want Jack – who seemed really confused – dwelling too hard on certain parts of the story. "Do we know why he was involved?"

"Money," Aric replied simply. "Lisa promised him a cut of what she was going to get from Ethan's life insurance if he agreed to help. He supplied the two guys who helped mess with the campsite scene and who forcibly drugged Ethan before letting him loose in the woods to wander and eventually die."

"And they thought stealing Charlie would help them get money?" Jack asked, wrinkling his forehead. "I'm not sure The Legacy Foundation would've paid a ransom. It would've for Chris, but he's family. Charlie is just an employee."

"I don't think it was the best thought-out plan," Aric explained. "They just wanted money and to get out of town. They knew Ethan would talk – and that it would be all over for Lisa in social circles even if she managed to get away with the poisoning – so they needed money in a hurry."

"It wasn't a very good plan," I agreed, widening my eyes when I realized Sami had silently slipped into the spot on my right. "Where did you come from?"

Sami's smile was mysterious. "I've been around." She grabbed the can of whipped cream from the counter and sprayed some in her mouth. "Can we order pizza, Dad? I'm starving."

"Ask your mother." Aric pinned her with a look that promised a serious conversation once they were alone. "Although, pizza does sound good." His expression softened. "If you order it, I'll pay."

"Yay!" Sami handed me the whipped cream before clapping her hands and hopping to the floor. "Meat lover's special?"

"Get the wings, breadsticks and that giant cookie thing your mom likes, too," Aric instructed. "You'll need something to bribe her with if you ever want to see the world beyond our property again."

Sami's smile slipped. "Whatever. I didn't do anything wrong."

"We'll talk about it later."

Jack slid me a curious look. "What's that about?"

"Oh, well ... ."

"Sami slipped outside during the excitement even though she was ordered to stay inside," Aric answered, his ease when it came to lying apparent. "She's going to be grounded once her mother has a free moment to talk to her. The pizza will be a last meal of sorts."

"Where is Zoe?" I craned my neck to look out the window. "Is she still talking to the cops?"

"She is," Aric confirmed. "She has some rather ... um, unique ... suggestions for punishment. I think she just wants to mess with Lisa and Fred a little bit. She gets her jollies by making people want to kill her."

I could see that. I exhaled heavily, blowing my hair up my forehead before focusing on Jack. "Do you want to go to the hospital and have your head looked at?"

"The paramedics checked. I have a lump the size of an orange back there, but no concussion. They said it was a small miracle that I didn't have more serious damage, but it appears I'm fine."

A small miracle ... or a woman with glowing blue fingers.

"I'm glad you're okay, but you didn't need to follow me," I supplied. "I only wanted to say goodbye."

"I know." Jack met my gaze. "I wanted to make sure you were okay. We've had a busy day and I knew you were tired. I wanted to make sure you got back to the inn safely. You tend to attract danger."

That was the understatement of the year. "I won't pressure you. I hope you know that. I was being a bit of a jerk earlier, but I know it's not fair to demand things of you. You can take all the time you want.

"And you don't have to follow me," I continued. "I've been taking care of myself for a very long time. I'm okay. I'll keep being okay."

Jack nodded as he ran his tongue over his teeth. "Yeah, well, here's the thing ... it became very apparent when you disappeared tonight that I want to take care of you. I at least want to be around when you take care of yourself."

"That's nice." Wait ... what was he saying?

"I actually figured it out weeks ago but didn't want to accept it," Jack said. "You drive me crazy and yet I can't seem to stay away. That is a simple fact. I'm incapable of ignoring how I feel when you're around ... or when I think of you ... or when I even hear your name."

My cheeks burned at his admission, my mind busy.

"Welcome to my world, man." Aric patted Jack's shoulder as he moved past him to stare out the window. "Oh, Zoe is doing a little dance to taunt the prisoners. She's such a gem."

I pressed my lips together to keep from laughing ... or crying ... at Jack's earnest expression. "I don't think I understand what you're saying, Jack," I said finally. "I need it spelled out."

Jack made a weary sound in the back of his throat. "Of course you do. I should've known you wouldn't make this easy."

"Women are never easy," Aric called out, his gaze still focused out the window. "But if you find the right one they're more than worth the effort it takes to keep up with them."

"Why is Mom singing?" Sami asked, appearing at Aric's side. "Does that mean she's in a good mood?"

"You're still grounded," Aric replied. "Don't think you're getting out of that."

"I ordered her a cookie and the cinnamon sticks."

"Well, that might work."

To my utter surprise, Jack smiled as he watched the interplay. "You need it spelled out?"

I breathlessly nodded.

"Okay. I guess that's fair. This might be the head injury talking – although I think it's a lot more than that – but I want to give it a try. I don't want to fight tooth and nail to stay away from you because it's become clear that I'm fighting a losing battle."

"So ... you and me ... um ... ."

"He's saying he wants to date you," Sami interjected, making a face. "How do you not get that?"

Aric flicked her ear. "Mind your own business."

"They're doing their business in my kitchen," Sami protested.

"My kitchen," Aric corrected. "We let you live here out of the goodness of our hearts. You're a tenant."

"And they're going to kiss." Sami stared hard as Jack leaned in close and stole my breath. "He's kind of hot, huh? I want a boyfriend who looks like him when I get older."

"You're not dating until you're thirty."

"Mom says I can date when I'm fourteen."

The last thing I heard as Jack's lips pressed against mine – other than the fluttering of my own heart – was Aric's growled response.

"You're definitely grounded, kid. I'm going to let your mother go nuts for a change when it comes to punishment."

"That's not fair."

"Life isn't fair."

I agreed with her. Life isn't fair. As I sank into the kiss, though, I had to wonder why I should care. Life often works in mysterious ways, and this was no exception.

It was time for an entirely new adventure, and I couldn't wait to see what was around the next corner.

Made in the USA
Middletown, DE
22 August 2023

37137796R00156